Death on the Rig

A Milt Kingston Novel in the

Uintah Basin Mysteries

by

T. S. Jensen

Death on the Rig

A Uintah Basin Mysteries, Milt Kingston Novel

Published by T. S. Jensen in Utah, U.S.A.

Visit **https://tsjensen.com** for more great stories!

For the roughnecks, EMTs, deputies, and Relief
Society sisters who keep small towns running
in all kinds of weather.

And for my parents, Keith and LaRue. You
taught me how to work, find my faith, and walk
through a trail of doubt without getting lost.

— T. S. Jensen

Books by T. S. Jensen

Uintah Basin Mysteries

Look for another Milt Kingston Novel

Coming Soon

Chapter 1

Steel Against Morning Snow

The scanner rode quiet under the dash as I turned off the county road onto washboard. Late winter dark pressed close on both sides, sage a smear in the headlights. Twenty minutes back, dispatch had said, "Oil rig fall out at Roosevelt Rig. EMS in route. Company safety on scene."

The company man would already have a story.

Floodlights bloomed ahead, a hard white island on the flats. Flares burned beyond, orange tongues licking at the clear black sky. No snow, no blowing anything, just cold.

I eased the truck onto the pad, gravel crunching, diesel and chemical odor pushing through the vents. Clara's unit rolled in behind me, lights off. We parked shoulder to shoulder, habit.

She climbed out, collar up against the wind. "You hear anything else?"

"Just 'fall from height.'" My breath smoked between us. "Let's go see."

A small knot of men stood near the derrick leg, hardhats bright under the lights. A body hung above, skewered midair.

Jared Pike didn't look like a man from down here. More like someone had thrown coveralls onto a twisted piece of pipe and left them. His harness line drooped slack. One arm bent back wrong, gloved fingers open to the cold.

A supervisor stepped forward as we came up. Late thirties, stocky, clean vest over his coveralls. Jaw muscle jumping. "Sheriff Kingston? Wade Garrison." He stuck out a hand, then thought better of it. "Rough night."

"Wade." I nodded at the hanging body. "That Jared?"

"Yeah." He kept his eyes on me, not the beam. "He went over from the catwalk. Should've been clipped in. Must've slipped."

"Walk me through," I said. "From before it happened."

He rolled right into it. "Routine checks, pre-dawn. He was up there fooling with valves. Hank here heard a shout, then... hell. We hit the kill, called it in. EMS said don't move anything till you got here."

Too smooth for the way his hands flexed at his sides.

Hank stood behind him, taller, shoulders hunched in his jacket. Shaggy beard, eyes rimmed red. He cradled a cigarette in shaking fingers. The unlit end carried a tooth mark.

"You Hank Dillard?" I asked.

He nodded once, throat bobbing.

"Hang on," Clara murmured. She stepped off toward the EMTs, notebook already out.

I tipped my head toward the ladder. "Show me where he started."

We mounted the first steel rungs, boots clanking. Cold bit through my jeans where the metal brushed. I'd climbed similar ladders when I was nineteen, before a badge and a belt. Back then, death was a story old hands told to scare us straight.

Halfway up, the wind found a tune through the derrick structure, somewhere between a whistle and a moan. At the top landing, work lights flattened every angle. The catwalk rail hit mid-chest on me. Beyond it, black nothing.

Blood had dried in a crooked path across the grated floor, darker where it had pooled by the rail. Spatter on the inside of the guard, not much outside.

"Where'd he go over?" I asked.

Wade pointed at a section of rail scuffed raw through the paint. "Here. Must've leaned out. Boots slipped. Wind kicks funny up here."

The air barely stirred against my face.

I stepped close. The beam that had taken Jared sat maybe twelve feet out and down, a crossmember thick as my thigh. From the way his body hung, he'd hit chest first then slumped. The angle bothered me. Men fall messy:

arms out, twisting, hitting whatever they meet on the way. This looked like someone had placed him.

"Where was his lanyard clipped?" I said.

Wade gestured at a safety anchor fixed to the rail. The carabiner hung empty. I squatted, joints complaining, and ran my gloved hand along the steel. Paint broke clean at the edge. A bright crescent of bare metal winked where something sharp had scraped hard and recently.

Fresh scrape. No rust, no dust.

Beside the anchor, the latch that should have held his lanyard sat partly open. At the hinge, the metal showed small, parallel bites, too regular for weather. Tool marks, tight and bright.

"Maintenance on this recently?" I kept my voice even.

"Just regular checks," Wade said. "We don't skimp on safety out here, Sheriff."

"Who signs those checks?"

"Colton. Safety." Wade jerked his chin toward the pad.

I straightened enough to look out. Below, a man in a cleaner jacket, company logo on the chest, stood off from the others near a truck, talking low into a phone. Shoulders loose, feet planted like he owned the dirt.

"Clara," I called. "Photos on this latch and anchor, close."

She stepped up beside me, already pulling the camera from her bag.

I moved along the rail, measuring with my eyes. From the ladder top to where Jared hung, the distance, the turn, the point where a slip would have thrown his body sideways, not straight down. I marked it all in my notebook: ladder height, beam location, angle.

We picked our way back down. My knees liked the descent less.

Out of habit, I counted back from the body to the beam again. If he'd fallen clean, the marks should've told a different story. This wasn't a bar fight, but my mind still cross-referenced.

Hank had drifted to the shadow near a truck, cigarette finally lit, ember flaring in small jerks. Sour whiskey rode his breath even from a few feet out.

"Had a long night?" I asked him.

"Long week," he snapped, then grimaced. "We worked swing. Couple beers after shift, that's all."

His knee bounced. He crushed the cigarette halfway smoked, grinding it into frozen gravel like it had offended him.

Behind us, the company man approached. Early thirties, maybe, clean-shaven, darker hair combed neat despite the wind. His coat looked more office than field. He stuck out a gloved hand.

"Sheriff Kingston? Colton Reese. Safety manager."

We shook. His grip was firm, not cold nor warm through the leather.

"Rough morning," I said.

"That's one word." His gaze flicked past me, up to the catwalk, catching for a beat on the anchor, the bright scrape, then dropping to Jared's grotesquely hanging body. "We take this seriously. Zero lost-time incidents last year. Jared knew better than to free climb."

"Tell me about him," I said.

"Good hand, when he wanted to be. Little too fond of roughhousing. One of those guys always writing things down, you know? Safety numbers, suggestions. Meant well. Sometimes that gets in the way of just doing the job."

Always writing things down. I filed it with the latch marks.

"Wind look like this when he fell?" I asked.

Colton tilted his head toward the sky, clean and star-pricked above the glare. The air felt sharp enough to bite. No snow, no mist, nothing to hide a thing.

"Hard to say," he answered. "These flats will surprise you. Could've kicked up a whiteout when he went over. We're in a bowl out here."

Whiteout. I followed his eyes up again. Not a cloud.

I pulled my pen, wrote on the margin: Sky clear. Dry. No snow. Underlined it.

Clara joined us. "Photos done. I'll get the ladder, anchor, rail, then body once they lower him."

"Make sure we get that latch from three angles." I spoke loud enough for Wade to hear. His jaw muscle ticked again.

Company crews moved like they wanted to be anywhere else. One young roustabout crossed himself quick when he thought no one was watching, then stiffened when my eye caught him. This wasn't just routine horror to them. Something extra rode the air.

"Who found him first?" I asked, turning back to Wade.

"Hank did," Wade said without looking at him. "He yelled; we all ran."

Hank flinched.

I wrote his name next to "first on scene." Underlined again.

By the time we finished documenting the beam and Clara signed off on EMS moving the body, my fingers had gone numb in my gloves. They eased Jared down with a winch, canvas rustling, metal squealing. The bag swallowed his shape, the outline of that impossible bend. Zip rasped; the sound never got easier.

I stepped back under the catwalk, notebook in hand. The bright crescent on the latch shone above me, too clean in all that dirty steel.

Pad noise swelled behind me, diesel hum, radio crackle, Hank cursing low, Wade answering some unheard question on his phone, voice flattened. Colton stood a little apart, still staring at the harness tag Clara had photographed, as if memorizing it for later.

Routine accident, dispatch had said. A man slips, a harness fails, paperwork follows.

I watched that scraped steel, the empty spot in Jared's rope, the clear, dry sky, and let the company story keep talking while I wrote the word that would change their morning.

Suspicious.

Chapter 2

Men in the Flares' Shadow

We pulled the main players into a rough circle at the edge of the pad, away from the worst of the noise. Floodlights hummed overhead, throwing long shadows that rocked when the wind nudged the towers. Steam from men's breath drifted, then vanished.

Clara flipped open a fresh page. I did the same.

"All right," I said. "This'll go quicker if each of you sticks to what you did and saw. We're not assigning blame out here. Just want it straight while it's fresh."

Hank shifted his weight from foot to foot, boot grinding gravel. Wade rolled his hardhat between his palms. Colton folded his gloved hands slow, like he had all the time in the world.

I started with the supervisor. "Wade, time you started pre-shift checks?"

"Three-thirty," he said. No pause. "Standard. I came on pad with the swing crew, signed the book, did a walkaround."

"And Jared?"

"He was on swing too. Should've been in the shack with the rest 'til I sent him out." Wade's gaze flicked toward Hank, then back. "Last I saw him before, he was at the lockers, grabbing his harness same as everyone."

I pictured the still-bagged replacement hanging there. "Harnesses all up to date?"

He didn't look away. "All current, Sheriff. We don't skimp on safety."

"My jaw tightened. "Logs will show that?"

"Yes, sir. Pre-use checks signed off."

I wrote: says all harnesses current. Locker: bagged replacement tagged Jared crew. I underlined the gap.

We moved to Hank.

"What were you doing right before you heard him?" I asked.

He rubbed his face with a dirty glove, leaving a smear across his cheek. "Was heading up to the catwalk too. He went on ahead. I was, uh, tying off some line, then I heard this yell."

"What kind of yell?"

Hank's leg bounced. "Scared one. Like... just a shout. Then metal. I looked up, he was already...." He swallowed. "You saw."

"Time?"

He blinked. "I don't know. Four? Four-thirty?"

"Closer to four-ten," Wade cut in. "Radio log'll show."

"Good," I said. "We'll pull it. Hank, you see anyone else up there with him?"

"No. Just him." A beat. "Shouldn't have been reading crap up there anyway."

I let that hang. Clara's pen stilled.

"What crap?" I said, keeping my voice mild.

Hank's eyes went wide like a deer in headlights. "Just, safety tags. You know. He always liked to act foreman. Reading all the postings, slowing us down."

There it was. Reading. Colton's comment about scribbling came back. Jared with a notebook on the catwalk, not a prank.

"Where were you when you keyed the radio?" Clara asked.

Hank licked his lips. "On the stairs. I hollered down, yelled at Wade, hit the button right there. Didn't leave the pad."

I sketched a small ladder in the margin, arrowing where the radio was supposed to be. Later we'd match the distance to his timeline. For now, the important piece was that word he'd snatched back.

"Did Jared carry anything with him?" I asked. "Tools, clipboard, anything besides standard gear?"

"Just his wrench," Hank said too fast. "You saw it up there. Nothing else."

I'd seen the wrench. I hadn't seen paper. That didn't mean it hadn't been there.

I turned to Colton. "Where were you when you got the call?"

He smoothed his gloves once. "At home. Phone rang about four-fifteen. Company duty officer. I grabbed my truck, came straight out."

"Who called you?"

"Dispatch. Then Wade here."

Wade nodded like they'd rehearsed it. I wrote the names, arrows connecting them, a small web building under Jared's.

"Your first impression when you saw him?" I asked.

"Tragedy," Colton said. "Man not clipped in. We drill them on that. This kind of carelessness makes all of us look bad."

"Carelessness," I repeated. He wanted that in the record early.

"Any reason Jared would bypass his clip?" Clara said. "Known for shortcuts?"

Colton hesitated just long enough for me to mark it. "He complained a lot. Thought some gear was old. Maybe he figured he knew better, trusted his boots. These guys..." He let the sentence trail off with a shrug.

"So you'd call this roughneck culture?" I said. "Not gear."

He smiled thinly. "Culture and conditions. Like I said, wind can turn on you. It was a whiteout mess when I rolled in. Hard to see ten yards."

I let my eyes travel over the pad, out to the bare flats. Stars watched, clear and cold. No drifting, no crust on the berms. My boots crunched dry, not packed.

"Funny," I said. "When we came in, I could count the bolts on your shack door from the road."

Wade huffed a laugh that died quick. Hank glanced up at the sky, checking his own memory.

Colton's jaw worked once. "Maybe it eased up by then. Point is, cameras don't always catch everything in that kind of weather."

There it was, laid out before I'd even asked. Cameras, weather, a neat little excuse wrapped in "point is." I wrote: Colton: "whiteout mess," claims cameras miss in snow. Note: sky clear, dry. Weather as cover?

Clara shot me a side glance. I figured she'd written the same.

We walked Hank back along the route toward the ladder, giving Wade and Colton a reason to stay put. The wind knifed sideways between units. Ice crusted the ruts, popping under our boots.

"Show me exact," I said to Hank. "Where were you when you last saw him on his feet?"

He slogged to a spot a few paces from the stairs. "Right here. He was already halfway up."

"So he passes you," I said. "You're on the ground. He goes up, you follow?"

"Yeah. He moves slower, 'cause he's always stopping, looking at..." Hank stopped himself again, sucked in a breath that whistled.

"Looking at what?" I didn't raise my voice.

"Nothing." He stared at my badge instead of my eyes. "I meant gauges. Whatever. He was... careful."

"You said 'reading crap,'" I reminded him.

"Safety posters." He forced a laugh that came out ragged. "He loves those."

The wind snapped the edge of the canvas on a nearby pallet.

"You two get along?" I asked.

He shifted again. "We drank sometimes. He thought too much. Slowed things."

"That make you mad?" Clara said.

"Everybody out here's mad about something," he muttered. "Doesn't mean we throw people off rigs."

I noted the word choice, throw, and let it pass.

Back at the edge of the pad, Wade was on his phone, voice low. Colton stood, looking up at the tower again, like he was replaying a board he already knew.

I gathered them once more. "Last thing," I said. "After we're done here, you'll all be headed back to the trailers. Clara and I'll walk with you. I don't want anyone disappearing before we get contact info and a little more detail in a calmer setting."

Wade bristled. "Sheriff, my men just watched a coworker die. They're in shock. Company's got protocols, "

"And the county's got one," I said. "You'll have lawyers and safety reports for months. I get one long walk."

He pressed his lips together, then nodded once. "Fine."

As crews drifted toward the man-camp road, boots sucking at thawing mud, I hung back enough to let Hank and Wade get a step ahead. Clara fell in beside another roustabout, asking about shift rotations, making notes.

We passed between trailers, sodium vapor lights buzzing. Generator drone vibrated through the ground. TV glow pulsed behind curtained windows. Out here, in half-shadow, men's shoulders finally started to drop; an ugly night was already slipping toward another story they'd tell later if no one wrote it down right.

Ahead of me, Wade grabbed Hank's elbow, fingers biting through the jacket. Their voices drifted back, blurred by wind and trailer walls, but one sentence came clean.

"You keep your mouth shut about that night he went through papers, you hear me?" Wade hissed. "It was nothing."

My boots kept moving, but inside everything locked.

Papers.

I slowed, fumbling my notebook, let them put a few strides between us, then called, "What papers, Wade?"

They both froze. Wade half turned, a tight smile already plastered on. "Safety sheets, Sheriff. Jared was just a worrier. Always double-checking stuff." His laugh came too quick and ended sharp.

I tucked the word into my notebook in capital letters, PAPERS?, next to his name. Cold slid under my coat, not from the air.

At the main row of bunk trailers, we split them. Clara took Wade to one side, his unit marked with a new grill and a pair of boots on the step. I steered Hank to his, a bare bulb throwing yellow over a cracked plastic chair.

He lingered on the top step, one hand on the frame like a man ready to slam the door if the wrong question came.

"Look," he said, voice dropping. "I didn't push him. I got mad when he slowed things, sure, but I ain't stupid."

"I didn't say you pushed him," I answered. "I said your timeline's fuzzy. Let's clear it."

We went over it again. Time he said he left the shack. Time he claimed he reached the stairs. At one point he mentioned a gas run, changed his mind, then changed it back. I let the contradictions pile in their own corner.

"So you left for fuel before the fall?" I asked.

"After." He ran a hand over his neck, scratching. "No. Before, I mean. Hell, I don't know. We go for gas all the time. You can check the card."

I would. Card readers didn't drink.

Across the row, under another porch light, Clara had Wade pinned gentle against his own story, hands in her jacket pockets, head tipped. Whenever Wade's answers stretched, Colton's name crept in, "Colton'll have that," "Colton signed off," "Colton does the cams." His jaw muscle ticked faster when she asked who actually made the radio call.

Later, back at the truck, she slid into the passenger seat and flipped her notebook open on her knees. The pad lights still burned behind us; diesel hum had fallen to a background growl. The scanner on my dash hissed and popped with some unrelated call halfway across the county.

"Well?" she said.

"Hank's all over the place," I answered. "Gas run sometimes before, sometimes after. Admits he's mad at Jared for slowing things down and 'reading.' Could be drunk, could be scared, could be both."

"Could be lying," she said.

"Could," I agreed. I wrote HANK, angry, drunk, resents note-taking. Timeline: gas run mismatch.

"What about Wade?" she asked.

"Smooth. Too smooth. Claims all harnesses current while a replacement with Jared's crew tag hangs in a locker. Jumps in every time Hank starts to talk about anything beyond 'he slipped.'"

"And Colton," she said, tapping the name where she'd circled it.

"Whiteout," I said. "On a dry, clear night. Brings up cameras before I ask. Watches the harness tag like it personally insulted him."

She leaned back, eyes on the faint glow of the derrick in the mirror. "Who's your primary?"

I looked at my notes. Under "Suspects," I'd listed three names. Hank's had the darkest underline. Wade's had a question mark about negligence. Colton's sat third, with a thin circle and the word "weather" in the margin.

"Hank, for now," I said. "Mad, drunk, first on scene, weird about papers. Plenty of motive, plenty of opportunity. Wade's got liability. Might've looked the other way on bad gear or worse. Colton...."

"Feels like the company," Clara said softly. "Not the hands."

"Yeah." I watched the flare burn against the dawn that wasn't quite here yet. "But the company man knows that latch better than most. And he's already building weather into the story."

I underlined my earlier note again: Sky clear, dry, no blowing snow.

Beside it I wrote: WX excuse, check record.

Then I opened a fresh page, wrote Jared Pike's name at the top, and, just under it, one word I'd circled once on the pad and would circle again before the day was over.

Careful.

Chapter 3

Casseroles and Questions

The casserole sweated under foil on the counter, leaving a damp ring on Eve's recipe card. I sat at the kitchen table with my notebook open, Jared Pike's name underlined at the top of the page. The scanner whispered from the living room, the same call signs looping through like it always did when the county settled in for the night.

Coffee steamed beside my pen. I wrote in block letters:

LATCH, FRESH TOOL MARKS   BAGGED HARNESS, UNUSED   HANK TIMELINE = SLOPPY

The dishwasher started its low churn, a kind of distant thunder. Eve moved between sink and stove in sock feet, stacking plates, tucking foil tighter around someone's "deep-dish lasagna" that could've fed a scout troop.

"Marie says she'll bring bread tomorrow," she said. "That's three casseroles today. We're going to die by cheese before this is over."

I made a mark next to Hank's name and didn't answer. Dish soap and leftover onions hung in the air. Behind me, Caleb's laugh bounced once from the hallway, then cut off. A bedroom door shut.

Eve rinsed a pan. "Sister Jensen said she heard it on the scanner. 'Such a shame, but those rigs are dangerous,' like that explains everything." She flicked water off her fingers. "How dangerous was this one?"

Steel through a man's torso. A harness that should've held. A bagged spare that still smelled like plastic instead of sweat and snow.

"Dangerous enough," I said.

She set a plate in the rack with a clack. "That mean you'll be out there all week?"

"Clara and I have more to do." I wrote "DOCS?, W & H" and circled it. Wade's hissed warning in the trailer corridor shoved back in: keep your mouth shut about that night he went through papers.

"Company's already calling it an accident?" she asked.

"Pretty quick to use that word," I said. I added: COMPANY REP: "TRAGIC ACCIDENT." Colton's neat jacket, his hand on the harness tag, his eyes not quite matching his mouth.

The furnace came on with a soft click and whoosh, warm air sliding from the vent under my feet. Grit from the rig still scratched inside my socks. My notebook paper had a smear of gray in one corner. I didn't rub it off.

Eve dried her hands, then wiped the same spot on the counter three times, though it already shone. "Rosa. That was her name?"

"Yeah." I let the picture of her at the rig edge come back: coat half-zipped, hair tangled, her hands flexing like they had nothing to hold now. "She drove in before we finished. Company man tried to usher her away. She wouldn't move."

"Good for her." Eve's voice went soft, then sharpened. "She have people? Ward sisters?"

"Some," I said. "They'll smother her with food like they did us." I wrote: ROSA, "HE WAS CAREFUL." DIDN'T DRINK. "SCARED LATELY."

The dishwasher thumped, changed pitch. From Abby's room, faint music leaked out, that same pop song on repeat.

Eve turned, dish towel in hand, and looked at my notebook. Her hair had slipped loose from its knot, a dark strand stuck to her cheek. "You writing up your report or writing yourself a sermon?"

"Trying to figure what I actually know, not just what people are saying."

"What people are saying is already getting loud," she said. "Sister Brown said at the door, 'At least it wasn't one of ours out there.' Like Jared doesn't sit three rows behind us when they can make it to church."

I underlined his name again until the paper almost tore.

I didn't like talking work at the table. Ben used to say, You bring too much blood home, it soaks your kids' shoes. But the rig clung to me. The angle of Jared's body on that beam, the clean edge of metal through flesh, the way the harness line hung useless.

Eve leaned her hip against the counter. "So. Was it an accident?"

"I don't think so," I said before I could tame it.

The word hung there between coffee steam and casserole smell.

She raised her eyebrows. "You don't think, or you don't want to think?"

I rubbed my thumb over Ben Latham's watch where it rested above my belt, the glass nicked at the twelve. "Latch was wrong. Harness wrong. Too many wrongs in one place for one bad step."

The scanner popped, a deputy checking in on a domestic that could wait for the night shift. My foot started a slow tap under the table.

"And?" Eve asked.

"And company wants it accidental. Ward will be happier with accidental. For paperwork, for tithing, for everybody's sleep."

She folded the towel, refolded it. "What do you want?"

The words on my page blurred. A trailer court years back drifted in: a woman with a split lip insisting she'd bumped into a cabinet, bishop at her elbow assuring me they had it handled. I'd written it up as "verbal only" and gone home. Two months later I stood in the same gravel, looking at a stretcher. Ben's hand on my shoulder had been heavy, his mouth tight. We both knew who'd failed her first.

"I want it to be simple," I said. "But it isn't."

The dishwasher finished a cycle and fell quiet. The house ticked and hummed.

Eve crossed to the table and sat opposite me. She picked up my pen, flipping it between her fingers. "You always say the law's only worth anything if it treats people the same," she said. "Does that stop at the edge of the rig?"

I swallowed. "No."

"Then this Jared," she said, saying his name like she was making herself learn it, "shouldn't get less of you because he works under flares instead of in town. Or because his paycheck comes from the same folks who sponsor the youth conference."

I watched her thumb press into the pen clip. Abby's footsteps creaked in the hall and stopped. Silence. Listening.

Eve looked toward the doorway, then back to me. "Milt, if it were our name on those papers..." She let that sit, corrected herself. "If it were your name. On some ledger. On something that put you on a catwalk you shouldn't have been on. Would you want the sheriff keeping the peace or telling the truth?"

The question hit my chest like a dropped wrench. I could see Colton's neat columns of numbers, the company logo printed at the top. Safety bonuses. Incident-free days. Metrics that turned into pay and callings and smiles at the diner.

I thought of our own mortgage, Eve's brother needing his job on another rig, the way ward members liked being able to say the sheriff sat on their pew. Thought of Rosa in her rental house with a plate of food she didn't want and a stack of forms she couldn't quite read.

"Truth," I said.

"Say it to yourself," she said quietly.

"Truth," I repeated.

She nodded once, like that was settled, then stood and grabbed another casserole from the counter. "We can freeze two of these. Unless they all label them 'eat soon.'"

I watched her move, the simple rhythm of rinsing, stacking, scraping. The same hands that passed sacrament trays down pews now batting away the idea that we owed anyone silence.

Abby ghosted through the hallway in my peripheral vision, hair coming loose from her braid, phone in hand. Her step slowed at the dining room opening. I kept my eyes on the notebook. She listened for a heartbeat, then slipped toward her room, her door easing shut without a click.

Eve flipped off the faucet. "You're not going to be able to make everyone happy on this one," she said.

"I know."

"But I need to know which side of that you're going to land on," she said. "For Rosa. For us."

The furnace cycled off. The house exhaled.

I turned to a fresh page. At the top, in letters a shade darker than the rest, I wrote:

OPEN HOMICIDE?

I underlined it twice. My fingers rested on the ink until a small black smudge marked my skin.

At the bottom of the page, on the right-hand margin, I wrote smaller: Peace or truth?

The scanner muttered. A school name. A mile marker. Nothing that needed me tonight.

Eve set the last pan in the fridge and wiped her hands. Then she reached over and closed the notebook halfway.

"You can work more in the morning," she said. "Come tuck your kids in."

She clicked off the main kitchen light. The glow over the sink and the thin blue from the living room TV bled together, leaving the table in dim amber. I slid the notebook into my shirt pocket, the cardboard edges pressing against the place above my heart where all this lived whether I wrote it or not.

As she walked down the hall, I sat a moment longer with my fingers on those two words. They felt heavier than the badge at my waist. Heavier than the casseroles lining our counter.

I stood, shut off the sink light, and followed the sound of my family's voices down the hallway.

Abby leaned in the living-room doorway with her phone, the lamp light soft on her face. Caleb sat cross-legged on the rug, a tablet on his knees, fingers tapping some blocky game. The TV was off. That alone told me they'd been waiting.

"Dad?" Abby asked. "Was that rig death your call?"

She said it like there were a dozen rig deaths to pick from. In the Basin, some weeks it felt that way.

"Yeah," I said. "It came over our scanner."

"Everybody at school's talking about it," she said, pushing her hair behind one ear. "Well, not everybody. But group chats." Her thumb twisted her phone case back and forth. "Somebody already posted the scanner audio with a picture from the paper."

Caleb glanced up, watched my face, then looked down again fast.

My legs felt heavier than they should as I walked in and sat on the edge of the couch. The furnace pushed warmth from the vent beneath me.

"What are they saying?" I asked.

"That he was drunk," she said flat. "Someone commented 'Another drunk roughneck' with, like, a laughing emoji. Under the link. Rosa's not even... I mean, his wife, " She stopped, jaw tight. "They don't even know him."

Eve wiped a dish in the doorway, pretending she wasn't listening. The towel went still in her hands at the word drunk.

My hand went flat on my knee, then stilled. "Did the article say he was drunk?"

"No." Abby shook her head hard. "It just said 'cause under investigation.' But people fill in the rest. They always do."

The rig bar fights I'd broken up. The DUIs. The small-town stories we called out half-true and let stand because they fit. I didn't want my kids learning their moral math from those.

"Listen," I said. "I was out there. I didn't smell alcohol on him. His locker didn't have bottles lying around. I talked to the men he worked with. I don't have evidence he was drunk."

"So they're lying about him already," she said.

"Some people like tidy stories," I said. "Drunk, careless, not like us. Makes it easier to sleep."

"Yeah, well, that's trash," she snapped. Her eyes were bright. "If they say he was drunk and he wasn't, that's like, killing him twice, isn't it?"

"That's why we check," I said.

Caleb's fingers stopped tapping. "Is his family okay?" he asked, voice small.

"No," I said, honest. "Not right now. But people are taking them food and checking on them. We'll help where we can."

Abby looked at me over the rim of her phone. "Are you going to say he wasn't just some drunk? Like, in whatever paper thing you write?"

I looked at the muted scanner in the corner, lights flickering. My notebook sat warm against my chest.

"I'm going to look at everything," I said. "If there's proof he'd been drinking, it'll go in. If there isn't, that'll go in too. Nobody deserves a lie on their record just because it's convenient."

She studied me like she was weighing the words, not just hearing them.

"One of the comments," she said quietly, "said, 'Those guys know what they sign up for. Hazard pay. You can't blame the company every time.'"

I could almost hear Colton in that line, polished and polite, turned casual for online use.

"Companies make choices," I said. "So do the people who run them. Part of my job is figuring where those choices line up with what happened to Jared."

"Will the ward be mad?" Caleb asked. "If you make the company look bad?"

Out of the mouths of eleven-year-olds. I glanced at Eve. She kept drying, but the dish towel didn't move.

"Some people might be uncomfortable," I said. "Some might be grateful. Mostly, folks will be busy with their own lives. Either way, I answer to the law first. And to God, far as I understand Him. Not to any one company."

Abby's mouth pressed thin. "And to us?" she asked.

The question cut deeper than she knew. Or maybe she knew exactly.

"And to you," I said. "Which is why I won't lie to you about what I see, even if it's messy."

She nodded once, then asked, "Did he have kids?"

"Yeah," I said. "Little ones."

Her gaze dropped. "Then everyone making jokes should have to look at them before they post," she muttered.

Amen, I thought.

From the kitchen, Eve said, "Abby, phone down in ten. Homework finished?"

"Mostly," Abby said.

"Mostly isn't finished," Eve answered.

Abby sighed. "I'll finish it." She started toward her room, then paused. "Dad?"

"Yeah?"

"You're not going to just say 'accident' because everyone wants you to, right?"

Her voice wasn't defiant. It was wary.

I pictured my fresh page. OPEN HOMICIDE? underlined twice.

"No," I said. "I'm not going to do that."

"Promise?" she asked.

"I promise I'll look at everything," I said. "And I won't let anybody rush me into a story that doesn't fit the facts. That's the best honest promise I can make."

She studied me a second longer, then seemed to accept it. "Okay." She turned, braid swaying, and disappeared down the hall.

Caleb kept staring at his screen without moving his fingers. "You going to be gone a lot?" he asked.

"Some," I said. "But I'll be home tonight. And tomorrow's church. I'm not disappearing."

He nodded, relief loosening his shoulders a fraction.

"Hey," I said. "If kids at school say stuff about this, and it feels off, you can always tell us. Okay?"

"Okay," he said. "I won't fight them. I'll just...tell you."

"That works," I said. I reached over and ruffled his hair once, then stopped before he could jerk away.

He didn't. Not this time.

Later, after they'd said prayers and brushed teeth and asked for water twice, I stood alone in the dark kitchen, looking out at the faint glow from town and the barely visible line of the river beyond. The scanner in the living room muttered about a traffic stop on Main. My notebook lay open on the counter where I'd set it down to grab a glass.

Under Jared's name, I wrote: Tell kids: he deserved better.

It was as much a note to myself as any report to come. Then I closed the cover, clicked off the last light, and went down the hall to bed with the weight of his name and my promises in my pocket.

Chapter 4

Paper Masks at the ER

The automatic doors sighed open on bleach-bright light and the stutter of monitor beeps. Hospital air hit me: disinfectant over tired coffee, that flat, recycled smell every ER carried. A toddler cried somewhere behind a curtain. A nurse at the desk wore a paper mask pulled down to sip from a Styrofoam cup.

Clara walked beside me, clipboard tucked under her arm, pen already clipped at the top. Her jaw worked like she was grinding through a list in her head.

"Let's start with intake," she said. "Then see if the doctor can spare five minutes."

"Dan Cho's on?" I asked.

She nodded toward the whiteboard behind the nurse station, where "Cho, Attending" sat in dry erase. "Lucky us. He doesn't fluff."

I stepped up to the counter. "Evening. Sheriff Kingston, Deputy Ray. We're here about the rig patient from earlier. Jared Pike."

The nurse's eyes went to my badge, then to the hallway behind us, like she was checking for cameras. "He's been transferred to the cooler already," she said. "Family's back in the room down there." She jerked her chin toward a short corridor. "Doctor's between patients. I'll page him."

"Appreciate it," I said.

We waited in the narrow space between chairs and hand sanitizer dispensers. The intercom called a code in another wing. Clara's pen tapped once on her clipboard, then stilled.

"You think Colton's already called admin?" she murmured.

"I'd bet a pan of funeral potatoes he has," I said. "Wants the paperwork to say 'fall from height.' Nothing more."

A curtain swished, and Dr. Cho stepped out from a bay, glasses sliding down his nose. His scrub top was patterned with tiny mountains, probably a gift from some nurse with a sense of humor. He looked tired, but his eyes stayed sharp.

"Sheriff. Deputy." He tugged his mask down. "Busy day on the pad."

"That's one way to put it," I said. "We just need a few minutes. Injury pattern, any labs you ran. Before company and OSHA start rewriting adjectives."

His mouth twitched. "Come on," he said. "We'll talk by the charting station."

He led us to a small alcove with a computer and a rolling stool. Monitor beeps from nearby beds made an irregular rhythm, like a nervous drummer. He pulled up Jared's file, eyes tracking lines faster than mine could follow.

"Male, late twenties," he said. "Impaled on structural beam. EMS note: pulseless at scene, CPR in progress en route." He scrolled. "We confirmed asystole here. No surprise."

"I'm more interested in before the beam," I said.

He nodded. "That's what I was thinking when I saw him."

He clicked into a different tab. "Penetrating trauma through torso, obviously. Massive internal bleeding. Also some things that don't line up clean with a conscious fall."

Clara leaned in a fraction. "Such as?"

"Bruising," he said. "Here." He pointed to a human outline, where he'd marked small circles. "Faint contusions around the neck, mostly posterior. One behind the right ear. Not the kind you get from flailing into a rail. More like compression."

"Choking?" I asked.

He shook his head slightly. "Could be from a hand, could be from something like a strap. I'm not the ME. But the distribution made me note it. Pupils were slightly unequal as well."

"Could the beam impact do that?" Clara asked.

"Some of it," he said. "But the timing..." He glanced up at us. "He came in with his jaw slack, tongue back, no sign of recent struggle. If he'd been awake and fighting when he went on, you'd expect more obvious defensive abrasions on arms, hands, face."

"What did you see?" I asked.

He tapped the screen. "Minimal scrapes on forearms. Scattered. More grease and dirt than torn skin. Clothes were intact except where we cut. No classic pattern of a man clawing at something as he falls."

Memory flashed of Jared hanging there, arms at odd angles, fingers loose.

I wrote in my small notebook: NECK BRUISING, BEHIND EAR. UNEQUAL PUPILS. DEFENSIVE MARKS MINIMAL.

"Bottom line?" I said. "If this was your brother, would you be okay calling it just a fall?"

He slid his glasses off and cleaned them on his sleeve, a stall to think. Shoes squeaked on polished floor as a tech pushed a cart past.

"If it was my brother," he said finally, "I'd want more pictures. I'll note 'possible pre-impact loss of consciousness' in my chart and flag it for the ME. That buys you room."

Room. Space between "tragic accident" and the truth.

"And toxicology?" Clara asked.

"Labs are drawn," he said. "Standard panel. State lab will take a while. Preliminary alcohol screen on serum here's not screaming high, but that's not definitive given blood loss. Don't quote me on levels yet."

"Fair enough," I said. "You know the company's narrative machine better than most. You comfortable with us quoting your 'possible pre-impact loss of consciousness' in an affidavit if we need it?"

He let out a breath. "Quote the chart," he said. "Not my name without paperwork. I have a mortgage too."

"I understand. Chart it is."

At the far end of the hallway, a man in a button-down and fleece vest sat on a plastic chair, phone in hand, leg bouncing. Clean, neutral look, like corporate people wore when they wanted to pass for locals. I didn't need a badge to know he was here on company business.

"Doctor," I said quietly. "Anybody from the rig company talk to you yet?"

"Admin asked for a summary earlier," he said, voice low. "Donor relations. I told them the same. 'Fall from height, injuries inconsistent with simple misstep.'" His lips thinned. "We have a faith-based hospital board and a budget. You know how that goes."

"I do," I said.

He clicked out of the chart. "The body's in the cooler. Belongings are bagged. Clothing's messy but intact enough for you to document. Harness fragments are with him. I made sure they didn't toss anything. Nurse Henson has the form."

He stood. "I've got to get back. But Sheriff? Don't let them talk you out of looking too close. I see enough 'accidents' that aren't."

"Appreciate it," I said.

He walked away, shoes squeaking, curtain swishing behind him. A monitor alarm chirped and then went quiet.

Clara let out a slow breath. "Neck bruising, behind ear, LOC," she said under her breath, ticking off on her fingers.

"Struck before he went over, or somebody held something around his throat," I said. "Either way, not a guy who just tripped."

"Pushes us into homicide territory," she said.

The word felt heavy but right. I thought of my fresh page at the kitchen table. OPEN HOMICIDE? The underlines looked thin now.

We signed the form at the nurse station and followed a tech through double doors to a colder corridor. Fluorescent lights hummed overhead. The air here smelled sharper, like metal and chemical fixative. A stainless-steel elevator door waited at the end, closed.

The tech, a young guy with tattoos peeking from his sleeves, rolled a covered gurney toward us from a side room. The sheet over Jared's body lifted once in the circulation.

"We're moving him down to the cooler," he said. "You can tag along now or meet him downstairs."

"We'll walk a bit," I said.

As he passed, the outline of a man under the sheet tightened my stomach. No beam now, no flares, just the plain shape of somebody who should've still been walking on his own.

I slid the chart copy with Dr. Cho's "possible pre-impact LOC" notation into my folder. The paper felt heavier than its size.

"Who's handling the ME work?" Clara asked.

"State pathologist in Vernal," I said. "We'll ask for extra photos of the neck and tissue samples. That'll slow release to the family."

"Rosa won't like that," Clara said.

"No," I said. "But I'd rather ask her to wait an extra day than tell her later we let them bury what we needed."

The elevator dinged as the tech hit the button. The doors slid open, bright light spilling from the car.

"Family room's this way," the nurse from the desk called from behind us. "Mrs. Pike's in there. Relief Society's on deck."

"I'll talk to Rosa first," I said. "Then you and I can go argue with the ME about angles."

Clara nodded. "I'll stay quiet unless you need me to prod."

We watched the gurney roll into the elevator, the sheet shivering once in the air. The doors shut with a soft thud. The hum of the hospital filled the space he left.

I turned toward the short hallway with the "Family Room" sign and the low TV sound leaking under the door. Time to trade charts and bruises for grief and questions nobody wanted asked, and to tell a widow, as carefully as I could, that I didn't think her husband just slipped.

As we walked, I slid my notebook from my pocket and, between steps, wrote one more line under Jared's name:

NOT JUST A FALL.

Chapter 5

The Widow's Dim Front Room

Eve and I parked half up on the snow-crusted curb. The little rental sagged under gray sky, the chain-link fence leaning toward the road. Through the front window a TV glowed, cartoon colors washing the curtains.

Rosa opened the door with a toddler on her hip. Another kid clung to her leg. Cold air and laundry detergent slipped out around them.

"Sheriff," she said, voice hitching once. "Come in. It's a mess."

"It looks like home," Eve said, stepping past me. "I brought muffins. You don't have to pretend to host anyone tonight."

That got the faintest smile. She set the toddler down; he toddled to the TV. On the cheap coffee table in front of the sagging couch sat one neat thing: a manila envelope with a ballpoint pen laid on top. Everything else, magazines, crayons, socks, had drifted sideways around it, like the room knew not to touch.

We took the couch across from Rosa's armchair. The furnace kicked on beneath the floor, metal clanking. From a back bedroom, cartoons played at low volume, enough to keep her kids from climbing the furniture.

"I'm sorry to bother you again," I said. "I promised at the hospital I'd come when things were...less fresh."

"They're not less." She folded and unfolded a tissue. "Just quieter."

Eve sat to my left, close enough that her wool coat brushed my sleeve. She didn't say anything, just watched Rosa like she'd watched our kids after fevers, reading the little flinches, how her breath caught.

"I need to ask some follow-up questions," I said. "Nothing fancy. Just trying to understand what Jared was dealing with. You can tell me to stop anytime. All right?"

She nodded. One of her boys wandered in, climbed up beside her, and hooked an arm through hers without looking at us. His eyes went straight to the muted TV.

"He was careful," she said, before I could ask anything. "I know I already said that. He checked ladders twice. Wouldn't even stand on a chair to change a bulb."

"I wrote that down." I tapped my notebook. "Tell me about the last few weeks. Before that night. When did his worry change?"

Her gaze went toward the kitchen doorway, then to Eve, weighing whether talking counted as disloyalty.

"After Christmas," she said. "They started pushing a new schedule. More nights. He'd come home saying, 'They want the numbers to look pretty for some chart.' He'd take his boots off at the door and just...sit. Didn't even turn the TV on."

I let the picture settle. "He ever say names with that? Supervisors, safety people?"

"Hank," she said. "He drank with Hank sometimes. Said Hank was in a hole with money but 'had a good heart.' Wake up at three a.m. and hear him muttering Hank's name like a cuss." Her mouth twitched. "Wade too. He didn't trust Wade's temper."

She smoothed her boy's hair, then her fingers drifted to the envelope. She traced the flap without looking.

"And the safety man?" I asked. "Colton?"

She flinched at that one. "The company one? He was always 'Mr. Reese' when Jared talked. Like you say 'Brother' for church. He came out once, walked around with a clipboard. Jared said he could see him doing math in his head about which ladder was cheaper to replace."

The furnace cycled off. In the stillness, faint road noise through the single-pane windows seemed louder.

"Back at the hospital," I said, "you mentioned a blessing from Bishop Cade."

Her hand dropped to her lap. She twisted her wedding ring.

"Yeah."

"If you still feel up to it," I said, "I'd like the words as close as you remember. You said he was scared of what 'they'd do if he talked.' I don't want to put words in your mouth."

Her eyes filled, but her voice stayed level.

"He went in there white as a sheet," she said. "Told the bishop he'd been writing stuff down about the rig. About the ladder, and a near fall. Said he was thinking of calling some number he'd seen on a poster. OSHA?" She worked around the letters.

"That's right."

"He asked for a blessing. Bishop put his hands on his head and told him..." Her gaze dropped to her lap. "Told him the Lord loved him. That fear wasn't from God. Then he said Jared should 'trust the brethren and keep things in the family.'"

I wrote it out slow: trust the brethren and keep it in the family.

"Those words?" I asked. "Pretty close?"

"Those words." She blinked hard. "Jared was different after. Like it twisted him. He kept saying, 'Which family?'"

Eve's sleeve hem slipped between her fingers; she straightened it, then let it go.

"Which family?" I said.

"Church family, company family, us." Rosa's laugh came out flat. "He'd point at the kids, then at his hard hat, then up at the chapel ceiling on Sundays and say, 'Somebody needs to pick.'"

The boy beside her shifted, pressing his face into her side when I said "rig."

"He ever show you what he wrote down?" I asked.

She shook her head. "Said it made me safer if I didn't see. But he kept that little notebook in his coat, the blue one. Wrote in it after the kids went to sleep. I'd hear the pen scratching while the TV was on." Her eyes went to the wall, like she could still hear it through plaster.

I thought of the half-torn page in my pocket back at the office, numbers lined up in careful hand, the word bonus next to Colton's name. Jared Pike hadn't been a drunk stumbling over a rail; he'd been a man building his own paper lifeline.

"Rosa," Eve said softly, "can I ask something?" She waited until Rosa nodded. "When you say 'brethren', did Bishop Cade mean church leaders, or did Jared hear it as company too?"

Rosa hesitated. "He said 'brethren' like from conference," she answered finally. "But Jared said after, 'They're all brethren. All those men sit on the same front pew.' He meant Cade, Joel, that safety man when he visits. Said they played on the same team."

I wrote Joel's name in my notebook margin. Assessor. Bishopric. Land board. Too many hats.

"The envelope," I said, nodding toward the coffee table. "Do you mind me asking about that?"

Her hand went back to it like a magnet. Fingers traced the edge of the seal.

"Came yesterday," she said. "A man from the company knocked right during dinner. Kids still had spaghetti on their faces. He had a jacket with the logo, not the hard hat. Smiled like he was bringing cookies."

"What did he say?" I kept my voice level.

"He said, 'We're so sorry for your loss, Sister Pike.' Like church, but with that badge." She nodded at my belt, then looked away. "Said the company wanted to 'help with the funeral and ease the burden' so I wouldn't 'have to worry about outside things.'"

"Outside things," I repeated.

"Lawyers." She swallowed. "He set this on the table and said there was a 'generous offer inside' so long as I didn't 'make trouble' or 'get outside folks involved.' Then he patted my oldest on the head and said his name wrong and left."

Cartoon laughter from the back room swelled, then dropped. My pen dug too hard into the paper; I eased up.

"You've opened it?" I asked.

"No." Her fingers tightened on the envelope. "I keep thinking if I open it, I've already said yes to something."

Eve shifted forward. "Has anyone from the ward talked about it?" she asked. "Bishop, Relief Society?"

"Bishop called this morning," Rosa said, gaze fixed on the envelope. "Said the brethren at the company were 'doing their best' and that it might be 'an answer to prayer' if it let me stay home with the boys."

Her jaw ticked on the word brethren.

"If the bishop says to keep it in the family," she whispered, "and the man from the company says the same, what family am I supposed to pick?"

That went straight through me.

"The law's job," I said, "is to find out what really happened. My job. Jared died on a work site in this county. That makes it our family business too. If he trusted you with what scared him, I need that same trust, at least long enough to look at everything."

She looked up then, eyes searching my face for the years I'd spent smoothing things over.

"And God?" she asked. "Because that's who I asked when I couldn't breathe at the hospital. 'What do You want me to say?'"

Eve answered before I could.

"God doesn't ask widows to lie for anybody," she said. Her voice stayed mild, but the words landed like a dropped wrench. "Not for companies. Not for bishops. Not for sheriffs, either."

Rosa's shoulders eased a fraction. She let out a breath that had been held since the ER.

"What do you need from me?" she asked.

"Right now?" I said. "Mostly your story, which you've given me. And your word that if someone hands you paper to sign, you'll let me or Eve or Marie down at the school look at it before you do. Even if they say it has to be right then."

She nodded slowly. "I can do that."

"And," I added, "I'd like permission to look through Jared's things at his trailer. I want to find that notebook, other notes, pay stubs. Anything that explains why he was scared. Nothing leaves my hands without a log; you can ask Clara about that if you want a second opinion."

She glanced toward the kitchen, toward a sink where dishes waited from some earlier attempt at order. "Kids need a diaper," she muttered, half to herself, and stood. "Give me a minute."

She disappeared down the hall. The leaky kitchen faucet dripped in the quiet.

I rubbed my thumb across Ben Latham's watch face. Her words lined up with Dr. Cho's bruising, with the latch marks on the rail, with that half-page of numbers. Trust the brethren and keep it in the family. Bonus, Colton. Generous offer if you don't make trouble.

"You okay?" Eve asked.

"I'm thinking," I said. "And trying not to tear that envelope in half myself."

"You can't be the one to do it," she said. "But you can make sure she's not opening it blind."

The faucet stopped. Rosa came back wiping her hands on a dish towel, shoulders set.

"You wanted to ask about the trailer," she said.

"I don't want to strip Jared's life for parts," I said. We stood near the front door now, kids in the back room wrestling over the remote. The fridge in the little kitchen kicked on with a soft buzz that filled the space between words.

"I know how this can feel, right after," I went on. "Like strangers hauling away what's left. I've screwed that up before."

Memory flashed: a different living room, a smashed picture frame on the floor, a mother sobbing while deputies boxed her son's things without asking. Ben's hand on my shoulder later in the truck, heavy as a verdict. We never went back there. She never answered our calls.

"I can't do this case right without seeing his notes," I said. "But it needs to be with your say-so, not just because I have a badge and a warrant form."

Rosa twisted the towel so tight it squeaked.

"What are you looking for?" she asked.

"Anything he wrote about the rig," I said. "Ladders, latches, near falls, guys giving him a hard time. Copies of logs he thought might disappear. Sometimes men like Jared write down more than they say out loud. If we find that, it helps prove he wasn't drunk or showing off. It shows he was trying to fix something."

"And if you don't find anything?" Her eyes narrowed, like she'd seen that outcome before from other men in uniforms.

"Then I still put in my report that you told me he kept a notebook," I said. "And I keep working the other pieces. This doesn't rise or fall on one scrap of paper."

She looked at Eve instead of me. "What happens if I say no?"

"Legally?" I said. "I'd have to go the long way around. Ask a judge, maybe fight the company about control of his personal effects. It would take time. Company lawyers are already moving. They'd like nothing better than for someone loyal to them to be the first one through that door."

"And for you?" she asked Eve.

Eve held her gaze. "If you say no, it just means you're not ready," she said. "We'll still help with food, rides, whatever. But if Jared wrote things down because he was scared, the only people who should decide what happens to that are you and the law, not a man with an envelope."

Rosa looked back at me. I waited, thumb resting on the cool metal of Ben's watch, keeping my face as plain as I could. I wasn't entitled to this. I'd already taken enough from her week.

She drew a breath that shook on the way in.

"If he wrote it down," she said, "he wanted somebody to see it. He wasn't the type to journal for fun." The corner of her mouth lifted, then fell. "Yes, Sheriff. You can look through his things."

"Can I write that?" I asked. "In my notes. Your permission. Date, time."

"Write it," she said. "Write that I said if he wrote it, it's because he was scared."

My pen moved: February, late afternoon, Rosa Pike states, "Yes, Sheriff, you can look through his things. If he wrote it, it's because he was scared."

"I'll have Deputy Ray with me," I said. "We'll photograph everything where we find it before we move it. If there's pushback from the park or the company, can we say you gave consent?"

"I'll call the trailer park manager," she said. "Told him if anybody messed with Jared's stuff before I decided, I'd change parks. He listened. He's got a nephew on that rig."

Eve let out the smallest breath of relief. Her shoulders dropped a notch.

"Thank you," I said. It felt thin compared to what she'd handed us, but it was what I had.

Outside, a car rolled past, tires hissing on wet pavement. The front door glass showed our reflections faint over the street: me in my county jacket, Eve in her coat, Rosa small between us, dish towel knotted in her hands.

"I'm not signing anything until somebody who isn't paid by the company or the church looks at it," she said suddenly. "Write that too."

I did. Verbatim.

"Rosa," I said, closing the notebook, "I can't promise you how this ends. But I can promise I'll treat whatever we find in that trailer like Jared speaking for himself. Not like junk to be swept up."

She nodded. "Just...don't let them say he was stupid." Her eyes shone. "He was scared. There's a difference."

"There is," I said.

Eve stepped forward and gave her a quick, solid hug. Rosa leaned into it, then pulled back, wiping at her face with the heel of her hand.

I opened the door. Cold air cut in, along with the distant sound of a semi on the highway. As we stepped onto the small concrete stoop, the porch light flicked on over our heads even though daylight still hung thin over the street. Inside, one of the kids un-muted the TV; canned laughter drifted out past Rosa as she hovered in the doorway, one hand on the knob, the other pressed flat on the envelope like she was pinning it to the table.

I tucked my notebook into my coat. Cade's phrasing and the company man's tidy script rode home with me, heavier than the badge at my hip.

Chapter 6

Notebook in the Thin Walls

The trailer park sat just off the man-camp lanes, rows of single-wides huddled under a sky the color of dirty ice. Our boots crunched over frozen gravel as Clara and I walked up to Jared's place. A neighbor's TV thumped through the thin walls of the next unit, laugh track cutting through generator hum.

The door stuck before it gave. When it swung open, a stale wave of old grease, coffee, and smoke rolled out into the cold.

"Time?" Clara asked, already pulling her phone from her pocket.

"Sixteen thirty-one," I said, checking my watch.

She snapped a picture of the doorframe, then one wide of the living room. Couch with sagging cushions, blanket thrown over one arm. Small table with a ring from a mug burned into the finish. Kids' drawings taped straight above the TV, stick people under a big yellow sun labeled DAD in a kid hand. A cartoon played next door, laugh track leaking through the shared wall.

"Entry at sixteen thirty-one hours," Clara murmured, scribbling on her clipboard. "Rosa Pike consent on file, plus warrant cover sheet for work-related effects."

I pulled on gloves. Linoleum creaked under my boots as I moved into the kitchen strip: sink full of dishes, a coffee maker with a stained carafe, a mug crusted on the rim. Nothing that smelled like liquor. Trash can half-full of takeout boxes and diaper packs, but no beer cans. No bottles under the sink, either, when I crouched to check.

"He didn't read like a man wasting out," I said.

"Neither did my last overdose," Clara answered. She was at the counter, snapping photos in a slow arc. "But yeah. This looks like stretched-thin, not spinning-out."

I nodded. We worked in a loose clockwise circle, staying out of each other's frames. I opened the cabinets one at a time: mismatched plates, cereal boxes, an extra tub of formula. Photo, close, then inventory line. The refrigerator hummed in the quiet, its motor cycling like a distant engine.

Down the narrow hall, the bedroom door stood halfway open. I palmed it with my glove and pushed.

The room didn't surprise me so much as confirm what Rosa had said. Bed unmade but not filthy. Two pillows. A kids' blanket crumpled at the foot, cartoon print worn at the edges. More drawings taped on the wall: a house with four stick figures, the tallest holding a square that might've been a book, might've been a notebook. A laminated saint card stuck in the mirror frame.

On the back of the bedroom door hung a coat. Canvas, faded blue, shoulders worn shiny. My eyes went straight to it.

"This yours," I called softly. Clara joined me in the doorway.

I photographed the coat in place, then the pockets, then the door hook. The floor under it was clear except for a pair of beat-up boots set heel to wall. Laces neatly tied. I bent, patted the coat down. Left pocket: crumpled receipts, burrito wrappers, a folded church program. Right pocket: smooth rectangle, stiff under cloth.

I eased it out enough for the camera, still in place.

"Item twelve," Clara said. "Document in right-hand coat pocket, bedroom door."

"Seventeen twenty-three hours," I added.

She snapped a close shot. I slid the folded page out fully and let it open in my gloved hands.

Half-torn notebook paper, ragged at the top where it had been ripped from a spiral. Lines of dates and dollar amounts in tidy ballpoint. February 3, 80. Feb 10, 60. Feb 24, 100. The sums didn't match any standard pay period. No regular check amounts, just these extra little bumps. Beside one mid-month line Jared had written in smaller letters: bonus, Colton.

The last two entries trailed off. March 2, 75. Next line: just a date, nothing after.

Clara leaned over my shoulder. "That's not on any stub we copied," she said quietly.

"No," I said. "But it will be on something with Colton's initials, or he's sloppier than he looks."

She nodded once and lifted her phone for another shot, catching my gloved fingers and the page.

"Item twelve, torn notebook page, right coat pocket by bedroom door, time seventeen twenty-three," she said for the audio on her own phone. "Subject: off-cycle payment list, includes entry 'bonus, Colton.'"

The neighbor's TV volume jumped for a second, cheering at some game show win, then dropped back down. Through the wall, a muffled voice cursed, followed by laughter.

I read the page again, slower. The handwriting was careful, numbers stacked dead straight. This wasn't a scratch pad. It felt like a ledger meant for one person's eyes.

"He tracked every side payment," I said. "Amounts, dates. No rounding. Rosa said he kept a little blue notebook. This is one of his copies. Insurance."

"Those are small numbers if you're buying a man's silence forever," Clara said.

"Small enough they stay off radar. Big enough to help with a broken truck or a medical bill." I thought of the envelope on Rosa's table. "When they stopped, he noticed. Right about the time Hal did that weld."

I flattened the page gently on the mattress and snapped a photo of it there, then one with my notebook open beside it, my pen underlining bonus, Colton in my own hand. My fingers stayed an extra second on the paper before I let Clara slide an evidence sleeve under it.

"Bag and tag," she said. She held the sleeve open while I tipped the page in. The plastic crackled. I sealed the flap and wrote along the edge: Jared Pike case, item twelve, torn page from pocket notebook, retrieved from coat in bedroom. Time and date. My initials. Her initials.

"This is where the company's lawyer says 'those were personal gifts, not pay,'" Clara said. "If we're lucky he'll say it in front of a recorder."

"He can call them birthday cards for all I care," I said. "Math on the ledger won't care what he calls it."

I sat on the edge of Jared's unmade bed. The mattress sagged under my weight. In my notebook, under Rosa's quote about fear, I wrote: Torn page w/ "bonus, Colton" in Jared's hand. Off-book "safety bonus" list?

I scanned the room. No porn stash. No pill bottles lying around uncapped. Top dresser drawer held socks rolled in pairs, work gloves, a folded picture of Rosa and the boys at some campground, fire ring in the background. Bottom drawer full of T-shirts and one neatly folded ward T-shirt from a service project.

"I keep waiting for the liquor or pills that make their story easy," I said.

"Companies like easy stories too," Clara replied from the doorway. Laughter from the next trailer bled through again. "We're not going to give them one."

We worked another twenty minutes. I logged the church program with Jared's name in the margin; Clara photographed a little spiral notepad by the microwave where he'd written grocery lists and, on one page, "OSHA number??" with a question mark. The DVD player on the floor held a disc in the tray: some kids' movie. Nothing with a horror label. This man's vice, if he had one, seemed to be cheap coffee and sore feet.

When we stepped back into the narrow living room, it felt smaller. The kids' drawings above the TV pulled my eye again. One showed a tall figure next to a square tower with little lines up the side, a child's version of a rig.

"Anything else you want to hit here now?" Clara asked.

I shook my head. "We've got what we came for. We'll tape the door and let the park manager know if anyone cuts it, I want a call."

Outside, the early dark was already coming on. Breath smoked from our mouths as we closed the door. Clara tore a strip of scene tape, stuck it over the jamb, and signed her initials across the seam.

"Man-camp canvas before we go back?" she asked.

"Quick passes," I said. "Nobody talks long out here after dark unless they've had too much or not enough. But the walls are thin. Sometimes that's enough."

By the time we hit the narrow lane between trailers, the generator drone had deepened. Porch lights flicked on in scattered units, puddling light onto mud and ice. A dog barked near the park entrance, then gave up and lay down again, from the sound of it.

I knocked at the first door on the row beside Jared's. No answer, though the blue flicker of a TV glowed behind drawn blinds. At the second, footsteps shuffled, then stopped. The peephole darkened.

"Sheriff's office," I said. "Just updating contact info for folks on this row. Not here to cause trouble."

A deadbolt turned halfway, then thought better of it. After a long beat, a man's voice came through the door.

"We already talked to company safety," he said. Accent from somewhere south of here, vowels rolled. "They said everything's handled."

"I'm not company safety," I said. "I can leave a card if you'd rather call later."

Silence. Then the door opened two inches, the chain still on. One eye, part of a cheek, and a hand gripping the edge.

"You the same sheriff from that morning?" he asked. "With the hat?"

"That's me." I stepped back so he didn't feel crowded. Clara hung a half-step farther, shoulders loose, pen already moving in her little notebook.

He glanced down the lane, then kept his visible shoulder behind the jamb.

"Can we keep this off the record?" he asked.

"I can listen without your name," I said. "If we need it later, we'll come ask. For now I just need to know what kind of man Jared was when folks weren't in ties and jackets."

A huff that might have been a laugh. Cigarette smoke drifted out through the crack.

"He was...quiet," the man said. "Did his job. Didn't drink much. Wrote all the time."

"Wrote?" I asked.

"Paper, man. That scratching." He lifted his free hand and mimed a pen. "I'm on the other side of that wall some nights; I hear it. Little TV, cartoons for the kids, and that scratch-scratch-scratch. Drove me nuts till I bought better headphones."

I pictured Jared at the tiny table, head bent, pen moving while some cartoon played in the background.

"Ever see what he wrote?" I asked.

The man hesitated. "Not...exact. One time, in the unit office, he had a log book open. Safety log. Ladder checks, near misses. He was copying stuff from it onto his own paper." He shrugged, the motion tugging the chain. "Said, 'Just in case the book falls in a puddle.'"

"Which book?" Clara asked, voice even. "Company log or his?"

"Company," the man said. "After one guy almost went down? Week before Jared?" He swallowed. "I was there. The ladder slipped, and he ended up dangling by his harness. Hank and another hand hauled him back. They wrote it in the log like 'minor incident.' Jared looked...sick. Said that ladder shouldn't have been up there at all."

"Did anyone fix it?" I asked.

He let out a breath through his nose. "Hal came, welded something, hammered on it a while. Boss man Wade was yelling about downtime. A week later, the same part breaks and Jared..." He didn't finish.

"Jared say anything about what if he disappeared?" I asked. "Anything like that?"

The man's hand tightened on the door edge. Knuckles went pale.

"He joked once," he said. "We were outside, smoking. He said, 'If I disappear, it wasn't the ladder.' Then he smiled like it was a dumb joke and went inside. Next week, the ladder eats him and now everybody says 'accident.' You tell me."

My thumb tapped the closed cover of my notebook, waiting for him to add Colton's name, but he didn't.

"You didn't hear that from me," he added quickly. "I got kids, man. They're not going to feed themselves if I get walked off for running my mouth."

"I'll write down that he was careful," I said. "And that someone was dangling from that ladder before he died. The rest stays between you and your conscience for now."

He snorted. "Conscience's been loud lately." The chain rattled as he eased the door shut a notch. "You get him some truth, Sheriff. He was a pain in the ass with those notes, but he didn't deserve that."

"We're working on it," I said.

The chain slid back. The door shut. Bolt turned.

Clara wrote the trailer number and time on her pad. Her pen moved fast, neat block letters that would look good blown up on a trial exhibit.

"Near fall, copied log, 'If I disappear, it wasn't the ladder,'" she murmured. "Unreported to OSHA, if the company's file dump wasn't a complete lie."

"Hal's weld receipt fits right between those dates," I said. "Jared watches a guy nearly die, writes it down, watches the weld, keeps writing, loses his 'bonus,' keeps writing, then ends up dead on the same structure."

"And the same phrase," she said. "'Better one bad fall than a full audit.' Hank half-spilled that in the parking lot. Somebody put that in their mouth."

Wind cut down the lane, carrying the smell of mud and diesel. A different trailer's blind slats clicked open behind us; I caught the glint of an eye watching, then the snap of plastic as it closed again. This place ran on rumor as much as on electricity.

We hit one more door. No answer, though movement rustled inside. At a third, a man opened with his jacket already on, keys in hand.

"Can't talk," he said. "Company said go through them."

"Door's open if you change your mind," I said, handing him a card. "You can call me from a pay phone in Vernal if that feels better."

He stared at the card, then at me. "You going to call my boss?"

"Not unless you want me to."

He slipped the card into his wallet. "We'll see," he said, and stepped past us into the cold.

Back at the truck, Clara slung her evidence bag into the back seat. The sleeve with Jared's torn page sat near the top, label bright under the dome light.

"You look like you dropped another rock on your own shoulders," she said, opening the passenger door.

"I'm just redrawing the picture," I said. "It's not Hank swinging a wrench in a blind rage anymore. It's a near fall, a weld, a hush-bonus that dries up, a man who won't stop writing, and a system that can't allow that notebook to exist."

"And 'bonus, Colton' sitting in your lap," she said.

"And that," I agreed.

We climbed in. The truck engine rumbled to life. As we turned out of the lane, the trailers slid past our windows, narrow boxes of yellow light and shadow. Somewhere inside them, men were doing their own math: kids' plates, rig schedules, rent, what a sheriff's card was worth against a supervisor's glare.

At the end of the gravel, the camp opened onto the county road. I eased onto the pavement and headed toward town, toward our little office with its burnt coffee and humming scanner.

The folded page and Rosa's words lay side by side in my mind, sharper than any photograph. I had her consent on paper, Jared's hand in ink, and one company man's name binding them together. It wasn't enough yet for a charge. But it was a line I could pull.

I touched Ben Latham's watch once, out of habit, and drove on.

Chapter 7

Coffee Steam on the Square

My coffee cup left a wet ring on the laminated menu. I slid it aside so my notebook could lie flat between me and Clara. The plate-glass window beside us showed Main in winter gray, a pickup idling at the curb, exhaust drifting up into the low sky. Inside, the grill popped and hissed, silverware clinked, somebody laughed too loud at the counter.

"Remind me why this counts as a day off," Clara said. She had the case file half-open, photos paper-clipped to reports.

"Eggs," I said. "Eggs make it a day off."

She snorted and pulled the notebook-page copy toward her. The one from Jared's coat pocket, the half-torn sheet with dates and dollar amounts, "bonus, Colton" written once in his careful hand.

I'd been trying to run a straight line through the last month. Near-fall, Jared's fear, the night on the catwalk, the way his body hit steel. Wade's story, Hank's, Rosa's. Nothing sat flat yet.

"All right," I said. "Timeline, not feelings. We start with the near-fall." I pointed my pen at a blank spot on my own notes. "Roustabout says a man dangled. No report filed. That's week one."

Clara tapped her phone screen, lips moving as she counted. "Weather that week: ice, wind advisory. That should be half a dozen line items in the incident log, minimum. They've got zero."

"Zero," I said. The waitress came by with the coffee pot; her nametag said MANDY in fading Sharpie. She refilled us, smile tight at the corners.

"How's it looking out there, Sheriff?" she asked.

"Cold," I said. "Same as ever."

She nodded but searched my face for more. When I didn't bite, she moved on, pot sloshing.

"They're all waiting to know if they still get to call it an accident," Clara murmured.

"I'm waiting to know that too," I said.

She pulled the payroll ledger photocopies closer, laid them beside Jared's page. "Okay. Look. Week of the near-fall." Her pen tapped a column. "Incident log: nothing. Ledger: no overtime bumps, no hazard pay. But here, " she moved her finger down ", off-cycle 'safety bonus' for Jared. Seventy-five dollars. Initialed C.R."

We'd seen a few of those oddball entries already. I'd half-written "hazard?" and "Christmas?" in the margins and left it.

"Next week," Clara said. "Bad weather again, according to the pad foreman's general log. They note icing on the stairs, mechanical delays. Incident log should spike. Doesn't. Another 'bonus' for Jared and two other names. C.R. again."

"Colton," I said.

She nodded. "Week after that, similar pattern. Crap conditions, clean incident log, off-cycle trickles." She flipped Jared's page so the numbers faced me. The graphite was smudged along the edges where he'd run his thumb. "He matched them. Date to date. You see it?"

Jared's neat hand: 1/6, 75, 1/13, 50. A few more down the line, then a blank space where the tear cut off the sheet.

"They stop here," she said. "Ledger stops too. No more bonuses for him after that."

The grill sizzled loud for a moment. Somebody called an order. Coffee smell curled up, cut through the grease.

"If I wanted my safety stats to look pretty without fixing anything," she said, "this is how I'd do it. Pay certain guys a little on the side to keep their mouths shut and not write every close call. Pick the ones who are detailed enough to notice things but need the money."

"Then cut off the ones who stop playing along," I said.

We stared at "bonus, Colton" until the letters blurred.

I saw that roustabout in the trailer park, eye at the crack of his door. Jared scratching late, copying log pages after a near-fall. The way he'd joked, if I disappear, it wasn't the ladder. My fingers kept time on the rim of my cup without meaning to.

"Somebody had to approve both piles of paper," I said. "Safety bonuses and incident logs. Same hands."

"Colton," Clara said. She twirled her pen once, then planted it hard against the ledger. "He signs off on crew training and on the log summaries. He recommends who gets what little pat-on-the-head check."

"Wade runs a sloppy site, Hank drinks too much," I said. "Easy to see them as the problem because they smell like it." My gaze stayed on Colton's name. "But this, here. That's clean hands on dirty numbers."

Forks scraped plates. The radio above the pie case hummed a soft country song about trucks and roads and leaving. Two roughnecks at the counter, boots muddy, shoulders hunched, went quiet when my voice carried a little too far.

I lowered it. "We can't say out loud that he's buying under-reporting. Not yet."

"Not yet," she agreed. "We can say we've got unexplained off-cycle payments and blank incident weeks during weather that should produce slips."

"Judge will ask why we care," I said. "Why it matters for a fall that maybe was just that."

"Because a pattern of lying about small injuries makes it more likely they'd lie about a big one." She shrugged. "It's not complicated."

It wasn't, and it was. Colton had sat across from me in that prefab office with his neat charts and his company mug, talking about family companies and stewardship. Same words Rosa had heard over Jared's bowed head in her front room, only dressed up.

"How many guys like Jared took the money and quit writing?" I asked.

"Enough that this shows up in the ledger," she said. "And enough that they thought they could stop his without him making trouble."

I pictured Rosa at her kitchen table, the torn envelope from the company. "They still think they can buy her quiet," I said.

"Maybe they can," Clara said. "Our job's to make sure we're not part of that deal."

The bell over the door jingled. A blast of cold air swept through. Hal Briggs stomped in, smelling of exhaust and shop heat, coffee-to-go already in his hand.

He spotted us, grinned, touched the brim of his cap with two fingers. "Sheriff," he said. "Deputy. You two live here now?"

"Cheaper than rent," I said.

He laughed and ambled closer. "You got room in your glamorous murder booth for a simple mechanic, or is that privileged territory?"

"Depends whether you're bringing receipts," Clara said under her breath.

I shut the file so case photos weren't staring up at him like a menu.

"Pull up a slice of vinyl, Hal," I said. "Tell me how my truck's doing."

Hal slid into the booth, bench groaning under his weight and his coveralls. Grease clung to the fabric, motor oil and cold air wrapped around him like a second jacket.

"Your truck's old but honest," he said. "Like some people I know. Brakes'll hold another season unless you plan on chasing folks up Diamond."

"I'll pencil that into the murder calendar," I said.

He laughed, let his gaze travel the room out of habit. His eyes skimmed the counter guys, Mandy at the coffee pots, a pair of women from the clerk's office splitting a cinnamon roll. When his gaze brushed my open notebook, he shifted his cup to block it.

"Busy week," he said. "Heard you been out at the site more than the crew."

"Lot of ladders out there," I said. "Hard to keep track."

"Yeah." He tugged at the bill of his cap. "Ladders."

Clara eased back, crossing her arms, letting me steer. That was our dance: I played dumb, she watched for flinches.

"You keeping busy yourself?" I asked. "Rig traffic slowing down any?"

"Enough to make me check numbers twice," he said. "Company's fussier about line items lately. Don't like seeing the word 'derrick' on an invoice if it ain't for a whole new one." He smirked. "They like 'miscellaneous structure' a lot better."

"Easier on the auditors," Clara said.

Hal's eyes flicked to her, then back to me. "Easier on whoever's got to sign the check, yeah."

A spatula scraped the griddle behind us. The low murmur in the room shifted when he said "derrick." Men heard words sideways.

"Speaking of miscellaneous structure," I said, "you do any work for Wade this month?"

"Define 'work,'" he said, but his hand went to the back of his neck under the cap. "He keeps my lights on, same as most of the pad boys."

"Specifically," Clara said, "any welds that didn't make the official maintenance list."

He took a sip of coffee, eyes going to the window like he might find an answer in the steamed glass. All he'd find was our reflection, blurred, the sheriff, the deputy, the mechanic in between.

"Now that you mention it," he said, voice dropping half a notch, "he did bring in a rung. Piece of one, anyway. Week or two before... you know."

He didn't say Jared's name. A lot of people didn't.

"Rung off which rig?" I asked, though we both knew.

"Roosevelt," he said. "Could smell it. Catwalk metal, not some backyard deer stand. Said it needed a quick zap. Didn't want to shut anything down long enough for paperwork."

His hand worked at the back of his neck again when he said it. My pen moved on its own.

"Quick zap," Clara repeated. "Did he say why it needed it? Crack? Rust?"

Hal rolled his cup between his hands. "Looked like stress at the weld where it meets the upright. Not snapped clean, more like somebody'd been bouncing on it. You know how those boys are."

"Those boys," I said. "Not you, of course."

He grinned. "I'm old. I use stairs."

"Date?" Clara asked, like people always kept that floating around in their heads.

"Mm." He frowned at the far wall. "Two Fridays before the fall, I think. Could dig the slip if you're bored one afternoon. I wrote it up as 'ladder component weld' or something bland so company wouldn't throw a fit."

"Receipt would be real boring reading," I said. "My favorite."

Hal's eyes swept the diner again. "Look. I don't want trouble with Wade. He pays his bills, mostly. But that rung... it was from up high. Could tell by the paint wear. Not bottom ladder."

"Same general area Jared went over," I said.

He didn't confirm, didn't need to.

"You see any of that rung still out there?" Clara asked. "Or did you send it back shiny and never think about it again?"

"Did my weld, ground it, sent it back," he said. "He picked it up himself. I figured they'd bolt it in, run a man up, call it good. Didn't think about it until I heard the scanner that night."

He looked at me when he said scanner. We'd both been on that channel long enough to hear the same tones, the same flat voices naming the pad.

"Company ask you about it after?" I asked.

"Nope," he said. "Figures. They don't like admitting their steel ever needs help." He lifted his cup, drained the last. "Like I said, I can dig the slip. Got it in the box with the rest of the month. If the accountant hasn't turned it into mulch yet."

"I'll take you up on that boredom cure," I said, letting weight ride on the words.

He heard it. His jaw tightened, then eased. "All right. Swing by the shop later this week. I'll have it pulled."

His gaze dropped to my notebook, to where I'd already written: Hal, weld on derrick rung, get receipt. His eyes moved over the date I'd jotted from memory, then he looked up and, for once, didn't joke.

"You gonna make that stick?" he asked quietly. "Whatever you're chasing out there?"

Rosa saying murder in her dim front room. Eve's question over dishes: peace or truth. Bishop Cade's hand on my elbow in hospital corridors.

"I'm going to figure out what happened," I said. "If it sticks, that's up to judges and juries."

He nodded like that answer hurt but fit. Then he rapped the edge of the table with his knuckles, light but final. "Well. Got brakes to bleed and transmissions to curse at. Don't let your eggs get cold, Sheriff."

He stood, tugged his cap down, and threaded back through the maze of tables. The bell over the door jingled as he stepped out. Through the fogged glass I watched him cross Main toward his shop, boots crunching on crusted snow.

Clara blew out a breath. "He offered that on his own," she said. "That tells me he's picked a side."

"Or two," I said. "Truth and staying in business. Hard combo."

I turned to a fresh page and wrote the line that had been circling my head since we sat down: bonuses lining up with blank logs. Under that, another arrow: Hal, rung weld, two weeks prior, contradicts Wade.

Beside Colton's name, I added: incident log approvals.

When we finally stood to pay, the window glass showed our shapes faintly in the steam: two tired figures under the neon OPEN sign. At the counter, the rig hands who'd fallen silent earlier bent over their plates again, backs rounded like they were riding out weather.

As I folded the checkered, pen-marked page and slid it into my pocket, the air from the door leaked cold along my neck. Curiosity, concern, warning, it all felt the same on skin.

Out on the square, the courthouse sat across the street, brick and windows catching what little light the sky offered. A place where words like accident and homicide turned into lines on paper, into charges and records.

We stepped into the chill.

"Two names circled," Clara said, flipping her collar up against her throat. "Wade and Colton."

"And a town full of people who'd rather I leave both alone," I said.

She glanced back at the diner. "That's not new."

"No," I said. "But the pattern is."

I thumbed Ben Latham's watch bracelet under my cuff and started toward the office, the taste of coffee and grease still in my mouth, the weld receipt already taking shape in my mind as the next solid thing to chase.

Chapter 8

Ward Voices in the Hall

We filed into the cultural hall like it was any other Sunday, even though it wasn't Sunday and the basketball hoops were folded into the ceiling. Metal chairs stood in neat rows on the glossy gym floor. The casket at the front looked smaller than it had in the ER, dwarfed by a podium and a microphone cord snaking across the stage.

Fluorescent lights buzzed overhead. The air smelled like casseroles waiting in the kitchen and floor polish. Abby and Caleb slipped ahead to sit with the youth; Eve and I took our usual row, third back on the right, close enough to see faces, far enough not to feel like we were on display. People nodded as we passed. Some held my eye. Some didn't.

The counselor conducting wore his best suit and his public voice. He talked about sorrow and comfort, about how Jared's "tragic accident" had shaken everyone. He used the word accident three times in as many minutes.

Beside me, Eve's fingers tightened around the folded program in her lap. The paper creased in on itself.

I let my gaze travel, not all the way around, too obvious, but enough to mark who'd come. Wade sat with his wife along the side, kids lined up in miniature dress clothes, his jaw set. Hank wasn't there. Company men filled a whole row, identical ties, faces solemn. Bishop Cade sat on the stand, hands folded, expression carved from the same wood as the podium.

Every time the counselor said "accident," I pictured the latch. Tool marks bright against dull metal. The replacement harness still bagged in the locker. Jared's body at an angle that didn't fit the story.

Hymns came and went. Hymnals thudded closed soft as people sat. Children rustled and were shushed. I only sang when the melody was one my mouth knew too well not to.

Rosa walked to the pulpit halfway through. She looked smaller in that big room than she had in her rented front room. Black skirt, borrowed maybe, blouse that had seen better days. Her hand clamped the edge of the podium; from where I sat her knuckles went white.

"My husband wasn't careless," she said. The microphone gave a little echo, sent her voice up into the rafters and back down. "He told me he was scared about something at work. I just... I just want the truth."

Her voice cracked on truth, but the word still landed heavy.

Silence followed. Not the rustle kind. The gym floor creaked as somebody shifted their weight. From the kitchen came the clink of a dish, fast, like someone had forgotten they were in earshot.

Then the counselor stepped forward, smile gentle, hand hovering near her back without touching. "We may not understand why the Lord calls some home," he said smoothly, "but we can trust His timing and those He has placed to watch over us."

Trust those placed over us. I'd heard that string already, in Rosa's front room, under Bishop Cade's hands.

Eve's grip on the program tightened until the edge dug into her palm. Later I'd see the faint line it left. For now, her face stayed composed, eyes on the stand. From the corner of my vision Abby looked back at me, eyebrows pulled in. A question there I didn't have room to answer.

My brain tried to do two jobs at once. One, sheriff: who sits where, who wipes tears, who doesn't. Two, member: sing, bow head, fit into the pattern I'd known since I was Jared's age.

The counselor called on a company man to speak. He talked about Jared as a "valued member of our safety family," about how the firm had a "long record of looking after our people." He used words like thorough investigation and standard protocols. He didn't mention welds or logs or bonuses. A company can say a lot without touching the facts.

When he stepped down, Bishop Cade rose. He spoke softly, as he always did, about trust and trials. About how this "accident" was a test of our willingness to rely on the Lord and on those called to lead in hard times.

He never said my name. He didn't have to. Every time he said lead, his gaze skimmed the congregation and paused on me for half a breath.

I thought of Eve's question over the sink, water running, plates in our hands: If it was our name on those papers, would you keep the peace or tell the truth?

The closing hymn started, another familiar tune. Voices rose and fell. I mouthed words my heart wasn't sure about anymore. When it ended, chairs scraped back all at once, a ragged chorus on the gym floor. People surged toward the aisles, toward Rosa, toward the casseroles.

I stayed seated a moment, watching. Relief Society sisters circled Rosa by the casket, arms out, tissues already in hand. They knew exactly how to do that part; they'd done it for car wrecks and cancers and crib deaths. This case fit their muscle memory as long as the word accident stayed nailed in place.

Over their shoulders, Bishop Cade stepped down from the stand and moved toward the side door. His pulpit face melted into something more watchful. He looked like a man going to put out a small fire before it reached the curtains.

Eve touched my arm. "I'm going to go hug her," she whispered, nodding toward Rosa.

"I'll be by the coats," I said.

She slipped away, quiet but decisive, weaving through the crowd until she vanished into that knot of women at the front.

I walked the other direction, toward the hallway and the coat racks. The noise followed, voices, kids, the high ring of a metal chair hitting tile. Behind the kitchen door, casserole dishes clinked as they were lined up on long tables.

The hallway felt narrower than usual. Bulletin boards along the wall held flyers for youth temple trips, canning nights, genealogy classes. Under the glass, a photo of Jared grinned from a ward picnic shot, paper plate loaded with food, kids climbing on a jungle gym behind him. They'd pinned it there for the funeral, probably. Or maybe it had been there already. I couldn't remember.

I stood by the coat rack, my back against a layer of Scout announcements and sign-up sheets. My notebook felt heavier in my pocket than paper should.

"Sheriff." The voice came from my right.

Bishop Cade approached, suit still crisp, silver hair without a strand out of place. Joel drifted a few steps behind him, assessor's badge pinned to his lapel from a meeting he'd come from. They looked like they'd stepped out of two different offices and into one hallway on purpose.

"Bishop," I said. "Joel."

"Quite a turnout," Joel said. "Shows how much folks cared."

"Shows how small the Basin is," I said. "Somebody dies, everybody knows their cousin."

Cade's hand settled on my elbow, light but firm. I knew better than to pull away. In this building, that hand carried more weight than my badge.

"Do you have a minute?" he asked. "We don't want to keep you from your duties, of course."

"I've got a minute," I said.

He steered me a half-step aside, out of the main river of people, but not so far anyone could accuse him of secrecy. That was the art here: privacy without walls.

"I just wanted to say," he began, voice pitched low, pastoral, "that we appreciate the care you're taking with all of this. It's a heavy load for a shepherd to bear when the flock is hurting."

I waited. Compliments were often the first layer on a sandwich.

"We've had visits," he went on, "from company brethren eager to reassure us they've conducted a thorough internal review. They've found nothing to suggest any foul play." His look managed concern and expectation. "In times like these, sometimes the most merciful thing we can do is accept a hard providence and let families heal."

He'd folded Rosa's plea and the company line into one tidy shape. That took talent.

Joel stepped in. "He's right, Milt. The firm's been good to this county. Jobs, tax base, donations." His smile stayed easy but his eyes had that assessor sharpness. "You know as well as I do our budget hangs on their checks. A homicide circus could spook investment fast."

There it was. Accident was doctrine; economics was scripture.

Behind them, in the stream of bodies, I caught a glimpse of Eve near the kitchen door, holding Rosa's youngest on her hip while Rosa hugged someone else. Eve's eyes met mine over the child's head. She shifted closer to the drinking fountain, as if to be within arm's reach if I needed an anchor.

"The company's looked into this thoroughly," Cade said again, echoing the man at the pulpit. "No need to drag everyone through more pain if we don't have to."

My jaw muscle jumped. I made myself unclench it before I spoke. "My calling," I said, choosing the word on purpose, "is to find out what actually happened. If the company's report lines up with the evidence, we'll all sleep better. If it doesn't, I can't pretend it does because it would be easier."

Joel's smile thinned. His hand went to his tie, smoothing it down faster than necessary. "No one's asking you to pretend, cousin. Just... be mindful of how hard this is on folks. Some wounds, you pick at them too much, they never close."

"Some wounds get infected if you tape them shut," I said.

Cade's hand on my elbow tightened the slightest bit. "We're all on the same side here," he said. "Wanting peace for Rosa and the children. Wanting stability for our people. The ward looks to you as a protector, both from harm and from unnecessary turmoil."

There was the heart of it. Not just protect from men with guns or bad brakes, but from questions that might ripple wrong.

"In my notebook," I said, "I've got a line: unexplained bonuses, missing incident reports, a tampered latch, a rung welded in secret. That's not turmoil. That's facts."

He glanced at my pocket like he could see the notebook through cloth. "And I'm sure you'll weigh them carefully," he said.

"I will."

A child cried somewhere down the hall and was hushed. The fluorescent light above us buzzed, reflected in the glass over a print of a temple hanging on the wall. Under it, a small typed card talked about eternal families.

"Sheriff," Cade said more softly, "sometimes the adversary uses contention to tear apart good things. I would hate to see this ward divided over speculation."

My temper wanted to answer that. My job didn't. I swallowed the heat and spoke from a cooler place.

"I don't deal in speculation," I said. "I deal in evidence. Right now, the evidence doesn't fit an easy accident."

Joel shifted, coat brushing the bulletin board. "Just... promise me you'll keep the bigger picture in mind," he said. "Jobs, tithing, county services. If this blows up, there's more at stake than one man's mistake."

I thought of Rosa's thin shoulders under Eve's hands. One man's mistake. I thought of Jared's careful numbers, "bonus, Colton" written like a warning for whoever came after.

"I've seen what happens when we decide some people's pain is too expensive to admit," I said. "Didn't sleep well that year. Not planning on repeating it."

Cade studied my face for a long second, looking for give. Whatever he saw there, he didn't like, but he smoothed it under a serene nod.

"Well," he said, releasing my elbow. "We'll pray that the truth comes out in a way that blesses the ward. If there's anything we can do to help families affected by, ah, whatever you find, please let us know."

"I will," I said. I meant the second half. Relief Society casseroles didn't fix conspiracies, but they kept kids fed while parents signed statements.

They drifted away, Cade to another knot of mourners, Joel toward a group of men talking county budgets near the clerk's office. Their suits merged back into the crowd.

I pulled my notebook out and flipped it open with my thumb against the spine. In the margin, under the list of suspects and the arrows tying Weld, Wade and Bonuses, Colton, I wrote a new line: Institutional peace = opposing force.

Eve stepped up beside me as I capped my pen. Her hand rested on the cool rim of the drinking fountain. Her knuckles were pale, too.

"What did he say?" she asked quietly.

"That I should accept the company's answer for the sake of mercy," I said. "Joel threw in the county budget for good measure."

She breathed out through her nose, slow. "And what did you say?"

"That my job's to match the story to the bruises and the steel," I said. "Not the other way around."

She watched my face as if weighing more than the words. Then she nodded once, small but firm. "Good," she said. "Because they're already telling her to stop saying the word murder."

My stomach tightened. "In there?"

"In there," she said. "Behind the hugs. 'Think of the children. Don't let bitterness take root. The brethren are handling it.'" Her eyes flicked toward the kitchen door where the sisters were still clustered. "She looked at me like she was drowning in blankets."

The urge to walk back in and pull Rosa out by the hand hit hard. I stayed where I was. There were kinds of rescue the badge covered and kinds it didn't.

"You okay?" I asked Eve.

She stared at the temple print for a moment, then at the scribbled lines in my notebook. "I used to hear those phrases and feel comfort," she said. "Now I hear muzzles."

The hallway hummed around us, coats rustling, kids' shoes scuffing, the occasional burst of casserole talk. From the cultural hall, the gym floor squeak drifted in as people moved chairs to eating tables. Life did what it always did: rolled forward, smoothing over the rough places if you let it.

I shut the notebook and slid it back into my pocket. The single new line there weighed more than any paragraph of statute.

"From here on," I said, "this doesn't just run through the courthouse. It runs through this building too."

"It always has," Eve said. "You're just writing it down now."

We stood for another minute under the fluorescent buzz, side by side, not quite touching, watching our people move around us. Some avoided my eyes intentionally now. Others looked at me longer than before, as if deciding what kind of sheriff they wanted me to be.

When we finally stepped back into the tide toward the cultural hall, the smell of funeral potatoes hit stronger, warm and heavy. Comfort food for a community hoping this was just another hard day that would pass.

For Rosa's sake, for Jared's, I knew I couldn't let it pass like that. Not this time.

Chapter 9

Static and Scribbled Names

The office felt hollow when I came back from the funeral. Fluorescents hummed over empty desks. The scanner muttered a traffic stop two counties over and settled into static. Burnt coffee smell clung to the air.

I dropped into my rolling chair, set my notebook down, and stared at the blank corkboard on the wall. The photo of Jared that had caught on the crossbeam, cheap paper, grainy copy, lay on my blotter. I clipped it to the board at eye level. Against the dingy beige he looked out of place, steel and blood frozen in institutional light.

Clara came in without knocking, coat half unzipped. "You really want to do this tonight?" she asked.

"If I go home now, I'm just going to lie there running it in my head," I said. "Might as well pin it to something."

She didn't argue. She set her notebook on the next desk and pulled a box of thumbtacks from a drawer. The plastic lid clicked open.

"All right," she said. "Start with what we actually know. Not what people want."

I wrote JARED PIKE dead center on a blank index card and tacked it up. Underneath I wrote: rig ladder / pre-impact bruising / notebook page / careful per Rosa.

"Victim," I said. "Late shift, off pattern on the catwalk. Ladder rung where Hal did that weld. Bruising at the hospital that doesn't match just a fall."

"And scared," Clara said. "Don't forget that. Rosa's words, not mine."

I nodded and tacked up a smaller card: "told Rosa he was scared," and drew a line back to his name.

We worked out in rings. HANK went up on one side. WADE on the other. Under Hank I wrote: debt, bar tab, first on scene, overheard fight. Under Wade: supervisor, logs, weld order, safety talk.

Clara added photos from our file. Hank, bleary-eyed on the man-camp porch. Wade on the pad, jaw set, hands in vest pockets. Thumbtacks snapped into cork.

"Where do you want Colton?" she asked.

I hesitated. The safety man had never swung a wrench in anger in his life, at least not that I'd seen. Collared shirt, calm voice, laminated posters behind his desk.

"Put him off to the side," I said. "He's got too much pen in this to leave him off."

She printed his name in block letters: COLTON REESE. She started to center it, then caught my face and shifted it a little away from the cluster, like we were afraid he'd overhear.

Scanner hiss rose and fell. Somewhere a deputy cleared a noise complaint. The rest of the Basin carried on like a man hadn't died on steel.

"All right," Clara said. "Walk me through it. If you had to testify right now, who are you pointing at and why?"

I uncapped my pen and flipped open my notebook. Pages of cramped handwriting. Weather note from the rig night: clear, dry, cold. Latch sketch. Little arrows to mark where the grease smear sat on the rail.

"We've got motive, means, and some opportunity on Hank," I said. "He owes Jared money, resents his note-taking. He knows the steel. But that fuel run receipt and dash-cam stills already start to chew into his window."

"And Wade?" Clara leaned against the file cabinet, arms folded.

"He's got the weld order," I said. "He signed off on logs calling that ladder sound. He's the one pushing production. But if his in-briefing really overlaps the best staging window, he's hard-pressed to be the only set of hands."

She nodded once. "So what's missing?"

"Someone who lives in both worlds," I said. "Steel and paper. Enough knowledge to weaken the latch and enough authority to steer the write-up after. Someone who cares about incident numbers more than any of these men."

I turned another page, back to my first notes from the scene. Mud, wind, work lights. Crew clumped in the yard. I'd written down small things, almost shorthand.

One line near the top snagged me.

colton, stared at harness tags longer than body.

The words sat there like I'd taken them from someone else. I leaned closer. The memory came back in a rush: Colton stepping into the locker area, hand brushing the bagged replacement harness, then his gaze locking on the little metal tag at Jared's gear. While Hank stared at nothing and Wade watched my face, Colton's attention had gone to numbers stamped on a strip of metal.

"He looked at that tag like it mattered more than the man," I said.

Clara frowned. "You didn't mention that earlier."

"I wrote it," I said, tapping the note. "Didn't think it meant much. Just... he checked the harness ID like he was reading off a badge number at a wreck. No one else gave it a second glance."

"Some safety guys are wired to think gear first," she said, but her voice had more question than defense. "Still. If you're right about deliberate latch damage, this stops being about some drunk shove and starts being about someone who knows the equipment inside out."

"Yeah." I looked up at the board, at Hank's photo. "Hank knows how to use it. But only one of these guys gets bonuses for how few accidents show up on the books."

I tapped my pen under Colton's name without quite meeting her eyes.

She caught that. "You think he's just cleaning up after, or planning ahead?"

"Don't know yet," I said. "He had that maintenance log for the camera gap ready to hand. Weather story's off. Now this harness-tag thing. He's either the unluckiest safety man in the county or sitting in the middle of every weird detail we've got."

I drew a light pencil arrow from COLTON REESE toward CAMERA GAP? and another toward HARNESS TAGS. Then I erased the question marks and wrote "control" above both.

"That's still thin," Clara said. "We go at him hard now, he lawyers up, and the company slams doors. Judge is going to want more than 'he stared too long at a harness tag.'"

"I know." I circled Wade's name and underlined WELD ORDER, BACKDATED?. Then I circled Hank and wrote: fuel run, coached? lie about papers night?

Every line felt like a choice. Hank at the top of the suspect column fit the story the ward wanted: roughneck with a temper. Wade below him fit the company's pattern: sloppy middle man. Putting Colton on the board at all meant admitting the man in the collared shirt wasn't just a witness.

"How far are you willing to take it if the arrows keep pointing up the ladder?" Clara asked quietly.

I thought of Bishop Cade's hand on my elbow in that hallway, Joel's smile talking about tax revenues, Rosa's fingers gripping the podium when she said "truth." I thought of Eve at the kitchen sink, water running, asking whether I'd keep the peace if it was our name on those papers.

"I'm not going to pretend the arrows go somewhere they don't," I said. "If they stop at Wade, they stop at Wade. If they keep going, we follow."

"That's a long way of saying 'I don't know yet,'" she said, but there was approval in it.

We added smaller cards: HOSPITAL BRUISING, pre-impact?; TRAILER NOTE, "bonus, colton"; BISHOP PRESSURE, "keep it in the family"; COMPANY SETTLEMENT. Lines ran between them like a child's maze. Scanner static filled the gaps in our talk.

By the time we ran out of tacks, Hank's name sat highest in the suspect column, Wade's just underneath. Off to the right, Colton's card hung with two light arrows and a question mark in my handwriting under his photo: tags / cameras?

Clara pressed her fingers into her temples when we circled back to the gap in footage again. "We need a clean timeline," she said. "Or we're just chasing vibes."

"I'll build one tonight," I said. "You go home. Sleep while you can."

"You?"

"I'll let the scanner sing me a lullaby."

She snorted. "You know that's not how lullabies work."

At the door she paused, looking back at the board. Her mouth twisted when she tacked Wade's picture a fraction higher.

"You sure you want Colton on there where anyone walking in can see?" she asked.

"Anybody walking in here tonight already knows we're not buying 'accident,'" I said. "Might as well be honest with ourselves."

She nodded once and left.

The scanner crackled about a stray dog. I sat awhile longer, pen in hand, eyes on the board. Hank's face, Wade's, Colton's off to the side. Three names, thin arrows, and one note under Colton's photo that just read "tags/weather?"

In the margin of my notebook I wrote, "Hank, Wade, Colton (?), don't forget the question mark." Then I closed it, the ink still damp.

I clicked the desk lamp on after everyone left and pushed the case file aside until it kissed the edge of the blotter. The rest of the office lay in shadow. Only the green of the scanner display at dispatch and the small clock over the hall ticking.

Yellow legal pad in front of me, pencil ready, notebook open beside it. Coffee in my mug had gone lukewarm; it still tasted burnt.

"All right," I told the empty room. "When could somebody have done it?"

I drew a vertical line down the pad and marked half-hour blocks along the bottom. 1800. 1830. 1900. Time anchors from my notes: scanner call at 2017, my arrival just after, first medic on scene at 2030.

I plugged in what we knew. Hank's fuel run time from the gas receipt. Wade's safety briefing start and end. The last camera check Colton swore his tech had done before the "static." I wrote each name under the blocks where they claimed to be.

Lines on paper made it plainer than words in my head. The most likely window to weaken a latch and move a body without a lot of witnesses, the gap between the last routine walk-through and the moment the crew "found" Jared, sat like a hollow square on the pad.

In that blank space I had, in earlier notes, penciled HANK? big and dark. Tonight, when I laid the receipt over the times, Hank's fuel run shaded most of it in. His truck on the highway, timestamped. The ugly weight of my earlier certainty eased a hair from my shoulders.

My pencil hovered over Wade's name. He'd told us the briefing ran long. Half the crew in a cramped trailer hearing about lockout procedures they'd all heard before.

If you were in a briefing, Wade, who was out on the steel?

I heard myself ask it out loud. The room gave me nothing back but scanner static and the soft rush of the air system.

I slid my finger along the blocks where Wade claimed to be in that talk. The overlap with the staging window was bigger than I'd liked to admit at first. Either his memory was off, or his alibi was better than I'd given him credit for.

"Can't be in two places," I muttered.

I underlined the empty stretch between the briefing and the call to dispatch. On the pad I wrote GAP in block letters and circled it hard enough to dent the paper. The pencil dug in deeper there than anywhere else.

Then I added another card in my head: CAMERA CHECK, Colton initialed. Maintenance log stamped right through that same gap.

Hands-on work with a latch and a harness doesn't take all night. Maybe not even half an hour, if you know what you're doing and you're willing to move a body that's already out.

Cold crept up my neck that had nothing to do with the thermostat. Cade's voice from the hallway pressed in again: spare the ward more pain. Joel's talk of jobs. Easy to go home, tell myself the math was fuzzy, pencil Hank back into that window.

Instead, Rosa's voice from the ER rose up: He told me he was scared.

I rubbed my eyes with the heel of my hand, then straightened and wrote in the margin: "Trust notes. Trust weather." On another line: "Company report ≠ scripture."

I checked my first scene note again: sky clear, stars out, breath hanging. Colton had tried to sell me "driving snow" when he explained his camera issues. My own handwriting undercut his story.

On the timeline I wrote, just under the hollow: "access to shack? who had key / badge?" Then, smaller: "Colton."

I added Hank's fuel run blocks in lighter graphite and drew a small arrow from Primary Suspect beside his name down to "complicit? coached?" Slimmer window for him on the steel; thicker line on "agreed to lie."

Wade's box I shaded around the briefing. Maybe he'd padded his times. Maybe he'd stepped out "for a minute" at the worst possible moment. But the more I stared at the math, the more the center of gravity shifted toward somebody whose movements didn't show up clean in crew chatter because he wasn't crew.

Alone like that, I let the fear surface. Not the rough fear of being shot at or hit by a truck, but the quieter dread of being wrong at the root. Of hanging a homicide case on a pattern only I could see, then watching it fall apart in front of a judge while the ward talked about mercy in the halls.

I pictured Cade again, telling me mercy sometimes meant accepting "hard providence." The word had tasted off even then. Mercy wasn't pretending a broken latch tightened itself.

My shoulders loosened a fraction when I penciled a thinner arrow from HANK toward that empty gap and a thicker one from COLTON in my notebook. Not proof. Not yet. But the story I'd been half telling myself, angry roughneck shoves his buddy, was already coming apart at the seams.

The legal pad now held three names along the bottom edge: Hank (fuel run), Wade (briefing), camera gap (Colton?). The blank above "gap" felt heavier than the filled spaces.

I drew a little X in that hollow and, next to it, wrote: "hands on latch / body." Then, under that, in smaller letters only I'd ever read, "management fingerprints, not just calluses."

When I finally pushed my chair back, my neck popped from too long leaning over the desk. I stood, rolled my shoulders, and looked one more time at the board across the room. Hank still at the top, Wade just beneath. Colton's card off to the side, question mark under his name.

In my head, his card slid a fraction closer to center.

I shrugged into my coat, picked up the mug, and snapped the lamp off. The legal pad lay in the dark with its crooked vertical line and the pressed-hard word GAP standing out like a bruise.

Out in the hallway the scanner hissed into another lull. I left it on. Some nights the noise felt like company. Tonight it sounded more like a metronome, ticking toward a point when that gap on my page would have to be filled with somebody's name in ink.

I locked the office door behind me and stepped into the cold, telling myself I'd sleep. Knowing I'd be back in here soon, running the same lines until they either lined up with the truth or refused to.

Chapter 10

Receipts in Grease-Stained Hands

Roosevelt's main drag sat under a flat gray sky when I turned toward Hal's shop. The bay door was half up, winter light slanting under it. A pickup on the lift clicked and pinged as its engine cooled, exhaust hanging in a pale cloud near the ceiling.

Hal stood at the counter, rag in hand. The rag had given up any claim to white years ago. He looked up when I came in, grin flashing, then sliding when he saw the badge.

"Sheriff," he said. "You tracking me down or my lousy handwriting?"

"Depends how bad the handwriting is," I said.

Oil and solvent smell wrapped the place, cut with the twang of country radio from a bench speaker. Grit crunched under my boots.

He dropped the rag on the counter, but his fingers kept working an invisible spot. "You here about that weld thing I ran my mouth about at the diner."

"About that," I said. "You said you had a receipt."

"I say a lot of things over coffee," he hedged. "Big company like that, they can take their work down the road if they get spooked."

"I know," I said. "And I know you got folks here who like eating regular."

He huffed. "That'd be nice."

I rested my elbows on the counter. "Hal, I'm not out to burn your shop down. I just need paper that shows what you already told me, that somebody called in a rung problem on that ladder before Jared died. Dates. Who ordered. What you did."

He looked past me at the open bay. Ratchets clicked as one of his guys loosened something under the lifted pickup. Out front, a truck rolled by on the highway, tires hissing on damp asphalt.

"You know if this gets back to them, they'll send their work down the road, right?" he said. "I even wrote it up how Wade told me so it wouldn't spook 'em."

"Long as what's in your book matches what's in my envelope, they can huff about the date all they want," I said. "It's still your weld on their bad steel. And if you don't hand it over now, odds are we end up in here with a warrant later, which nobody enjoys."

He winced at the word. The rag started moving again, wiping the same stretch of laminate. His eyes didn't quite meet mine.

"Paper's paper," he muttered. "But my name's on that paper."

"Yeah," I said. "So let's make sure the story that goes with it is the one you actually lived, not whatever the company wants to paste over it."

He stared at me a second, then sighed like air out of a bad tire. "Hell, Milt. You always did know how to ruin a guy's nap."

He turned into the little office nook behind the counter and hauled a bound repair log off a shelf. The covers were stained and curling, carbon copies bulging where they'd been torn.

His fingers tapped a stack of loose invoices a beat before he yanked the right one free.

"This is the carbon I gave Wade," he said, bringing it back. "And this here, " he flipped to a page in the bound log, "is where I first wrote it down."

The carbon copy was slick with grease on the corner. Date at the top, circled in ballpoint. Description: "derrick ladder rung repair, Roosevelt site." In the "ordered by" box: W. GARRISON, his name underlined. Work done after dark, note about limited access, "welded crack, advised full replacement."

The date said three months back.

"Night I did it, I wrote it clean in here with that night's date," he said, tapping the log page. "Next day Wade comes back, says for their 'paperwork' he wants it to look like older maintenance. Asked me to write an earlier date on the carbon, make it match some inspection they had. I grumbled, he looked nervous, I did it. Figured it was their mess if they wanted to play pretend with timing."

He slid the bound log closer. Real date, neat in his cramped hand. Beneath it, the same language as on the carbon, down to the way he drew his Ys. The only difference was the top line on the slip in my hand, month and day written in with a heavier stroke.

"Can I photograph the book page?" I asked. "Whole spread, so we've got context."

"Yeah." He rubbed the back of his neck. "Take a picture of the grease too while you're at it, so nobody says I made this up last week."

I smiled a little. "You don't get artistic control over my evidence photos, Hal."

He snorted. "Worth a shot."

I took pictures, wide shot of the log, close on the date, then on the carbon, and in my head I started cataloging details for Clara later. Order of entries. Same pen. Hal's thumbprint faint in the corner where he'd grabbed the page.

"Why'd Wade want it aged?" I asked.

"Say it made the company feel better to think it'd been looked at awhile back, not just right then," Hal said. "Said if it looked fresh they'd start asking why he didn't shut the rig down to do more. You know how they are about hours."

"Yeah," I said. "I do."

I slid the carbon into an envelope I'd brought. My hand lingered on it an extra beat before I sealed it. It felt heavier than a scrap of paper ought to.

"You understand this means I'm going to end up asking you to swear to this, under oath, someday," I said. "That you wrote the real date in the log the night you did the work, and you changed the date on the carbon at Wade's request."

He rocked back on his heels, rag hanging from his hand.

"I get it," he said. "I also get Jared was my customer same as any of them, and he tried to be careful. So... yeah. If it comes to that, I'll say it. Just don't let 'em make me out like I'm the mastermind here."

"Nobody who's seen your coffee thinks you're masterminding anything," I said.

He barked a laugh. Some tension slipped from his shoulders.

"You need anything else?" he asked. "Got a brake special this week."

"I'll let Clara know," I said. "For her cruiser."

He shook his head. "That woman scares me. In a good way."

"You and me both."

On my way out to the truck I glanced back through the smeared glass. Hal stood with his elbows on the counter, rag dangling, watching me go. The manila envelope in my hand felt like more than a weld order. Behind him, the ratchet started up again in the bay, business resuming. But whichever way the company decided to jump later, there was no rewinding what he'd just handed over.

Out by the curb, diesel grumble reached from passing rigs. I tucked the envelope into my inside pocket and patted it once, like checking a heartbeat, before starting the engine.

Instead of heading straight back to the office, I let the truck idle along the square once. Courthouse steps on one side, oil-company pickups on the other, logos bright even under cloud.

A gust of wind flapped a county meeting notice on the bulletin board by the courthouse door. Above it, a glossy flyer about "community partnership" carried the same logo as the trucks. From where I sat, the courthouse and that sign lined up in a single frame. Law and benefactor sharing brick.

Coffee and grease from the diner seeped through the truck vents. Door chimes jingled as people went in and out, ranchers in ball caps, clerks in cardigans, two men in collared shirts with company badges clipped to their belts.

They crossed toward the courthouse together, talking low, not looking around. I rested my forearms on the steering wheel and watched them climb the steps that led to the courtroom where we'd be arguing warrants before long.

Hal's receipt in my pocket, Rosa's half notebook page in my file, the ledger entry with "bonus, colton" scrawled next to Jared's name, they all started to braid together in my mind.

Jared copying papers in his trailer, Rosa said. Hal crawling up a ladder he didn't like the feel of. Wade ordering a weld and then asking for the date to be moved. Payroll ledger showing safety bonuses signed off by Colton that stopped not long before Jared died.

Evidence liked patterns. That was one of Ben Latham's lines. Men like Wade lived between instructions and reality; men like Colton lived where numbers became praise or punishment.

Under my breath, watching the company men disappear inside the courthouse, I said, "If you're signing checks to keep mouths shut, Mr. Reese, we're going to need to look at your pen."

It was just air in the cab, but saying his name there, in the same breath as "we" and "look," stiffened something in me.

I thought of the easy path: build the whole case around Wade. Sloppy supervisor, ordered repair, lied about it. Maybe that alone would satisfy a jury. Maybe the company would offer up his job like a burnt offering and call it justice. Hank would take a misdemeanor on the chin for bad statements. Ward would talk about forgiveness.

But the half-page from Jared's notebook wasn't going away. The "bonus, colton" scribble matched numbers in the ledger Clara and I had copied. Hal's dated weld said somebody knew that rung was bad days before the "accident." And in every one of those documents, the man who signed off lived in an office with safety posters on the walls.

Out here, away from files, the shape of it felt clearer than when it sat in manila folders. A bad rung. A scared roughneck who wrote too much down. A safety man whose metric depended on quiet.

I climbed out, boots crunching grit on the street. The wind cut through my coat and flapped the meeting notice again. As I walked toward the sheriff's door, my hand went to my jacket pocket and touched the envelope, as if to make sure it hadn't vanished.

Inside, under fluorescent buzz, I'd be back to persuading a judge with citations and timelines. Out here, walking between the courthouse and company trucks lined up like they owned the curb, it boiled down to a choice: follow the paper where it pointed, even if it pointed upstairs, or stop at the first foreman who lied and tell myself I'd done enough.

My steps up the sidewalk were slower than usual. But by the time I reached the door, I knew two things. First, we weren't going to just hammer Wade and call it a night.

Second, before any company lawyer could lean on Hal to "lose" a page, we'd get his log under oath and in copy.

Inside the office, the case board waited with its three names and thin arrows. In my head I drew another line, this one between Hal's weld slip and the ledger in our file, both running through the same initials: C.R.

Documents and warrants, not just bar interviews and rumor. That's where this was going now. I opened my notebook and, under the line where I'd written "Institutional peace = opposing force," added a fresh one: "Follow the paper above Wade."

Chapter 11

Beer Glass Alibis

The bar sat halfway down Main, neon beer signs buzzing against the plate glass. Fryer grease and stale lager hit me as soon as the door shut behind me. TV sports mumbled over the bar, the jukebox leaking a country song from the corner.

Hank Dillard hunched in a back booth under a beer sign, safety-yellow jacket draped over the seat beside him. The fabric caught the light like it still remembered rig work. He watched me in the mirror behind the bar before he turned his head, hand tight around a sweating pint.

I crossed the sticky floor, gas-station receipt folded in my pocket, pump log times copied in my notebook. Part of me wanted this to be easy: one drunk roughneck with a bad temper and worse judgment. Easier than edging closer to the glass offices and the stake hall.

His knee bounced under the table when I slid in across from him.

"Evening, Hank."

"Sheriff." He tried for a grin. It slipped. "You want a beer?"

"No, thanks." I set my notebook on the table and laid the folded receipt next to his glass, keeping my hand on it. "We need to straighten out your night when Jared went over."

"I told you already." His answer came fast, too loud. "We were all on the pad. I turned around, there he was on the beam. End of story."

"Funny thing," I said. "Gas pumps don't drink. Their memories hold up better."

He stared at my hand. A drop of water slid down the side of his glass and pooled against the paper.

"You got that from the station?" he asked.

"Receipt from the clerk. Time-stamped. Pump three. Truck plate scribbled in the corner. Looks a lot like the one out front of your trailer." I slid it toward him.

He wiped his palm on his jeans before he touched it. His eyes moved along the line with the time. His jaw worked.

"So what, Sheriff, you gonna arrest me for fueling up wrong?"

"No," I said. "I'm going to stop wasting time pretending you were on the pad when Jared went over. Which means if you're not my killer, you're either a witness or a patsy. You get to choose which."

The word hung between us. Patsy. His eyes flicked up at me, then around the room, like he could spot who'd hear it and report back. Nobody cared. Two guys argued about a game at the bar. The fryer popped in the kitchen.

His shoulders sagged. The fight went out of his voice before the words changed.

"I took the truck," he said. "Wade told me fuel was low and he didn't want the night shift screwed. Told me run down, top off, back in twenty. No big deal."

"You'd sworn you were on the pad that whole time."

"Yeah, well." He swallowed. "Wade said keep it simple. Said if we started talking about runs and breaks, people'd get mixed up. Cops like simple stories, right?" The edge in his voice was bitter.

"Depends," I said. "Simple lies or simple truth."

He snorted. "It don't ever stay simple."

I let that sit. "Receipt's time," I tapped the paper, "has you at the pump right in the middle of the twenty-minute window the doc thinks Jared was put on that beam. That takes you out of physical hands-on. You understand what that means for you?"

"I wasn't up there," he muttered. "Couldn't have been. Hell, I couldn't see half the pad from the road. Snow and all."

"It wasn't snowing that night," I said. "Clear, cold. Stars sharp. You remember."

He flinched, like he'd repeated somebody else's script and heard it wrong for the first time.

"Okay," he said. "Okay, fine. I remember it clear. Whatever."

I leaned in a little. Grease from the kitchen clung to my jacket, same stink as the man camp. "Let's talk about why you lied."

Hank's knee rattled the table again. His voice dropped.

"They told us not to stir it up," he said. "Right after. Safety meeting in the trailer, Wade up front. Said company said this was a tragic accident, and that was that. Said nobody wanted auditors crawling over everything. Said we all liked our paychecks."

"'They' who?"

"Wade. But he kept saying 'he said.'" Hank wet his lips. "Like he was quoting somebody. 'He said better one bad fall than a full audit.'"

The phrase landed heavy. Too polished for Hank. Too neat. My mind slid it next to the welded rung, the camera log, the ledger with Colton's name.

"Who's 'he'?" I asked.

Hank blinked hard, suddenly wary he'd stepped too far. "I don't know. Wade just kept saying it. Like a saying they handed down from upstairs. 'One bad fall.'" He stared at his beer. "Didn't sound right even then."

"You lied in a sworn interview," I said. "You understand that puts you in your own kind of trouble."

"I know." He lifted his eyes to mine, raw. "But what you want me to do, Sheriff? You ever had a foreman tell you if you screw up his numbers, you can find yourself hauling pipe in North Dakota? I got a trailer here. My folks up the road. I got...debts."

"You got a conscience too," I said. "You could've told me this the first time."

"You showed up out there with him still stuck on that beam," he said, voice rough. "Everyone buzzing. Wade looking at me like he could skin me alive through my coveralls. Company man staring holes in that harness tag. Bishop calling my phone asking if I was okay. I ain't proud, but I ain't stupid either."

"Which company man?" I asked.

"The safety guy. Reese. Suit with the hardhat. You know." Hank's fingers traced a ring of water from his glass. "Stood there looking at the latch, not us."

"He talk to you directly?"

"Not that night. Later, when they did that big group talk. He said accidents happen on rigs, that's just the work. Said making a federal case out of every slip would shut the whole Basin down. Asked us to remember Jared like a brother, not like...like some courtroom exhibit."

There it was again. Exhibit. Audit. Falls reduced to cost.

"You ever hear those exact phrases before the death?" I asked.

Hank hesitated. "Wade's used 'em. Same kind of words. 'Don't make a federal case. Don't stir it up.' I figured it was just...the way bosses talk."

"You and Jared," I said quietly. "You ever fight up there? Folks at the camp say you two drank together sometimes."

He winced. "We argued. He was always writing stuff down. Every little thing. Ladder creaks, near slips, who was late, who didn't tag in right. I told him he was gonna get one of us canned. He said somebody had to tell the truth." Hank's voice thinned. "Night before it happened, we jawed a bit. Nothin' serious. I never laid hands on him, Sheriff. I swear."

Receipt times and badge swipes spun behind my eyes. I could already see the affidavit paragraph: fuel run confirmed, opportunity narrowed.

"Wade know Jared was writing?" I asked.

Everyone knew. That look told me that. He still answered.

"Yeah. He caught him one night in the office, going through copies of the incident log. Lost his mind. Next day Jared was on the crap jobs, cleaning sludge. Still writing though. I told him to knock it off. He said, 'If I disappear, it wasn't the ladder.' I thought he was just bein' dramatic."

"He ever say Colton's name to you?" I asked. "About the bonuses, about notes?"

Hank's eyes slid toward the TV, away from me. "He said 'safety man' a few times. How the bonus checks had his signature. How they'd dried up. Jared said it meant the game changed. Whatever that meant."

"So when Wade told you to keep the story simple," I said, "you went along."

"You ever had a bishop sit you down and say keeping the peace is God's work?" he asked suddenly, meeting my eye. "Feels real close to your boss saying the same thing, even if he don't use the word God."

Memory drifted in from my own kitchen. Eve at the sink, water running over plates. If it was your name on those papers, she'd said, what would you want done?

I took a breath. "Right now, Hank, peace looks like a straight statement that helps me put this on the right desk. You keep backing their lie, you're the one holding it up."

His hand shook as he picked up the receipt. "If I change my story, they'll can me."

"If you don't," I said, "and this goes to trial, that paper and that pump log will make you look like a liar under oath. Judges don't like that. Neither do juries."

He swallowed. "So what do I do then? March into court and say, 'Yes, Your Honor, I took a gas run and then came back to find my buddy hanging like meat'?"

"You sit down with me and Clara at the office. We record you correcting your statement. You tell us exactly when you left, when you came back, what you saw, and who said what in that safety trailer after. We make clear you were under pressure when you first talked. That won't erase lying, but it'll weigh different."

He stared at the blank patch of table where the receipt had been before he lifted it.

"You really think I didn't push him?" he asked, voice small.

I thought about the angles on that beam, the bruises, the tool marks on the latch. A sloppy drunk could do a lot of harm, but the staging had a colder hand behind it.

"No," I said. "I don't think you did. I think you helped them sell the story after."

He shut his eyes for a second. When he opened them, something had shifted: still scared, but less sullen.

"He said better one bad fall than a full audit," he repeated. "You write that down right, Sheriff. Don't let them pin them words on me."

"I will."

I slid the receipt into my pocket and rose. Hank watched it go like it carried his future with it.

"You call in tomorrow," I said. "We'll set a time with Clara. Don't talk to Wade alone in the meantime. If he wants to talk about this, you tell him to bring his lawyer."

Hank huffed out a laugh that wasn't amused. "Men like us don't got lawyers on speed dial."

"Then you let him talk to mine."

His knee finally went still. "You're really gonna make this a...what'd he say...federal case?"

"I'm going to make it the case it already is." I nodded once and slid out of the booth.

He didn't touch his beer as I walked away.

Outside, the cold hit clean, stripping the fryer haze from my nose. The door thunked shut behind me, cutting the jukebox mid-chorus. In the glass I caught one last glimpse of him rubbing his forehead, hunched over the empty space where the receipt had lain. Less like a killer. More like a man who'd finally seen the story was bigger than the break room.

I didn't head straight for the truck. I walked down Main with my hands jammed deeper into my coat pockets, boots loud on the sidewalk. Neon reflections smeared in the puddles along the curb, red and blue rippling in the blacktop.

Airbrakes sighed as a semi rolled past, wind tugging at my collar. Grease smell clung to my jacket. It followed me even when the bar lights fell behind. The town felt mostly asleep, one late customer leaving the diner, laughter spilling for a moment when the door opened, then gone.

I replayed Hank's words in order, like shuffling cards back into a stack. Fuel run. Snow that never fell. "He said better one bad fall than a full audit."

Under a flickering streetlight I stopped. The words lined up in my head the way they hadn't in the bar. That kind of neat phrase didn't grow in a bunkhouse. It came from a memo. A safety-meeting slide. A man used to selling ugly math as wisdom.

In my notebook, upstairs on the case board, Colton's name already sat with arrows from ledger, from camera log, from that email about "trial exhibit A." Now another arrow formed in my mind, from Hank's booth to the polished office where slogans like "family companies" and "zero incidents" glared from glossy posters.

One bad fall, I thought. One body on a beam so the auditors stayed home. My own compromises flickered alongside it, the times I'd rounded corners to spare a bishopric embarrassment, the incident years ago when I'd trusted church assurances instead of a battered woman's eyes. I'd told myself then I was keeping the peace. The bruises that came after had cured me of that story, but the habit of wanting quiet ran deeper than I liked to admit.

If Colton had said that line, he'd stood on the same ground I had, only farther out.

"One bad fall for who, Colton?" I said, out loud to the empty street.

My voice sounded strange. Calling him by his first name moved him in my head, from abstract corporate title to a man I might one day have to read charges to under fluorescents.

My pace slowed as I walked on. Gravel crunched in the gutter. A truck rolled through the light at the intersection, turn signal clicking. Behind me, the bar's neon hummed on, indifferent.

By the time I reached my truck, my cheeks were numb and the anger that had flared at Hank had cooled into something tighter, more focused. Fuel receipt said he'd been gone right when Jared must have been moved. That knocked a big hole in my first-week theory of a drunk fight gone too far. It also meant the hands-on work belonged to someone with more control over time and cameras.

I climbed into the cab, shut the door, and sat in the dark a moment with my breath fogging the windshield. The scanner murmur was low tonight, farm calls and a traffic stop out past the river. Ordinary trouble.

I flipped open my notebook and, by the light of the small flashlight I kept in the dash, turned to a blank page. At the top I wrote: "Hank: off pad entire 20-min window, gas run confirmed." Under that, in block letters: "Phrase: 'better one bad fall than full audit', WHO SAID?"

I drew a small hook beside the question mark, the way I sometimes did when something felt like it would come back to snag us later.

Hank's name, on the suspects list in my head, thinned a little. Still tangled in lies and fear, still due some reckoning for going along with "accident" talk. But less likely the man who put Jared on the beam. The arrow from his name now pointed harder toward Wade, and past him, toward whoever had put those phrases in Wade's mouth.

The case had started on steel and blood. For a few days I'd let myself believe it might end on a barstool. As I put the truck in gear and pulled away from Main, I knew better. This wasn't going to be about one bad hand with a wrench. It was about the people who decided "one bad fall" was a cost of doing business and taught men like Hank how to say it.

The question mark on the page stared up until I shut the notebook. It sat there in the dark like a hook waiting for a name.

Chapter 12

Safety Posters and Polished Lies

The oil company's field office squatted at the edge of town, prefab walls and a fenced equipment yard, badge reader blinking a green eye by the front door. Inside, HVAC hum and printer noise filled the bright hallway. Coffee and toner mixed in the air.

The receptionist buzzed me through. "Mr. Reese is expecting you, Sheriff."

I walked past glossy safety posters, "ZERO INCIDENTS: OUR FAMILY GOAL" in big font over smiling hardhats. One near the conference room door read, "TRUST OUR FAMILY COMPANIES," the word family repeated like it could turn liability into kinship.

Colton Reese waited in a glass-walled conference room with a company mug and a curated stack of binders. A manila folder sat to one side. He stood when I stepped in, smile set to "approachable."

"Sheriff Kingston," he said, offering his hand. "Appreciate you making time. Coffee?"

"I'm good, thanks." His grip was firm and dry. No grease in these offices, only paper.

We sat across from each other. I set my notebook on the polished table. The laminated safety poster on the far wall reflected in the glass, words backward and still legible.

"I wanted to circle back on a few points," I said. "Training logs, camera coverage, how incident reporting flows. Since the preservation order, IT has most of your systems locked down. This is more about your recollection."

"Of course." He slid the manila folder toward me with two fingers, like a dealer presenting a clean hand. "This is a convenience copy of the maintenance log entry we preserved after your initial visit. Camera three static check, as we discussed."

The form inside matched what I'd already seen digitally: "Cam 3, lens static / snow interference, quick maintenance check." His initials crouched in the margin. The time window bracketed Jared's death almost exactly.

"You initial every maintenance entry personally?" I asked.

"For anything that touches safety systems, yes." He flashed a practiced smile. "Keeps us accountable. We care about our guys out there."

I looked up. "Tell me again about that night," I said. "Your involvement from afternoon on. Just walk me through it."

He leaned back, hands resting lightly on the binder edges. "Routine safety audit," he said. "I was onsite earlier that evening, did a walkthrough, checked harness tags, ladder points, the usual. Weather was already turning. Driving snow, you remember. I headed out before midnight, no issues flagged that couldn't wait for daylight."

Driving snow.

In my notebook from that night, now burned into my memory, I'd written: "02:15, clear, bitter cold, stars sharp, breath smoke in rig lights." No precipitation. Roads dry, if icy.

"You're sure about the snow?" I asked mildly. "My patrol log from the response notes clear and cold, no precip. We rolled up within the hour of the 911."

He blinked. Just a heartbeat too long. His fingers tightened on the binder before he loosened them.

"Well, you know how it is out there," he said, recovering quick. "Nights run together. Might be thinking of another storm. But lens static's lens static. Wind and grit can do it same as snow. Point is, camera three was experiencing interference, so we scheduled a quick check."

"You did the check yourself?"

"I authorized it, initialed it. Techs handled the physical side." He flipped the binder open to a tab, showing rows of codes, all neat, black ink. "As you can see, nothing unusual. Routine."

His words flowed smooth, all policy and process. "We care about our guys" came out twice in five minutes. "Family" three times. Jared's name, once.

"How often does a camera go down for that long?" I asked. "Same night as a fatal incident. Same corner of the pad."

"Sheriff," he said, patient now, "we're talking about a remote site in rough weather, aging infrastructure. A little static during a big storm isn't exactly a conspiracy." Smile again.

"Still wasn't a storm," I said. "And your badge logs show you in the control shack during that static window."

He nodded easily. "Had to confirm what the techs were reporting. Last thing I want is blind spots." He spread his hands. "We're on the same side here. Nobody wants a repeat of that tragedy."

I counted, in my head, how many times "tragedy" had been the word of choice from company, church, and county. None of them liked "homicide."

"What do you remember about Jared that night?" I asked. "You said you did a walkthrough."

Colton frowned thoughtfully, gaze just distant enough to look sincere. "Hard worker," he said. "Quiet guy. Signed all his safety sheets, never missed a training. I don't recall anything unusual in his posture or behavior."

No mention of the notebook, of him copying logs, of the way his name sat on the far end of the bonus ledger. I watched his eyes. When I said "Jared," they stayed flat. When I said "camera three," there'd been that long blink.

"You checked harness tags yourself?" I asked.

"Standard practice on a walkthrough. Glance at dates, make sure nothing's out of compliance." He said it like it was nothing. "You know how OSHA can be."

On the night we'd found Jared on the beam, out under the rig lights, everyone else had stared at the body. Colton had stared at the harness tag, fingers brushing it like a man checking a serial number. I'd circled that in my notes days ago without knowing why it bothered me. Now, with the maintenance log and Hank's "one bad fall," the itch sharpened.

I laced my fingers to keep from showing it and leaned back.

"You mentioned last time the cameras are our best neutral witness," I said. "I agree. That's why I'm interested in anything that clouds them. You can appreciate that."

"Absolutely," he said quickly. "Which is why we responded as soon as we saw snow, static, on the feed. Frankly, Sheriff, we're just as interested as you are in learning from this. We take safety seriously. This isn't just about bonus structures; it's about sending our guys home."

Bonus structures. The ledger in the courthouse vault had his signature next to Jared's last payments, then a hard stop weeks before the fall. "Bonus, colton" in Jared's own hand. He knew who controlled the spigot.

"You ever tell your foremen," I asked, "anything along the lines of 'better one bad fall than a full audit'?"

He laughed, small and controlled. "That's quite a phrase. No, Sheriff, I prefer not to talk about any falls at all. Audits are part of the business. We work with them."

He nudged the manila folder closer, page edges perfectly aligned. "Look, I'm happy to walk you through our safety-training program. We really do care about our guys, and I'd hate to see rumor undo trust between your office and us. We're on the same team."

There it was again: team, family, us. Words I'd heard in bishopric interviews and commission meetings, now under fluorescent glare on a poster. My own ward leader had told Rosa to "trust the brethren and keep things in the family." Colton's poster told the whole town to trust "family companies."

"Trust has to be earned, Mr. Reese," I said. "Right now I'm still collecting receipts."

He adjusted his tie knot. Small motion. Smile froze a fraction, then thawed.

"Fair enough," he said. "You'll find we've been nothing but cooperative."

"You have been responsive," I said. "I appreciate you making a convenience copy here that matches what IT froze under the preservation order. Makes it easier to tell a judge your records are consistent."

He heard the word judge. Another micro-pause.

"We have nothing to hide," he said. "Our incident rate's one of the lowest in the region. Folks in this town rely on that rig staying open. I'm sure you understand the bigger picture."

I thought of Rosa's kitchen, Hal's receipt, Hank's twitching knee, Wade's panic in the diner lot. Bigger picture looked less like a sturdy frame and more like a net.

"I understand the rig feeds a lot of families," I said. "I also understand one of those families is planning a funeral for a man your own email called 'trial exhibit A' when he wouldn't stop taking notes."

His pupils tightened just a shade. "That was a poor choice of phrasing in a private email," he said. "Frustration, nothing more. You know how internal venting works."

"Sure," I said. "Same way bar venting works. Only the men at the bar don't control cameras."

We let that sit. Printer whirred in the next room. Somewhere down the hall, a phone rang twice and stopped.

"We done for today?" he asked smoothly. "I've got a regional call in ten."

"For now." I tapped the maintenance log. "I'll be following up with some weather data folks, double-checking that snow. Might reach out again once I've reconciled your story with my notes from that clear night."

He inclined his head, like he respected diligence. "Whatever you need."

As I stood, his fingers settled on the binder edges again. Anchoring more than paper, I figured. Image, metrics, future promotion.

Out in the parking lot, winter light bounced off the office windows. Through the glass I saw him turn back to his computer, face lit blue as he typed. The big wall slogan near his door, TRUST OUR FAMILY COMPANIES, caught the light.

Leaning against my truck, I flipped my notebook back open and underlined "driving snow" where I'd written it down in the room. I drew a thin arrow to the earlier note from the rig night: "clear, dry, stars out." Then I wrote his initials beside the maintenance log entry time the IT kids had frozen under my order.

One lie about weather doesn't sink a man. But when the man lying controls cameras, logs, and safety slogans, it turns into weight. Add Hank's phrase, Jared's ledger, Hal's weld receipt, and the hook in my notebook had more than one line on it now.

Before I went back to the office, I swung by my desk at dispatch and called the state road station and the weather service office we used for accident reconstructions. I asked for archived conditions for the night Jared died, precipitation, visibility, road surface, from their log and the nearest highway camera feed, and flagged it under the case file number.

By the time I hung up and got back behind the wheel, I already knew what they were going to say. Two hours later, when the fax curled out of our ancient machine, "no recorded snowfall in the period 0000, 0400; clear, subfreezing; roads dry", it just gave paper to what my own breath and windshield had told me that night.

Back at the office, I flipped on my desk lamp and laid Colton's copied log flat, smoothing the corner he'd creased with his nail. The evidence room door clicked shut somewhere behind me; the scanner hissed about a calf in the road, then went quiet again.

Coffee in the break room smelled burnt. Paper on my desk smelled like toner and company spin.

I took my pen and boxed the weather discrepancy, a neat square around "snow interference" with a note to pull and file the official records from the state station we'd just requested. In the margin I wrote, "STATE WX / HWY CAMS, clear, no precip, contradicts log," and drew an arrow back to Colton's initials. Beside those initials on the maintenance entry, I ran my thumb once over the ink, then circled them hard.

On a fresh margin I wrote three bullets under his name:

", camera 3 log, his initials (matches preserved entry) , weather lie (blizzard vs clear, contradicted by NWS / road cams) , 'family companies' poster = Cade blessing echo"

I drew an arrow from "family companies" back to Rosa's living room in my memory, Bishop Cade's hand on Jared's head. Trust the brethren. Keep things in the family.

Same tune, different choir.

Going over his answers, part of me still wanted to slide his snow flub into "busy man, bad memory" and move on. Men like Colton were easy to like in chambers and stake halls, knew their scriptures and their spreadsheets, made donations, talked about feeding families.

But pairing his slogan with Cade's blessing words made my stomach tighten. If the same language was being used to sell settlements and to bless frightened workers, this wasn't just one ambitious safety manager. It was a web.

I set my pen down, then picked it back up long enough to jot a line I'd heard my own voice say earlier: "Trust has to be earned, Mr. Reese. Right now I'm still collecting receipts."

Corny on paper. But it was also likely what I'd say in chambers when I asked a judge to let me behind his glass walls.

My fingers tapped the notebook cover, once, twice, then I snapped it shut harder than I needed to. The desk lamp threw a small circle of light over the maintenance log and the clipped-on weather fax, now stapled to the back of the entry. Outside that circle, in the dim office, the scanner muttered and the town went on doing its math.

Colton's name on my board darkened a shade.

He wasn't at the top yet. Wade still sat heavy under "complicit," Hank under "pressured." But now the line from cameras, from ledger, from coached phrases, from the maintenance entry, and from weather itself, backed by state logs, not just my memory, ran through a single man's initials.

It was time to stop treating his cooperation as a favor and start building the warrant that would make it mandatory.

Chapter 13

Man-Camp Corridors

Generator drone vibrated under my boots as Clara and I walked the row, aluminum boxes on both sides like a forgotten storage yard. Cold diesel and cigarettes hung in the air. A game show cackled behind one door, volume snapping down as whoever was inside understood it wasn't another hand coming off tour, it was the sheriff.

I wanted three things before we left: Jared's habits from the men who lived beside him, anything concrete on fights with Hank or Wade, and something that tied his scribbling and that half-page of numbers in my notebook to real incident logs. Company records already had a preservation order hanging over them. Words off these porches would tell me how brave I needed to be pushing for more.

I rapped on the first door. TV murmur, then footsteps, then the door opened two inches, chain still set. A man in long underwear and a team cap eyed my badge like it might stain him.

"Evening," I said. "Just following up on Jared Pike. Got a minute?"

He sniffed, eyes sliding past me toward the pad. "Already talked to Wade. Hank too. Company said, "

"Company isn't the coroner," I said. "You work with him regular?"

"Different shift." Chain slid a half inch. "He kept to himself. Quiet guy. That's it."

Behind me, Clara let out the sort of sympathetic sound she used on ER nurses stuck on overtime. "You boys all keep to yourselves when you're off?" she asked. "Every time I've been out here, I hear more about sore backs and junk coffee than quiet."

The man's mouth twisted, not quite a smile. "We complain. That don't mean we say names."

"Not asking for gossip," I said. "Just whether you ever heard Jared talk safety. Ladders. Harness checks. Falls that could've been worse."

He shook his head fast. "He wasn't here long enough to get in fights," he said, which answered nothing. Then the chain hissed and the door eased shut.

That set the tone. Two more trailers gave me the same mix: "Good hand, real shame" and "didn't see nothing." Eyes lingered on my patch, then skidded to the pad where work lights glowed past the berm. I could feel the company's warning in every polite sentence, keep your mouth shut if you like a paycheck.

By the third door my patience thinned. Static from a TV and forks on plates bled through the wall. No answer to the first knock. On the second, Clara leaned in.

"Hey," she called. "We're not here to get you fired. We just don't like when decent men go over railings and folks pretend it's the weather."

Laughter inside cut off. The door opened a crack. A younger roustabout looked out, bare feet, T-shirt hanging off one shoulder. Kid couldn't have been more than mid-twenties. I remembered his face from the pad, leaning on a tool crate while Wade barked.

He gripped the door edge hard enough his knuckles blanched. "You the ones been asking about Hank?" he asked.

"Hank, Jared, anybody on B-tour who can help me keep an innocent man from taking a fall he doesn't deserve," I said. "You Josh?"

His throat worked. "Maybe."

Clara stepped where he could see her badge and the scar on her jaw. "You're out here twelve hours at a clip climbing steel," she said. "You get hurt, you want somebody with sense writing it up. That starts with us understanding what really happened to Jared. We're not here to print your name on the front page."

He glanced past us toward the strip of sky above the berm. Wind cut down the lane, rattling cheap blinds on a far unit. Somebody peeked, then let them clack shut. I held still and let the silence sit.

"Look," he muttered finally, door opening enough for us to see the clutter behind him, muddy jeans on a chair, an overflowing ashtray, company-logo parka hanging crooked on a hook that rocked in the draft. "Everybody says you ruin men's lives if they open up to you."

"The sheriff?" I asked. "Or the company?"

He gave a joyless laugh. "Both."

He kept his hand flat on the door, fingers white. "Jared was...particular," he said. "Messed with everybody's rhythm, always writing stuff down. Ladders. Near-misses. Stupid things."

"Stupid?" I asked.

Josh's jaw tightened. "That's what they said. He took one slip on that east ladder a few weeks back. Didn't go over, but he caught himself hard. Woke up the whole floor with the cussing. Next day he starts copying pages out the incident log at lunch, like that was going to change anything."

"How you know he was copying?" Clara asked.

"Because he told me when I told him to knock it off before somebody made him disappear." He tried to smirk and couldn't hold it. "He had that little notebook. Kept saying if he disappeared, it wasn't the ladder. Like it was a joke."

"You thought he was joking," I said.

"I thought..." His eyes ran past my shoulder toward the rig. Light from the pad flickered off the trailer skin. "I thought he'd transfer or something. Not, " He made a helpless motion.

Generator vibration came up through the steps, steady as a heart that refused to admit trouble. I pictured Jared on that ladder weeks before, boot slipping, fingers clawing, anger masking how scared he'd been. I'd seen that mix on farmers' faces after bad rollovers; bravado covering the knowledge they'd just nearly died.

"You see him with the company logs," I said. "Actual binder, not just his notebook?"

Josh nodded once. "Hank left it on the doghouse bench after safety meeting. Jared's running his finger down the column, muttering about near-miss codes and how some never make it on the page." He swallowed. "He said if they weren't gonna pay folks for taking the hits, they could at least mark it right."

"Anybody else there?" Clara asked.

"Wade walked in at the tail end. Told Jared he wasn't paid to be a bookkeeper. Called him 'OSHA' like it was a joke name. After that...Jared kept his copying to off-shift stuff. Saw him hunched over that notebook plenty, though."

"Ever hear him name who he thought was cooking the books?" I asked. "Hank? Wade?"

Josh's hand tightened on the door again, eyes flicking to Clara like he needed to check whether what he said next would get him shot or saved.

"He just kept cussing about 'Colton's bonus math,'" he said. "Said numbers never made sense if you liked living past fifty." His gaze dropped to a chipped threshold. "And he said, 'if I disappear, it wasn't the ladder.'"

My pen itched in my pocket. "Whose ladder was he worried about?" I asked. "Hank's, Wade's, or the company's?"

Josh wet his lips. "Didn't say. Just…'up the ladder.'" He gave a small, miserable half-laugh. "Another joke."

Up the ladder. The phrase settled in my chest. Same direction as every other arrow.

In my head I saw the half-page from Jared's notebook, dates, dollar amounts, "bonus, Colton", and Hal's grease-smudged receipt with Wade's signature and a backdated weld on that rung. Add in a near-fall weeks earlier and a man muttering he'd disappear.

"Anybody from the office come out after that?" I asked. "Safety folks. Colton."

Josh shrugged with just one shoulder. "He was around more. Poked at harness tags like they owed him money. Had some meeting in the trailer over there." He jerked his chin toward a unit three doors down. Curtain shifted in its window and froze. "I'm not saying they killed him, Sheriff. But Jared scared somebody by writing things down."

"That somebody isn't you," I said. "What you've told us stays here until we need to put names on paper. If that day comes, we'll talk to you first."

He snorted. "You won't get me back on a stand when the company's lawyers start calling."

"You don't have to decide that tonight," Clara said. "You helped more than you know. Get some sleep when you can."

He nodded, shoulders easing a touch, and closed the door softly.

We finished the row, each trailer another version of the same story: Jared was careful; Jared was stubborn; Jared had his nose in papers; Jared worried more than most. No one wanted to say who'd told them it was safer not to remember.

Walking back toward the truck, mud slicks shone in the weak yard lights. Somewhere onions fried; smoke stung my nose. A curtain I hadn't noticed before snapped shut, blinds clacking like teeth.

I took my notebook out and wrote the kid's line exactly the way he'd said it: If I disappear, it wasn't the ladder. Below that I added: near-fall weeks before; copying incident log; "Colton's bonus math," up the ladder. I drew a line from those words to Colton's name and pressed the pen down hard until the tip bit the paper.

The generators' hum followed us out of the camp, loud enough to drown out just about anything a man didn't want to hear, including his own doubt.

Hank stood under a porch light, cigarette cupped against the wind, breath fogging in short bursts. His parka hung from a hook beside the door, rig logo fluttering when the wind gusted down the lane. Gravel crunched as men drifted past, not looking too long in our direction.

He watched me walk up like weather he couldn't outrun. "You done talking to everybody?" he asked.

"Everybody who'd open a door," I said. "You got a minute?"

He looked at Clara, then back to me. "She staying?"

"She knows the case as well as I do," I said. "You want straight answers, you're better off with both of us."

He took a drag, ember flaring red, then stabbed the cigarette into a coffee can full of butts. "Fine. I'm too tired to play games."

"That makes three of us," I said. "We've cleared up your fuel run pretty well. Cameras, gas receipt, dash-cam stills. You were on the highway when Jared went over that rail."

For just a second something like relief flashed across his face, loosening his shoulders. I didn't let him enjoy it.

"Thing is," I went on, "not being on the pad doesn't mean you're finished with this. There's the part where you helped write a story that doesn't square with weather, welds, or what I'm hearing in these trailers."

He scratched the back of his neck, eyes sliding away toward the dark pad. Folks lied in that direction; I'd come to recognize it. "I told you what I saw," he muttered.

"Maybe you left some pieces out." I held up the note page from Jared's trailer. "You know he was copying incident logs after a near-fall on that ladder a few weeks before he died."

I watched his reaction. It wasn't surprise. Irritation flashed first, brow creasing, lips pulling tight, aimed at the world in general and probably me in particular.

"Who told you about that?" he asked. "Josh? Kid don't know when to keep his mouth shut."

"So he's right," I said. "Jared took a slip. Started copying log pages. Complained about the way bonuses got handed out, near-misses disappearing. That ring a bell?"

He ground the heel of his boot into the gravel. "Jared made a big deal over everything," he said. "You know the type. Reads the posters like scripture."

"The kind of man who lives long enough to raise his kids," Clara said.

He flinched.

"Look," he said. "We all knew the logs were...flexible. You write up every stubbed toe, nobody cashes a check. Guys get real unhappy when their Christmas money disappears over some dropped wrench."

"So you shaved a few things off the edges," I said. "Who told you to?"

He stared at the coffee can. "Nobody has to tell you that kind of thing. It's in the air. You feel it in safety meetings."

"Fun thing about air," I said. "It carries words. I want the ones you heard."

He tugged at the cuff of his sweatshirt. "You ain't gonna let this go, are you."

"Man died out there," I said. "Not planning on it."

Wind pushed down the lane, rattling the hanging parka and bringing the metallic clank of someone still working late on the pad. Hank's shoulders sagged a fraction, like he'd run out of places inside himself to stash the guilt.

"At a briefing couple months back," he said finally, voice low, "we were bitching about OSHA and auditors and all that. One of the suits laughed and said, 'One bad fall is better than a full audit.' Whole room chuckled. Everybody knew better than to write it down."

The words dropped into me like a stone. I kept my voice even. "Whose mouth did that come out of?" I asked. "Yours?"

He shook his head fast, boot grinding gravel until it squealed. "Wasn't me. I might be dumb, Sheriff, but I ain't suicidal. Came from up the ladder." His eyes flicked toward town, not the rig. "Way over my pay grade."

"Name," Clara said.

He rubbed his neck again, fingers digging hard. "It was in a meeting with the safety guy and Wade and some others. They all sit together in those chairs up front. They talk the same. After a while you can't tell which one said what, you just...remember the lines."

He lied there, but not about everything. I could feel the shape of the truth underneath, fear wrapped around a specific syllable he didn't want to let loose.

"In that same breath," I said, "did they mention audits and paperwork? Camera coverage? Incident codes?"

Hank huffed out something that wasn't quite a laugh. "Always. They talk like calculators. 'Incident rate per thousand man-hours.' 'Loss-time events.' All that. We just know when the board's red or green."

I pulled the gas receipt copy from my pocket, tapped it against my palm. "Here's what I know, Hank. This puts you off-pad when somebody moved Jared's body. Tool marks on that latch and lab work on the bruising point away from a spur-of-the-moment fight and toward planning. You're not the architect here."

His eyes met mine for the first time since I'd walked up. Raw gratitude bled through the shame.

"But," I said, "you still called Rosa to steer her toward accident. You signed onto a story that helps the man who said 'one bad fall' sleep at night."

He swallowed. "What was I supposed to do? Tell a widow I thought her husband got helped over the rail because he made too many notes? What's she supposed to do with that? Sue? Lose the house when she can't prove it? I've seen that movie too."

"So you told the one that lets the company write a check and everybody go back to work," Clara said.

He nodded once. "I'm not proud of it. But it's what we do out here. You think I ain't asked myself what kind of man that makes me?"

I believed him. The bitterness in his voice had teeth.

"I think," I said, "it makes you the kind of man who can still choose what he does next. Which is decide whether you're going to stay a shield for somebody way up that ladder, or help me pull them down where the law can see them."

He looked at the dark pad again, then at the trailer door behind him. I thought of the stories he told himself at two in the morning to justify staying on this crew. None of them held much weight up against a body on steel.

"If I talk," he said, "I lose this job. Maybe every job like it. You know that, right?"

"I do," I said. "I also know Jared's daughter will someday ask what folks did when her dad tried to tell it like it is."

Silence stretched thin. A man walked by without looking up, lighter flaring as he passed.

Hank reached for another cigarette, then stopped, palm resting on the pack like it weighed a ton. "You got that gas receipt," he said. "Proves I wasn't there. Remember that when they start saying I pushed him."

"I will," I said.

He finally pulled a smoke, lit it, and dragged deep. Ember glowed, then faded as he ground it out right away in the coffee can, like he didn't deserve the breath.

"'One bad fall,'" I said quietly. "Those exact words?"

He nodded. "Those exact words. You probably got 'em in his emails or whatever you took from his office." He shivered once, whether from cold or the thought of written proof I couldn't tell. "I ain't saying his name on your recorder. Not tonight."

"Not tonight," I agreed. "But if I see that line on paper above somebody's signature, I'm coming back to ask whether you're ready to say it out loud."

He stared at the gravel. "Way over my pay grade," he whispered again, more to himself than to me.

We walked back toward the truck. Behind us, Hank stayed under the porch light, shoulders hunched, not looking our way.

The man-camp hummed around us, generators and TV laugh tracks and the far-off clank of tools. Under my ribs the words "one bad fall" sat like a splinter. My suspect list had just shuffled again: Hank sliding out of the top slot, still dirty but less bloody, and Colton's name rising, weighted now with math, cameras, and the way his words lived in other men's mouths.

Chapter 14

Scanner Hiss and Cold Coffee

I left the overheads off in the office and clicked just my desk lamp on, letting its yellow circle carve out an island in the empty bullpen. The scanner muttered about a loose calf on Forty, then slipped back to hiss. Burnt coffee clung from a pot that had cooked too long on the hot plate.

On the desk I spread what the last weeks had given me: Hal's backdated weld receipt; copies of the maintenance log with Colton's initials; Rosa's statement; Hank's gas receipt; my own scribbled notes from the rig, the man-camp, Colton's conference room. All the noise I'd been carrying around in my head.

I pulled a legal pad toward me and drew a straight line across the center. Time on paper always looked cleaner than time in real life. I wrote 2100 at the left edge and 0100 at the right. Four hours. Somewhere in there they turned a man into an incident rate.

At 2100, I marked Wade's shift change and the safety meeting he loved to brag about. Next, Hank's fuel run:

out-gate swipe at 2205, gas receipt at 2222, dash-cam still with his truck headlights sliding past a pump island at 2224. Back-gate swipe at 2248.

I added Hal's weld, order rushed through a week before Jared's death, timestamped mid-afternoon. That job didn't sit on this line, but the memory of sparks on that rung did.

Camera 3 maintenance log next. "2200, 2300: static check, weather interference, C.R." I wrote it under the line and underlined Colton's initials twice. On the pad, that hour turned into a shaded block of convenient blindness.

Above the line, I marked the 911 call from the rig at 2317. I could still feel the cold of that night, clear sky, stars sharp enough to hurt under the derrick lights. No snow piling on camera housings. No blizzard.

Jared's last known alive sighting had wobbled between statements. Wade swore he'd seen him heading back up the ladder "sometime after ten" to check a gauge. Hank had first put it closer to ten-thirty, then backed away once the gas receipt pinned him elsewhere. The kid at the bar remembered Jared leaving around nine, talking about "one more hour." None of it gave me a clean minute.

I stared at the line until my eyes blurred. When I shoved the rumors aside and just looked at hard marks, a pattern started to crawl out of the mess. I leaned back, the chair creaking, and rubbed a thumb over Ben

Latham's watch on my wrist. The metal stayed warm from my skin.

If the camera was officially down from 2200 to 2300, and Hank's truck was off-site until near eleven, then anyone using that window to move a body had the advantage of darkness, static, and one less witness. Wade, by his own account, was in the doghouse with his crew for a safety brief that "ran long." Long into what?

I wrote "Wade brief" above the line and stretched its block from 2145 to 2245, the way he'd described it in his first interview, "about an hour, maybe a little more; you know how these things drag." That put the tail end of his meeting right over the camera gap and the time Hank's truck headlights were two towns away. Hard to be everywhere at once.

I added a box at 2230 marked "near-fall weeks prior," a note from Hal's receipt and Hank's offhand comment, Jared taking a slip on that ladder, jolting his shoulder, cussing up a storm. That memory didn't give me a timestamp for the death, but it told me the ladder wasn't random. Somebody had seen how close it could come and filed the feeling away.

On another sheet I wrote three headings: HANK, WADE, COLTON. Under each I listed what they had: motive, opportunity, hands on steel.

HANK: debt; drunk fights; first on-scene. Then, crossed out: fuel run during window; gas receipt; dash cams; coached but scared. Next to his name I wrote "cover-up, not push?" and drew an arrow down.

WADE: falsified logs; rushed weld; replacement harness order never installed; pressure from above on incident rates; gambling debt to maintain. Under that: "briefing at time of likely staging"; "present for body discovery, shapes first story."

COLTON: controls bonuses; signs off safety metrics; "trial exhibit A" email; maintenance log covering camera gap; weather lie; eyes on harness tags at scene; "up the ladder" phrase echoing from Hank, Rosa, Josh; badge logs in a separate stack showing his card used in the camera shack that night.

When I stacked those columns side by side, ink heavier under one, the line I'd been resisting stared back at me. I'd been trying to keep a roughneck or a crew boss as my hands-on man because it made a cleaner story in a county where everyone knew what corporate suits meant at Christmas but didn't stand next to them on steel.

The line on the pad didn't care about my habits.

The scanner crackled to life with a welfare check out on the east road, then went quiet. My pen tapped twice against the legal pad before I forced it still.

Part of me kept wanting to tuck the uglier pieces under Wade's name. He'd lied, after all. He'd let Hal backdate that weld, let the replacement harness sit in a bag. Men like him were easier to picture with blood on their hands. They yelled. They drank. They made fists in bar parking lots.

Colton wore a tie and talked about "our family companies." Sat in glass offices with safety posters framed behind his head. Answered weather questions with a smile and a bad memory I'd already proven wasn't memory at all.

I bent over the line again and boxed the thirty-minute stretch from 2215 to 2245: camera down; Hank on the road; Wade in his own version of a captive audience; Jared unaccounted for except in the mouths of men who needed him where he didn't end up.

In that box I wrote C.R.

Eve's kitchen question from that first night came back under the HVAC hum: If it was our name on those papers, would you keep the peace or reveal the facts?

It wasn't our name on the logs, but it was on the land under those rigs and in the ward minutes when they blessed the project. Paper tied families to steel they'd never climbed. I looked at the page until the words blurred, then underlined Colton's initials a third time, hard.

"Clear and cold," I said into the empty room. "No blizzard."

My voice sounded small against scanner hiss and ticking clock. I read Colton's maintenance entry aloud the way he'd written it: "Camera 3 static check, 2200 to 2300, weather interference, C.R."

I drew an arrow from that block to the weld receipt. Another from the weld to the half page out of Jared's pocket notebook. From that to Josh's words about "Colton's bonus math." A crooked triangle of ink, dead man at the center.

I thought about the judge I'd need to go back in front of. The one who'd already signed my preservation order with barely concealed irritation at dragging a company through more hassle over "one tragic accident." This time I wouldn't be asking to freeze things the company said they were happy to share; I'd be asking to pry open mailboxes and server logs they'd rather keep to themselves.

Outside the office, the hallway lights clicked off on their timer, leaving the glass dark. My reflection floated faint in it, tired man in a badge with too many arrows pointing at someone he'd shaken hands with last week on the square.

I tapped the pen once more, then wrote at the bottom of the timeline: HANK, cover-up; WADE, fraud / pre-knowledge; COLTON, primary: cameras/bonuses/gear.

Under that I added: need paper: payroll detail, incident ledger, emails, badge logs, harness inventory. No more polite requests.

My thumb found Ben's watch again, circling the metal, feeling the faint scratch at twelve where he'd once dinged it on a cell door. Ben had taught me that suspicion without proof was just a story you told yourself in the truck. Tonight the proof was close enough to see its outline; I just had to be willing to draw it dark.

When I finally pushed back from the desk, the legal pad held a boxed-off window circled in ink, Colton's name written through the middle like a fencepost through old wire. Hank's name had drifted to the margin in smaller letters. Wade's sat in the middle with an asterisk that would matter later, just not in the way folks on the rig thought.

I clicked off the lamp. The room dropped into darkness except for the green glow of the scanner, static whispering into the empty air as I walked down the hall. The Basin didn't sleep when I did, and neither did the stories men told to keep their jobs. Tonight I'd stopped pretending those stories lived only in bunkhouses.

Tomorrow they were going to court.

Chapter 15

Blessings and Budget Sheets

The clerks' room door clicked shut behind me with that hollow church-door echo, and the smell of funeral potatoes still lingered in the hallway. Inside, it was just fluorescent hum, a battered folding table, and stacks of welfare forms laid out like a paper fence.

Bishop Cade sat at the far side, jacket off, tie loosened a notch. He smoothed a stack of tithing envelopes with careful fingers. Joel leaned against the filing cabinet, manila folder in hand, like he'd only stepped in to grab reports.

"Sheriff," Cade said. "Thank you for making time. I know you're pulled a dozen ways."

"This is your building," I said, taking the metal chair opposite him. "I'm just borrowing a corner."

Joel gave me a small-town grin and set the folder on the file cabinet. "I've got the updated ward budget sheets, Bishop, if you want—"

"Set them there for now," Cade said. "We can look after we visit."

He folded his hands, the name tag on his white shirt catching the light. Primary sang down the hall, kids' voices rising and falling through cinderblock.

"We're worried for Sister Pike," he began. "Spiritually, of course, but temporally too. These things—sudden deaths—shake folks. I wanted to ask how she's doing, whether there's anything we as a ward aren't seeing."

"That's why I came," I said. "Well. That and to make sure nobody's crowding her about paperwork."

"She mentioned some papers." Cade's thumb ran along the edge of an envelope. "The company's been generous. Settlement, they're calling it. I told her the Lord provides in many ways."

Joel shifted, the manila folder's spine tapping his thigh, soft but steady. "Those jobs out there keep a lot of lights on, Bishop. Not just Rosa's."

There it was, slipped in early.

I set my notebook next to a stack of fast-offering slips. "Rosa's grieving," I said. "She's also clear she doesn't want to be pushed into signing anything she doesn't understand."

"Of course," Cade said. "Agency is sacred. We only counsel."

He smiled, pastorally neutral. "Jared was a good man. None of us understand why the Lord takes some early.

Sometimes it's just…life in the Basin. Accidents. Harsh places."

The word accident hung there, polite as a hymn.

"The latch on that catwalk didn't fail on its own," I said. "Whatever this ends up being called, it wasn't just 'life in the Basin.'"

Something tightened along Joel's jaw. Cade's smile thinned a fraction.

"Brother Kingston," he said, "forgive me if I'm stepping beyond my stewardship. But I do worry about contention. Our people are tired. Companies are nervous. We've been blessed, truly blessed, to have family companies steward this land for generations. They've kept men employed, funded chapels and youth programs. Trusting them, keeping things in the family—that's part of how the Lord keeps peace in a place like this."

There it was. Steward. Family. Same cadence Rosa had used in that dim front room. Same tone as the safety poster in Colton's office.

Joel nodded, flipping his folder open like he couldn't help himself. The header on the top sheet read: BUDGET – STAKE CENTER – DONATIONS/TITHES.

"We run these programs on tithes, Bishop," he said. "And on what the county can scrape together. Taxes, royalties, donations. It's all braided. If this gets dragged out in court, folks are going to feel it. Less in the welfare fund, less for activities, more folks needing help."

His eyes came to me. "You know the numbers as well as I do, Milt."

I did. Roof replacements, camp funds, fast-offering deficits. I also knew what it cost to put a man's name on a death certificate as "accident" when it wasn't.

"Budgets don't decide cause of death," I said. "Evidence does."

Cade's fingers smoothed the top envelope again. "No one is suggesting you ignore your duty. Heaven forbid. We sustain you in that. But I'd hate to see this—one tragic fall—turned into something that tears the ward. Sometimes, trusting the brethren, trusting the good people who've stewarded our livelihoods, is the way we show faith."

Trust. Brethren. Stewarded. I almost didn't need the pen.

"My badge doesn't know kinship, Bishop," I said. "It just knows latches and logs. Would you rather I trust the paperwork or the posters?"

Joel's throat cleared, sharp in the little room. Cade took a slow breath.

"I would hope," he said, "that both tell the same story. We've always tried to keep things in the family. Settle disputes around tables, not in courtrooms. That's kept the Basin from flying apart more than once."

"Including this?" I asked. "Keeping it in the family?"

He glanced at Joel before he answered. Just the quickest flick of eyes, but it was there.

"Our focus," he said carefully, "is on Sister Pike and her children. If the company can provide for them, and the county can close its file knowing it's done its work, that seems...merciful. Doesn't it?"

Mercy for whom sat unsaid.

Primary sang a snatch of "Families Can Be Together Forever" down the hall. Out in the gym, a folding chair scraped the waxed floor.

Jared's notebook page came back to me, cramped figures and that neat little "bonus – Colton" crammed along one edge. Hal's grease-stained receipt. Colton standing under that safety poster: FAMILY COMPANIES, FAMILY VALUES, over a photo of a rig at sunrise.

"Rosa told me about the blessing you gave Jared," I said. "About 'trusting the brethren' and 'keeping things in the family.'"

Cade's ringed hand paused on the envelope edge.

"She must be hurting deeply," he said. "Grief colors memory."

"Maybe," I said. "But you just used the same words, so either her memory's sharp or both of you got them from the same place."

Joel shifted. "Milt, nobody's scripting anybody. It's just...we all talk the same way. We grew up with the same stories."

"That's part of what I'm looking at," I said. "Same stories. Same words. From the blessing couch to the office poster to this table."

Silence, except for the fluorescent buzz and Cade's measured breath.

"If you charge someone from the company," Joel said finally, "and it goes south, there's going to be backlash. Jobs, donations, legal fees. Folks will ask why you didn't just call it a tragic accident like the report can."

"Reports can be wrong," I said. "Or written to sound like peace."

Cade's gaze softened, like he'd decided to treat me as a struggling soul instead of a stubborn sheriff. "You're tired, Brother Kingston. We all are. I just ask that when you weigh things, you remember the bigger picture. The Basin needs unity. These family companies need room to keep stewarding. We can't afford to have every mishap turned into a crusade."

Every mishap. Jared's body hanging off steel, rebranded as a mishap.

"I'll remember the bigger picture," I said. "And the smaller one. The size of a notch in a latch, the length of a camera gap."

He smiled sadly, folded his hands again. "We'll keep praying for you. For wisdom. For Rosa. For...everyone involved."

"I appreciate prayers," I said. "I'll also be asking a judge for warrants."

Joel's pen clicked in his hand. "Just...keep us in the loop on anything the ward needs. Welfare checks, rent help for Rosa. We can't carry it all if the county pulls the rug out on jobs."

"If someone killed him," I said, "the rug was already pulled."

I stood. My chair scraped the floor louder than I meant.

"Thank you for your time," Cade said. "Truly. We want the same thing, you and I. Peace."

I walked to the door, hand on the knob. Peace. On their terms.

"Peace built on truth holds better," I said, without turning. "We'll see which way this one leans."

In the hallway, noise washed over me: kids laughing in the gym, a piano plinking out the tail end of a hymn, the faint clatter of dishes near the kitchen. Behind me, the clerks' room door closed with a soft thud.

I stepped under a bright fluorescent by the bulletin board, flipped open my notebook, and wrote Cade's phrase down word for word—family companies stewarding this land—before the ward's buzz could sand it smooth. Then I flipped back through earlier pages. Rosa's front room: "Trust the brethren. Keep this in the family." Colton's office poster: FAMILY COMPANIES STEWARDING THIS LAND SINCE 1954. Now Cade, fresh ink, nearly the same sentence.

Blessing to widow to bishop's counsel to poster. Same cluster of words doing the same work everywhere I turned. I didn't need to win a doctrinal argument. I just needed to show a judge, someday, that when people in this building said "trust" and "family companies" in the same breath, they weren't just bearing testimony. They were reinforcing a story that made widows sign faster and roughnecks shrug off bruises.

My faith, whatever shape it had left, was going to have to survive me writing a bishop's words down the same way I wrote a suspect's. If it couldn't, I wasn't sure what it was worth.

Cold air met me at the doors, sharp and clean after the recycled building. Out in the lot, trucks idled and people laughed, not knowing or not caring what was scribbled under my elbow. I pulled my collar up against the chill and walked toward my truck, already turning over how this cluster of words would look on a warrant affidavit—lines bridging ward minutes and a company memo under the same thin fluorescent light.

Chapter 16

Ledger Ghosts

The records-room door in the courthouse basement opened on cool, dry air and the thin whine of a dehumidifier. Rows of gray rolling shelves ran away from us under buzzing fluorescent tubes, lit like a tomb for old paper.

The clerk, a woman I knew mostly by face from the square-side coffee counter, handed me a sign-in clipboard. The pen rattled in my hand as I wrote my name, case number, reason: OSHA-ledger review – payroll / incident logs.

"Thank you for coming down yourself, Sheriff," she said. Her voice had that careful evenness people used when they were trying not to pick sides. "We pulled what you asked last night."

Behind her, Clara already had a gray cart in motion, stacked with thick green ledgers and cardboard boxes. The metal wheels squeaked.

"Appreciate you staying late," I said.

"Judge's order's pretty clear," she answered, eyes sliding to the envelope on my belt and back. "Just...try not to take the whole room apart."

"We'll put everything back where we found it," Clara said. "Promise."

We parked the cart at the central table. Clara flipped open the top ledger, the heavy cover landing with a soft thump that echoed more than it should. The smell of old paper and cardboard breathed up—ink, dust, a hint of mildew the dehumidifier hadn't quite beaten.

Columns ran down the pages in neat, faded lines: EMP ID, HOURS, GROSS, DEDUCTIONS, NOTES. Rows of numbers marched like headstones.

"This is all local payroll?" I asked.

"Field office copies," the clerk said. "Master records are scanned, but these are what they send over quarterly. I've got incident logs in the second box."

She clicked her pen, an anxious little metronome, then retreated to a desk near the door, pretending to check email while she listened.

We started with January and worked forward. Fingers on pages, eyes tracking. Most entries were straightforward—overtime, per diem, standard deductions. Boredom set in before the second page, that dull glaze that always came with ledgers and lab reports.

I'd learned a long time ago that the glaze was dangerous. That was when you missed the ghost in the column.

After a while Clara shifted to another ledger, flipping until she found the right heading. "Here," she said. "Site seven. That's Jared's rig."

The dehumidifier hummed. Somewhere above our heads, a gavel thudded faintly and stopped.

I moved closer. At the far-right side of the sheet, a narrow column carried a different label, in someone's tidy handwriting: Safety Perf. Bonus – Site 7.

My stomach gave a slow, sinking twist.

"Look at the pattern," Clara murmured.

Not every name on the page had an entry in that column. When they did, the amounts were small, irregular. A hundred here, two-fifty there. Scattered over months.

She tapped one row with her pen. "Employee 1427. That's Jared, right?"

I checked my notebook. 1427, J. PIKE. "Yeah."

"Bonus, bonus, bonus..." she said quietly, sliding her finger down dates I already knew too well. "Then nothing."

The last bonus by his number sat three weeks before his fall. The dollar amounts beside earlier dates—$200, $150, $200—matched almost exactly the figures I'd copied from the torn notebook page we pulled from his trailer.

"C.R.," I said.

Each bonus entry had those same initials hanging off the edge of the column.

Clara's pen tapped twice on the letters. "Colton Reese. Could be someone else, but I doubt it."

Jared's line ended in that empty stretch of boxes. Under his, two other hands—numbers I recognized from crew rosters—kept collecting little hits of cash, all the way up to and past the date on the death certificate.

I thought of Hank's muttered "better one bad fall than a full audit," Wade's tight jaw, Colton in his clean office talking about safety metrics like they were sacrament.

The clerk's breath caught at her desk, a sound too small to be deliberate.

"Let's not say names out loud," Clara said, softer now. "Sound carries."

We worked across to another month. Same pattern. Bonuses only for certain IDs. Same initials.

"Incident log," I said. "Let's see if dates match."

The clerk brought the second box over without being asked this time. "These are copies," she said. "Originals are out at the office, but they're supposed to send everything. I'm not vouching for what they actually do."

"That's why we're here," I said.

We spread the incident book next to payroll. Clara turned to the tabbed section for Site 7. Near-falls, minor injuries, equipment hiccups—most coded as resolved with "no lost time," signed by shift supervisors.

She traced one with her finger. "Date of that near-fall the roustabout told you about."

I matched it across to payroll. Safety Perf. Bonus for Jared that same week. Another bonus for a different hand, smaller. Colton's initials on both.

A heavier quiet pooled between the fluorescent buzz and the soft rustle of pages. Boredom had shifted to that other feeling paper gave you when it turned—dread with edges. Once you saw the story numbers told, you couldn't unsee it.

"He set this up like a reward program," I said. "Keep incident rates pretty on the books, you get a little extra. Don't make noise about the weak rung, sign off on 'no lost time,' and here's two hundred cash through payroll."

"Looks like it," Clara said. "And right there, three weeks before the death, Jared stops taking the money."

"Or stops being offered it," I said. "Either way, he goes off script."

I pictured that torn half-page again. Dates, dollar amounts that hadn't matched his stubs. Bonus – Colton.

"He started copying logs," Clara said. "He told people, 'If I disappear, it wasn't the ladder.' He was keeping his own ledger of their ledger."

"And somebody up the chain noticed," I said. "The same somebody who initialed these."

The clerk's pen stopped clicking.

By the time we closed the last payroll ledger, I had a list of employee numbers and dates in my notebook. Jared's bonuses rising, then cutting off like a road at a washout. A couple of other hands still walking that road, maybe still swallowing their fear for a line item.

Clara slid the book back onto the cart and I left my palm on the open page a heartbeat longer, over that column label and the blank where Jared's last bonus should have been.

"This enough for probable cause to go after the rest of Colton's systems?" I asked quietly.

"Combined with Hal's weld receipt, the camera gap, Hank's coached line?" Clara said. "Yeah. We've got dollars, dates, initials, and a dead man who stopped taking the money right before he went off a ladder that shouldn't have failed."

She paused, fingers still on the ledger's spine. "But we need to talk about scope before you walk into Harper's chambers."

"Scope?"

"You're going to want everything. Emails, badge logs, the full camera server. I can see it on your face." She kept her voice low, but there was a set to her jaw I didn't usually see. "If we go in asking for the whole company's digital footprint, Harper will trim it himself, and we lose control of what he cuts. We need to draw the box tight—Reese's accounts, Site 7, six-week window. Let the first warrant prove the second one."

"That feels like leaving money on the table," I said.

"It's strategy, not timidity." She met my eyes across the cart. "You give a judge a rifle shot, he signs. You give him a fishing net, he rewrites your warrant over lunch and hands you back something useless. I've seen it happen."

I wanted to argue. The pattern on that ledger made me want to rip every drawer in Colton's office out by the runners. But Clara had spent more hours in front of judges than I had, and the flat certainty in her voice wasn't bluster. It was experience.

"Fine," I said. "Rifle shot. But the moment that first warrant comes back dirty, I want the second one drafted and ready to file."

"Already planning on it," she said. "I'll have the template on your desk before you get to Harper."

I took my county phone out and snapped a quick photo of the page with Jared's ID and that empty run of boxes. The shutter sounded loud in the basement.

The clerk swallowed. "You're going to copy those officially, right?"

"Certified copies," Clara said. "You'll get a receipt."

"I'd like that." The clerk rubbed her thumb along the edge of another ledger, not quite meeting my eye. "My cousin works out there. Folks have been saying it's just a tragic accident. That we've got to trust the family companies, or the ward'll be hurting for years."

Trust. Family companies. Again.

"So if a judge sees these," she went on, "that's on the judge. Not on the girl who opened the vault."

"It's on the man who initialed 'C.R.' all the way down that column," I said.

She let out a little breath she probably didn't know she'd been holding.

We boxed up copies under her supervision, each page slid into a manila envelope, signatures and case numbers going on the labels. The overhead lights flickered once, then steadied. Somewhere above us a door slammed and voices rose, then faded.

As Clara pushed the cart back toward the shelves, I stood a moment longer at the table, thumb rubbing the envelope's metal clasp. The ghosts on those pages weren't just Jared. Every bonus line was a man learning that keeping quiet paid, and that going off the schedule might get him noticed in all the wrong ways.

We thanked the clerk, signed the log again, and stepped out into the stairwell. Fluorescent light spilled up from the basement, cold concrete stacking above it like a narrow canyon. At the top of the stairs a thin slice of daylight painted a line on the wall.

"I'll start a clean timeline document tonight," Clara said as we climbed. "Dollars, dates, initials, cross-referenced with incidents and that maintenance log. You give the judge story spine; I'll give statute. And I'll draft the scope language so you don't have to argue it on the fly."

I shifted the envelope higher under my arm, feeling its weight against my ribs. It wasn't just photocopies in there.

It was a map—from a replacement weld to a rig deck, from a blessing couch to a glass office, from a dead man's cramped handwriting to a neat little column labeled SAFETY PERF. BONUS.

We pushed through the basement door into the courthouse hallway and walked toward the front doors and the strip of sky beyond them. For the first time since Jared's body swung on steel, I felt the case leaning from "maybe" toward "prove it."

Chapter 17

Kitchen Light on a Warrant

The dishwasher thumped and hissed behind me like it had opinions. I cleared the last cereal bowl off the kitchen table and dropped the manila envelope on the scarred laminate. Ledger copies fanned out, gray and grainy under the yellow lamp. Hal's weld receipt, my notes about latch marks, Hank's "one bad fall" line—all spread like a losing hand of cards.

Ben Latham's watch sat by my pen. I thumbed the crystal once, uncapped the pen, and wrote at the top of the notebook page: "Basin Energy – Site 7."

Eve rinsed a pan in the sink. Dish soap and cooling coffee mixed with the faint cold off the river through the cracked window.

"More homework?" she asked, not turning yet.

"Just trying to see what story the paper tells," I said.

Which was only half it. The other half was whether I was going to pick a fight with a company that paid half the ward's tithing and gave my brother his job.

I laid the ledger copy square in the light. "Safety Perf. Bonus – Site 7." Dates, employee numbers, dollar amounts. Clara had penciled Jared's number in the margin. Line of payments, then a clean stop a few weeks before his body hit steel. Colton's initials hung off the edge of every one.

Under that I set Hal's receipt, the one that should have lived in some forgotten file instead of my kitchen: weld on that rung, dated a week before Jared "slipped," then backdated on paper to make it look older. Same week Jared got his last bonus.

"You're muttering statute numbers," Eve said. Dishes rattled as she slid them into the rack.

"Trying to decide if this is enough for probable cause," I said. "For a warrant on their systems. Cameras, badge logs, emails."

"And?" The dishwasher door thunked shut. Suds smell thickened the room.

"And judges don't sign warrants because something smells off. They sign them because you put black ink under it."

I looked at Colton's initials in the ledger. Looked at Hal's looping signature. Saw Cade in the hallway at church, asking me to "spare the ward more pain."

Eve shut off the water and dried her hands, slow. She hadn't come to the table yet. I could feel her listening.

"If we push for their emails, cameras, everything," I said, "company lawyers come in hot. Donors call Tessa. Cade starts talking about jobs in elders quorum. It won't just be Colton. It'll be the whole outfit. People hear my name at fast and testimony meeting and think 'lawsuit.'"

"Is that what you're weighing?" she asked. "Or are you weighing whether you're sure enough Colton's the one?"

I tapped the ledger with the pen. "Every weird piece goes through him. Bonuses he signed. Camera he controlled. The gap in footage he wrote up as weather that didn't happen. But if I overreach, we look like we're on a fishing trip. Judge narrows it, or worse, denies it. Then he knows exactly what I'm after and has time to clean up."

The words sat there. The dishwasher rumbled and the scanner murmured from the living room. Nothing dramatic on the air—just some deputy running plates, another domestic on the west side. The county kept on running while I stared at numbers.

Eve dried a plate and finally crossed over. She didn't sit. She stood at my shoulder, looking down. Her fingers smoothed the ledger's edge.

"Show me," she said.

I walked her through it: Jared's number marching along the bonus column, then dropping away. The matching figures from his pocket notebook. Hal's weld receipt dated before the fall and then written over. Hank's line about "better one bad fall than a full audit" matching the way the ledger neatens up after Jared stops taking money.

"And this one?" she asked, pointing to the maintenance log copy Clara had printed. "Cam 3 static check, 21:40 to 22:05. Weather interference."

"That's Colton's write-up," I said. "Same window the rig camera goes to snow. He told me that first week it was driving snow. I wrote down stars and dry cold in my notebook that night."

She went quiet. The river outside hissed louder in the pause than any sermon I'd sat through. Her hand shook when she traced the column where Jared's money stopped.

"You keep saying, 'if we push,'" she said. "Like the pushing itself is what you have to justify."

"It kind of is," I said. "Legally, we have to show the judge we're not just mad. Politically, I have to live in this town tomorrow."

She set the dish towel on the table, flat. "If that line right there," she tapped Jared's cut-off entry, "had our name on it—if the column said 'Kingston' instead of 'Pike'—would you be telling yourself it was enough just to know why it stopped?"

My throat worked before anything came out. I stared at the ink, thought about my own paycheck, about Joel in Cade's office talking budgets and land. Thought about Rosa on her sagging couch, kids climbing her like furniture.

"If it was your bonus," she went on, voice softer but harder, "and somebody cut it off right before you went off a rig, and the safety guy who signed it also happened to be the one who turned the camera off and lied about the weather—would you want your sheriff to shrug and say, 'We know in our hearts what happened, that's enough'?"

"I'd want him to knock on every door with that man's initials on it," I said. The answer came up before I could sand it down. "I'd want him to make that man hand over every scrap of paper and byte of data he'd touched."

Eve let out a breath. "Then that's what you do."

My gut settled in a way my brain hadn't caught up to. The list on the page stopped feeling like a maybe and more like marching orders. Probable cause wasn't a feeling; it was this list, plus my notes, plus Hal's receipt. It was the camera gap logged as weather that didn't come.

"It's going to cost," I said.

"Everything we've ever told the kids about honesty already costs," she said. Her fingers rested on my wrist, warm. "If we back off now that we know, they'll learn the other lesson instead."

That sat with the ledger and the envelope and everything else I'd been trying not to name.

The dishwasher hummed into its drying cycle. In the other room, the scanner crackled: a traffic stop, nothing special. The Basin ticking along, unaware that one corner of ledger paper had just tipped me from thinking to acting.

I pulled the notebook closer and wrote across the top of a clean page: "Affidavit re: Basin Energy Site 7."

Underneath, I set three headings: "Physical Evidence," "Financial Records," "Surveillance Gaps." Beneath each, bullet points in my tight, neat script.

"Which judge?" Eve asked.

"Harper first," I said. "He'll fuss about jobs but he reads." I added his name in the margin like a reminder of the audience.

Eve's shoulders lifted. "Then write like you're explaining it to Rosa," she said. "Plain and narrow. You're not trying to take down the whole company. You're asking to look at one man's fingerprints."

I nodded. The old urge to tuck the envelope in a drawer and call it enough thinned out, enough that I could hear my pen again.

"You sure about standing in that hallway on Sunday?" I asked. "When the cold shoulders start."

She smiled, tired and fierce. "I'd rather have them angry at us for telling it like it is than have to live with Rosa's eyes if we don't."

Her hand squeezed my wrist once, then she turned back to the sink to stack the last plates in the drying rack. The lamp over the table haloed the pages in front of me. Outside, the river ran on, indifferent.

—

The house went quiet once the kids were in bed. I stayed put, elbows on the table, notebook open where I'd written "Affidavit" in block letters.

The air cooled; the furnace cycled low. The river's hush slipped in clearer through the bathroom window somebody'd left cracked. The scanner in the living room talked to itself in bursts, other people's trouble passing through.

I drew a line under my headings and started filling them in. Tool marks on the safety latch, corroborated by photographs. Replacement harness still bagged in the locker. Ledger entries with amounts matching Jared's notebook page, all approvals initialed C.R., cut off weeks before his death. Cam 3 static logged as weather interference by C.R., contradicted by my own contemporaneous note of clear, dry conditions.

I made myself stick to what we could prove without lab results. No speculating about choke holds or unconsciousness yet; that would go in another affidavit down the line.

As I wrote, a pattern sharpened I'd felt but not laid out this clean: every item on the page had "C.R." tagged to it. Bonuses. Camera. Maintenance note. Safety meeting minutes I'd shoved in a folder from the first interview. I boxed his initials each time they showed, ink cutting a little harder with every pass.

This wasn't just the system being crooked. The weak spots lined up under one man's pen.

That steadied my language. I crossed out "pattern of corporate negligence" and rewrote it: "pattern of decision-making and documentation controlled by safety manager Colton Reese." Judges read that differently.

"Concerned about pattern of dishonesty" turned into "Reese has documented conditions contradicted by independent evidence." That was enough; a judge could draw his own conclusion about honesty.

I could hear Harper's questions before he asked them, his dry voice in chambers. "Sheriff, are you asking me to haul the whole company's records in here, or is this about a specific individual?"

Clara's voice from the courthouse stairwell came back to me: Rifle shot, not a fishing net. So I answered Harper on paper: "Scope: Limited to electronic accounts, badge logs, and camera maintenance records assigned to or accessible by Mr. Reese and supervisory staff at Site 7 on date of incident and in six-week window prior. Not seeking full corporate financials at this stage."

Under each bullet, I put how we got it: subpoena, consent, OSHA pretext. Chain of custody was as much a character in this as Colton. The facts on the page didn't care who sang in the choir.

When I outlined the final paragraph—"Affiant respectfully requests a warrant authorizing seizure and forensic imaging of the above-described electronic accounts and logs"—my shoulders dropped a half inch I hadn't noticed they'd been holding.

Eve crossed behind me and rested her fingers a moment on my shoulder. No words, just that touch.

"You coming to bed soon?" she asked.

"In a minute," I said. "Just going to box this up."

I snapped the notebook shut and laid the manila envelope on top, smooth. Together they made a single, weighty rectangle. I pictured carrying it up the courthouse steps, Harper's pen over the line, Colton's face when he heard the word "warrant" instead of "follow-up."

"You've already crossed the line you were staring at," Eve said from the doorway.

She turned off the living-room lamp as she went, leaving the scanner to mutter in green and the kitchen light to burn over one small bright island of paper. I sat another moment, thumb rubbing Ben's watch, then killed the lamp and carried the stacked packet to the shelf by the door where I kept things I didn't want to forget in the morning.

Chapter 18

Maintenance Log Mismatch

The field office's front door sighed when the receptionist buzzed us in. Fluorescent light flattened the framed safety posters on the wall, hardhats, smiling crews, "Zero Incidents, Zero Excuses." The badge reader clicked and the lock thunked.

Colton came down the hallway with a paper coffee cup and his practiced neighborly smile.

"Sheriff. Deputy Ray." He shook my hand with the same grip he'd used at Jared's service, like none of this was personal. "What can we help you with today?"

"Clearing up some paperwork," I said. My affidavit outline sat heavy in my inside pocket. "Thought we'd grab a few follow-up logs while we're in town. Keep you from having to deal with subpoenas if we can avoid it."

He laughed, easy. "We're all for cooperation. Saves everyone trouble."

His eyes flicked to Clara's notepad, then back to me. He gestured toward the offices. "Come on back. We can use the conference room."

The HVAC hummed in the hallway. Phones rang behind closed doors, a printer started a job somewhere, spitting pages we weren't allowed to see. As we walked, Clara murmured, just loud enough, "Maintenance logs, camera service, week before and after," like a grocery list.

Colton opened a glass-walled conference room, all table and stackable chairs. The far wall held a whiteboard with half-erased arrows about "Safety Culture Goals."

Clara and I took seats on the side that faced the door. Habit.

"So," Colton said, staying standing a second too long, "what specifically are you hoping to look at?"

"Full maintenance logs for Site 7 cameras for the week around the incident," I said. "Anything related to Cam 3 especially. Figured we'd start with what you've already got handy."

He nodded, too quick. "Sure thing. We've got all that in the back. Give me a minute to pull it so I'm not dragging you through the file room."

He slipped out, leaving coffee smell and toner.

Clara glanced at me. "He's feeling you for what's in your pocket," she said quietly.

"Let him wonder," I said. I opened my notebook, blank page ready.

Through the glass I could see part of the hallway. A woman from HR walked past, clipboard hugged to her chest, eyes flicking toward us before she moved on. People knew when the sheriff was in the building.

Colton reappeared a couple minutes later with a clipped stack of paper and a frown of concentration. He carried the log with two fingers at the corner, like it might smudge.

"Here we go," he said, setting it between us. "Camera maintenance logs, week before through the night of. You'll see we documented the static event just like we're supposed to."

He took the head of the table, sideways, where he could watch us and the door.

Clara slid the top page toward herself, pen poised. I leaned in. The entries marched down in tidy blocks: date, time, camera, issue, action, initials. Most were routine: "Cam 1 lens wiped, dust" or "Cam 2 alignment check."

Three lines up from the bottom on the last page, there it sat: "02/, /, , 21:40, 22:05, Cam 3 static check, weather interference, action: monitor, no hardware fault. Initials: C.R."

My fingertip landed under the time block before my mouth said anything. The window matched almost exactly what we'd pulled off the copied footage: snow on the screen from just after nine forty until a few minutes past ten. The same window Jared went off the steel.

"Remind me," I said, voice light, "that static check, that was the same night as Pike's fall, right?"

"Yes, Sheriff," Colton said smoothly. "Nasty little squall came through. Knocked it out right in that window. We logged it, same as always. Nothing out of the ordinary."

Out of the corner of my eye Clara's pen paused just above the paper for half a beat.

"You remember snow that night?" she asked, casual as you please. "I just remember cold."

There was the tiniest hitch, the blink of someone editing as they went. Then he smiled like we were swapping weather tips. "Out there, you get microclimates. Might be stars in town, flurries on the pad. That's why we don't take chances. We log it."

My notebook back at the office had "clear" underlined twice. I didn't argue weather here. Not yet.

"Looks thorough," I said instead. I turned a couple of pages back, scanning. His initials weren't everywhere. Other techs had handled small things. The only entries with his initials in that week were a safety meeting sign-off and this static window.

"When you say 'monitor, no hardware fault,'" Clara said, "does that involve anyone going out to the unit, or is that just watching the feed from here?"

"Depends," he said. "In this case it was clearly weather-related interference. White-out snow. Signal fade. Once it cleared and came back clean, there was no reason to put somebody on the ladder in the dark."

His fingers stayed on the tabletop, not quite still. He looked more at me than at her. I tapped once by the "weather interference" line.

"You logged that from here?" I asked. "From the control room?"

"Well, yes," he said. "Our safety policy is we don't send somebody out in active weather. It's all time-stamped if you need to see it."

"I'm sure we will," I said. "Appreciate you having this ready."

Clara flipped to the back page. "Mind if we copy this?" she asked.

"Of course," he said. "I'll have reception run a set."

He reached for the stack. As he did, I said, "One more question while you're here, Mr. Reese."

He settled back, hand on the paper.

"Your earlier incident summary talked about 'driving snow' during that timeframe," I said. "This says 'weather interference.' Just tracking language. Anything else you'd want to add now, while it's fresh?"

He gave a tiny shrug. "Sheriff, we're not meteorologists. We describe what we see on the screen. It was white static. That usually means snow. We log it. If you want the exact inches, that's more your department."

"It'll be the state's, actually," Clara said lightly. "We'll pull the official records to match. Just making sure we all use the same words."

He smiled wider, but the muscles around his eyes didn't. "You do what you have to. We'll keep doing our part."

The printer whirred out in the workroom, a little burst of mechanical noise. It sounded like the sound in the records basement, where ledger ghosts had first put his initials in front of me.

"Anything else today?" he asked.

"We're good for now," I said. "Like I said, we're trying to keep this cooperative. If we need more, we'll go through your counsel."

He didn't miss the shift in pronoun. His eyes flicked to my coat, where the notebook with "Affidavit" lived.

"Understood," he said. "If you need anything else, just have your office email us and we'll route it through legal. Keep everything clean."

On the way out, reception handed Clara the copied log. She slid it into a thin folder, only the corner of the "Cam 3 static check" line visible through the paper when the light caught it.

Out in the parking lot, winter sky stretched clear and pale over the asphalt. No sign of the storm he'd woven into his story.

We climbed into the truck and I let the engine idle until the heater quit blowing straight cold.

"Microclimates," Clara said. "That's a new one."

"He doubled down," I said. "He could have said he'd misremembered. Instead he added flurries."

She flipped the folder open on her lap, pen ticking a quick circle around the static entry.

"It's not just that he lied about the weather," she said. "He formalized it. This isn't a slip in conversation. It's a written, logged event."

"Initialed by the same man who turned Jared's money on and off," I said. The words tasted like metal. "He might not know I wrote down the sky that night. But he knows we're close enough that he wants legal in the loop."

"Which helps us," she said. "Judges don't like liars. Especially ones who sign logs."

I pulled out of the lot, eased us around the office building, and pointed us toward the square.

We circled the square once instead of pulling straight into the sheriff's slot. The courthouse windows glowed; the diner's neon sign buzzed pink and blue. A couple of trucks idled by the curb, exhaust marking the air.

I slipped into a space facing the courthouse steps, left the engine running long enough to tick the heater down, then killed it. The truck's metal pinged as it cooled. Through the windshield, the courthouse's fluorescent spill made the sidewalk look whiter than the sky ever had that night on the rig.

Clara pushed the visor down and tucked the copied log behind the elastic strap. The word "static" showed faint through the thin paper.

"So," she said. "Where do we put this in the affidavit? Centerpiece or one tile?"

Anger itched under my ribs, wanting something direr than careful phrasing. I pictured slamming the log down on Colton's desk until he dropped that smooth act. Pictured Rosa's face if this ever got boiled down to "weather glitch."

"We treat it like what it is," Clara went on when I didn't answer right away. "A documented lie in a system he controls. Not a smoking anything. A credibility problem that opens the door."

I let my hands rest on the wheel, knuckles going tight before I made myself loosen them.

"We reframe it as: 'Mr. Reese has already been shown to falsify maintenance circumstances surrounding this incident,'" she said. "That justifies looking at his entire digital footprint for the site. His emails, his camera-access logs, his badge swipes. Pattern, not one-off."

I nodded. "So we don't put all the weight on this page," I said. "We set it next to the ledger, Hal's weld, the bonus cut-off, Hank's line. Show that every time the story bends away from accident, his name is sitting there."

"Exactly," she said. "If we oversell this as the magic key and Harper pokes a hole anywhere, we look like we were reaching. If we treat it as another brick in a wall, he sees structure."

The courthouse door opened. A clerk stepped out, hugged her cardigan tight, hurried to a sedan. Her breath showed in a faint puff then disappeared.

I pictured Harper on the bench upstairs, flipping through my affidavit. "Ledger entries initialed by Reese." Turn page. "Backdated weld receipt." Turn page. "Maintenance log entry for Cam 3 static, falsely attributing interference to snow that confirmed records show did not fall."

"Have you confirmed the weather yet beyond your notebook?" Clara asked.

"Not formally," I said. "State data's there; we just haven't pulled it."

"Then that's our next stop before you swear to anything," she said. "Scanner interlude: weather nerd edition. We give Harper printouts from the state station and your contemporaneous note. No 'I'm pretty sure.'"

I blew out a breath, watched it fog faintly on the glass. The anger in my chest settled into something heavier but steadier. "We've got enough," I said, and heard myself believe it. "Even if we never got another piece, this is probable cause on his systems."

"Then we act like it," she said. She smoothed her notepad flat against her knee. "We tweak the draft tonight. Make sure the log language is quoted exactly. Then tomorrow we check weather, talk to Tessa about the political storm she's going to pretend she didn't see coming, and go upstairs."

The courthouse fluorescents hummed across the square. Somewhere inside, the judge's chambers light would still be on; he worked late more often than he'd admit. Through another window I could see the outline of the clerk's counter, stacks of files like low mesas.

My mind jumped ahead: the short walk from our side door to his, the sound of his pen on paper, the low sigh he'd give when he saw a donor's company name in the caption. The moment his ink crossed the line.

"Let's go convince a judge we're not crazy," Clara said.

I picked up the keys. The folded log crackled as I slid it from the visor down into the manila envelope with the ledger copies and Hal's receipt, the packet thickening into something that might finally outweigh all the quiet pressure to let it go.

We stepped out into the chill. Her door thunked shut, echoing off the brick. She tucked her hands into her jacket pockets and looked up at the courthouse windows, jaw set.

I fell into step beside her, envelope under my arm, the square's neon and sodium lights painting long, thin lines across the truck's hood behind us, more ledger marks on a town that had been balancing jobs and safety in the dark for too long.

Chapter 19

Threadbare Sunday

Snowmelt slicked under my boots as we stepped through the glass doors of the stake center. Warm air rolled over us, heavy with perfume and leftover funeral potatoes. Two boys in clip-on ties shot past, racing for Primary like the building might sprint away without them.

Eve paused beside me, smoothing her skirt once, then again. Abby and Caleb shrugged out of their coats. I shook mine, drops pattering onto the entry mat, and took in the long hallway.

Same cinderblock, same bulletin board with flyers about temple trips and canning classes. Same faces. Different angles.

Some eyes met mine and held, with small nods. Others slid off, as if somebody down the hall had just whispered their name. My shoulders hitched. I rolled them loose. Smile. Handshakes. Routine.

"Hey, Sheriff." The other bishopric counselor, Mark, clapped my arm. "Busy times at the office, huh?"

"Always," I said. Not one word about Jared, or Colton, or the rumors everyone had chewed on all week.

Abby slipped a program from the stack and twisted one corner between her fingers as we walked into the chapel. Our usual row, three from the front on the right, sat half-empty. The family that always beat us there, the Nielsen kids with the loud laugh, stood farther up, sliding into a row they'd never claimed before.

Abby tugged my sleeve. "Since when do they sit with the Harts?"

"Since today, I guess."

"Uh-huh." She watched them a beat longer. Mrs. Nielsen glanced back, met my eye, then steered her husband all the way to the middle of the row.

We slid into our spot. Eve's hand rested on my knee under the hymnbook as people settled around us. On the far side, a sister I'd home-taught for years rose halfway, purse in hand, like she meant to cross over and join us. Someone tapped her shoulder, and she sat back down two rows behind.

Hymn numbers flipped on the board. The organist ran a few practice chords. Programs rustled, a soft, papery wind.

I watched patterns, like at a scene. Who came late and chose a different door. Which kids made it up to our bench and which got a quiet hand on the shoulder, turned toward the other side.

Bishop Cade stood to welcome everyone. He talked about fasting, about unity and trusting "those called as stewards," the word hanging there like a nail between us. He never said the word rig. He didn't have to. Half the men in the room smelled of it.

Abby leaned my way during the sacrament hymn. "Mom, can I sit with Cass?" She tilted her head toward her friend two rows back.

"If Cass's mom says yes," Eve murmured.

Cass looked eager enough. Her mother's eyes cut forward to me, then back. A tiny shake of her head. Cass's shoulders rounded. Abby's did too.

She stayed planted.

Sacrament passed. Talks blurred, a high councilor on faith, a teenager on scripture study. My mind kept slipping sideways, running timeframes and warrants. When my thoughts drifted toward Colton's office, Abby's fingers twisting her program snapped me back.

On the last hymn, a boy behind us sang too loud on purpose, like always. Most weeks his dad grinned at me over the top of his head. Today his gaze bounced past, landed on the bishop, and stayed there.

After the closing prayer we funneled into the hallway with everyone else. Folding chairs scraped in the cultural hall as deacons lugged them out for a later meeting. The gym floor squeaked under their sneakers. Kids in patent-leather shoes skidded and laughed.

Sister Green touched Eve's elbow. "We'd love to sit with you for Sunday School," she said, voice bright. "But I promised my sister we'd catch up about girls camp." Her eyes slid to me, then to the nearest exit.

"No worries," Eve said, that same brightness pasted over something tighter. "Next week."

We drifted toward Gospel Doctrine. My name floated twice in low conversations that stopped when I came close. A brother I'd once hauled out of a ditch on Christmas Eve nodded past me to Caleb. "Hey, bud. How's the Lego city?"

"Good," Caleb said. The man's gaze never came back to my face.

In class, Eve and I took two metal chairs at the edge. Abby headed for Youth. Caleb wandered down the hall with his Primary class, glancing back when one boy he usually sat by ducked into the bathroom instead of walking with him.

The lesson ran on New Testament verses about love and charity. Comments on kindness, on "assuming the best" when we don't know everything. A woman in the back said, "Sometimes we just have to trust the people the Lord has put in charge and let them handle the hard things. Otherwise, we pick at wounds that could be healing."

Heads nodded. My jaw ached.

The teacher caught my eye. "Brother Kingston, anything to add?"

A dozen answers flickered. Jared's name. Rosa on her sagging couch. Hal's grease-stained hands holding that backdated receipt. The maintenance log with a storm that never happened.

"Truth and healing aren't opposites," I said. "Sometimes you've got to clean a wound before it can close. That hurts, but leaving dirt in there probably isn't a good idea."

Silence sat with us a moment. Then someone changed the subject to service projects.

When the block ended, the hallway filled again. Sisters swapped casserole pans. Kids lined up at the drinking fountain. I squeezed past two men from elders quorum who had been calling the office all week about "how long this thing is going to drag on."

"Afternoon," I said.

They both answered, "Sheriff," and pivoted toward Bishop Cade, who shook their hands and said something I couldn't catch over the carpeted hum.

Abby slid up beside me. "You see that?" She tipped her head toward the chapel. The Nielsens were back in there, tidying hymnals with the bishop's wife, laughing at something he'd said.

"They're helping, that's all," I said.

"Sure." Her voice went dry. "Guess nobody wants to be in your splash zone when this blows up."

"It's not about a splash zone, Abs."

She stopped by the coat rack, blocking my path. "Then what is it? Because Mrs. Green used to hunt us down if we sat in different rows. Today she acted like we had cooties."

Eve came up, hand on Abby's shoulder. "People are nervous," she said. "They don't know where this ends yet."

Abby looked between us. "Do you?"

Cold from the exterior door bled through the glass into my back. I thought of the affidavit on my desk, the maintenance log in Clara's careful handwriting, the ledger copies Eve had watched me spread on our table.

"No," I said. "I don't know every stop between here and done. But I know where it started. Up on that steel. That's not going away."

Abby pressed her lips together, not quite satisfied, but she didn't push. She pulled on her coat, arms jerky, and headed toward the exit with Caleb trotting behind her.

Eve and I lingered a moment by the coat rack. The cultural hall lights snapped off in two banks, leaving us in the dim glow from one last row of fixtures. Through the glass door, the parking lot looked washed-out, cars lined like teeth. In the reflection I saw more of our family's outline than anything outside, a cluster of four against the door's dark.

Eve slipped her hand into mine. "You okay?" she asked.

"I will be." At the far end of the hall, Bishop Cade bent his head toward a knot of men in work coats. Their faces closed up when they glanced our way. "Just need to stop telling myself we can keep this out there." I nodded toward the square, the rigs, all of it. "It's already in here."

She squeezed my hand once, firm. "Then we deal with it here too."

We walked out together into the flat winter light, the gym squeak and casserole smell fading behind us, and the thin ice of our standing flexed under my boots.

—

By evening the smell of leftovers filled our kitchen. Same table that had held ledgers and receipts last night, now set with reheated roast and potatoes. The scanner murmured from the counter, picking up some deputy runabout on the far side of the county. The furnace kicked on, warm air humming through the vents.

Caleb poked at his plate. "Can I give the dog the fat?"

"After you eat something that's not pure salt and gristle," Eve said.

Abby sat back in her chair, arms folded, staring at the meat like it had offended her. The corner of her napkin curled under her thumb.

We bowed our heads for a quick blessing, Eve's voice steady as she thanked God for food and asked for "wisdom in hard days", then fell into the kind of silence that isn't peaceful.

"So," Abby said finally. "Church was weird."

"That's one word," I said.

Caleb looked between us. "Did we do something wrong?" His fork stopped halfway to his mouth.

Eve's answer came before mine. "No," she said. "You did nothing wrong. Your dad is doing his job. Some people are scared of what that might mean. That's on them, not on you."

"And on me if I get it wrong," I added. My voice caught a hair before the next words. "But we're not going to lie just so folks don't have to think about how Jared died."

Abby's gaze flicked up, sharp. "So you are going after their computers." She nudged a pea into a line. "When you do that, is that when everybody stops talking to us? Or is this just the warm-up?"

I cut a piece of roast that tasted more of worry than meat. "Some people have already decided how close they want to stand," I said. "You saw that."

"Yeah." She snorted softly. "Pretty loud decisions for people who never said anything out loud."

Caleb pushed his potatoes into a little mountain. "What if my friends stop coming over?"

"Then we talk about it," Eve said. Her hand slid under the table to rest against my knee. "And we remind them and their parents they're welcome here. Some won't pull away. Some will and then drift back later when they calm down. People are more than one Sunday's reaction."

"They didn't look like it," Abby said.

Her jaw had that set I knew. Sarcasm to sand down the raw parts. She was old enough for understanding reality. Pretending everything would slide back to normal would feel like a lie.

"I'm not going to tell you this won't cost us anything," I said. "It already has. It probably will more, especially once Judge Bishop signs off and we show up out there with a warrant."

"So you are sure." Abby's eyes pinned me.

"Sure enough to put paper in front of a judge," I said. "Sure enough to stand up in that courtroom and swear I believe a crime happened, with these facts to back it up."

"Sure enough to lose friends?" she asked.

Hal sliding that weld receipt across his counter. Rosa holding her kids close on a sagging couch. The bishop's careful words about trusting stewards and sparing the ward pain.

"I hope we won't lose the ones that matter most," I said. "But if the price of keeping some folks happy is pretending Jared just slipped, then yes. I'm that sure."

Abby dropped her gaze, traced the rim of her plate. "Okay," she said quietly. "Just...don't act surprised when people show it."

"I won't," I said. "And when they do, that's not your job to fix."

She gave a small, humorless huff. "Could've fooled me. Half the Relief Society looks at Mom like she's supposed to smooth everything over with a casserole."

Eve's mouth twitched. "Well, casseroles are my spiritual gift," she said. "But I'm done using them to cover lies."

That pulled the faintest smile out of Abby. Caleb's shoulders eased a notch.

"We'll be okay," I said.

Abby lifted a brow. "Define okay."

"We'll still be here. We'll still have a roof and this table. We'll still be able to look each other in the eye."

Silence again, but a different kind. Less brittle.

The scanner crackled, a traffic stop out on the highway. Background noise to the heavier call in front of me.

"Tomorrow," I said, "Clara and I go see Judge Bishop. We lay out what we've got: the latch tool marks, Hal's weld receipt, the ledger bonuses, that fake storm in the maintenance log. We're going to ask him for a warrant that lets us copy certain company records. Not everything under the sun, but enough to see who changed what and when."

Caleb's fork paused mid-air. "Can they say no?"

"The judge can," I said. "If he thinks we're fishing or asking for too much. That's why we've built this careful. This isn't about hating the company or wanting to make trouble. It's about proving what happened to a man who didn't come home."

"And if he says yes?" Abby asked.

"Then we go get the records," I said. "By the book. Chain-of-custody forms, copies, receipts. No kicking down doors. But it'll be public enough that people will talk more. Company folks, ward folks, maybe neighbors. You deserve to know that's coming."

Abby pushed a piece of potato around. "You sound like you're giving us a briefing," she said ruefully.

"Maybe I am." I set my fork down. "I don't want this to be something I do off in a corner while you all pretend life is normal. That's how bad choices get made."

A memory surfaced: a younger me in this same kitchen, different table, listening to Ben Latham say he'd taken a bishop's word on a husband's temper and then driven by a house with every window broken out. His face set like dried mud as he'd told me, "Silence feels like peace until the yelling starts again behind closed doors."

I looked at my kids. At Eve, watching me steadily.

"This warrant," I said, "isn't just my project. It touches all of us. So if you've got questions, this is when you ask."

Caleb lifted his eyes. "Are they going to be mad at you at work?"

"Some already are," I said. "Some aren't. Same at church. Same at the diner. That's going to be true the rest of my time in this badge. What I can promise is I'll do my best to keep us safe. I won't go looking for fights just to pick them. But I also won't walk away because it's inconvenient."

Abby studied me, testing the words against whatever picture she'd had of me as sheriff when she was eight. She finally nodded once. "Okay," she said. "Then if people give me grief at school, I'm not going to pretend either."

"You don't have to," I said. "Just don't punch anybody. That complicates paperwork."

That earned me a real, if short, laugh.

We finished dinner in small talk, Caleb's science project, Abby's English essay. Afterward, Abby and Caleb carried plates to the sink. Abby stacked them with more enthusiasm than care. Caleb fed scraps to the dog, who thumped his tail against the cabinet.

I rinsed dishes while Eve leaned against the counter, arms folded, watching the kids move through their chores.

"You didn't soft-pedal," she said quietly.

"Didn't feel like we had that luxury."

"Good." Her hand brushed my back. "They can handle it."

"I hope so."

"They'll handle it better than being lied to."

The scanner murmured behind us, voice after voice chasing small emergencies in a county that thought it knew where all the danger lived. In our kitchen, heat from the dishwasher fogged the window, turning the darkness outside into a dull mirror. Four shapes again, together.

Tomorrow I'd walk into Judge Bishop's chambers with our affidavit. Tonight, at least, the warrant belonged to all of us.

Chapter 20

Judge's Pen on the Line

The courthouse hallway smelled like paper, old dust, and somebody's reheated lunch. My boots echoed on scuffed wood as Clara and I walked toward Judge Bishop's chambers, manila envelope tucked under my arm. The affidavit inside had been handled enough that the edges felt soft, almost warm.

"Remember," Clara murmured, low enough that it wouldn't carry past the next doorway, "probable cause, not closing argument. We're not here to try the case."

"I know." I still mentally ticked through the list as if I might forget it between the elevator and the judge's door: latch tool marks, backdated weld, ledger bonuses, maintenance log with the fake storm, Jared's pocket note, Hank's "one bad fall" phrase.

Mayor Tessa Kline waited on a chair outside the chambers, legal pad on her knee like a shield. She stood when she saw us, blazer neat, expression already caught between welcome and worry.

"Sheriff. Deputy." She nodded. "Judge asked me to sit in."

"Afternoon, Mayor," I said. "Appreciate you making the time."

Her gaze flicked to the envelope. "Let's hope it's worth the trouble."

The bailiff cracked the heavy door and motioned us in. Chambers were small, lined with shelves, sunlight slanting from a high window and catching dust motes above the judge's desk. A faint smell of stale coffee came from a mug near his elbow.

Judge Harlan Bishop sat behind the desk, reading glasses halfway down his nose, our affidavit open in front of him. He looked up as we entered, expression neutral.

"Sheriff. Deputy Ray. Mayor." He gestured to the chairs. Leather creaked as we sat.

"Afternoon, Your Honor," I said.

He tapped the edge of the affidavit with his pen. "You both swear this is complete and accurate to the best of your knowledge?"

"Yes, Your Honor," Clara said.

"Yes, sir," I echoed. My thumb rubbed once against my notebook in my inner pocket.

"All right." He leaned back a bit. "Walk me through it. Plain language. Start with the latch."

So we did. I laid out the physical scene: the safety latch that should've caught Jared's harness, fresh tool marks on the metal where someone had pried or ground it, the replacement harness still in its bag in the locker. Clara slipped a photo across the desk, edges catching the light.

Judge Bishop studied it, pen tapping lightly in a steady rhythm. "And Mr. Garrison swore the equipment was current and sound."

"Yes, sir," I said. "Then we got this." Clara slid Hal's weld receipt beside the photo. "Work done on that rung a week prior, backdated."

He flipped the paper so the ink faced him. "Mr. Briggs vouched for this timing?"

"In person," I said. "He knows it might cost him contracts. We corroborated his shop log and card receipts."

Pen tap slowed. He turned a page in the affidavit. "You're not asking me to arrest anyone today."

"No, sir," I said. "We're asking for limited access to company records and Colton Reese's materials so we can see who ordered what and when."

Tessa shifted in her chair. "Your Honor, if I may, "

"In a minute, Mayor," he said without looking up. "Let's finish the facts."

Clara pointed to the next exhibit. "Payroll ledger," she said. "Safety bonuses authorized by Mr. Reese for certain crew, including Jared, ending abruptly a few weeks before his death. Amounts match the figures in Jared's pocket notebook." She laid a copy of that scrap beside the ledger page, faint pencil against lined paper.

The judge's eyes tracked from column to column. "And the company explanation?"

"They described them as routine incentives," I said. "What we heard from the man-camp is that they were hush bonuses. Extra to keep people from calling in minor incidents."

He nodded once, neither agreeing nor disagreeing. "Which brings us to the cameras."

I walked him through the maintenance log: "Camera 3 static check" initialed C.R., timed to cover the gap where our footage turned to snow. "Weather interference" scribbled in the note line. I laid my own weather note next to it, dated and timed. "I wrote this on the tailgate that night," I said. "Clear, dry, stars out. We've since pulled state weather data backing that up."

"So Mr. Reese documented a storm that didn't happen," Bishop said. "On a log he controls."

"Yes, sir," I said. "And he repeated that storm story in an interview here in town. Said driving snow. I remembered crunching through dry gravel and seeing my breath plume in the clear air. That's when I checked my note."

Tessa's pen made a small circle on her pad. "Judge, nobody's saying this isn't concerning," she said. "But we're talking about hitting the main employer in the county with a warrant. Every time that building feels heat, the phones start ringing in my office. Contracts get spooked. People worry about their mortgages."

"I'm aware," Bishop said. He glanced her way, then back at us. "But I sign on probable cause, not economic forecasts." His gaze settled on me. "Sheriff, you're asking me to authorize a search of company emails, badge logs, safety files. That's not nothing. How do these pieces hang together in your mind?"

I took a breath, counted the steps like fence posts. "We've got a physical mechanism that doesn't match accident," I said. "We've got a weld receipt showing prior work on the rung that failed, contrary to sworn statements. We've got a money trail where safety bonuses stop right before a man dies. We've got a maintenance log with a fabricated storm and Mr. Reese's initials on the exact camera gap that hides the fall."

I thought of Hank in the diner parking lot, voice shaking when he said, Better one bad fall than a full audit. "We also have phrasing," I added. "A roughneck told me his foreman said, 'better one bad fall than a full audit.' We later saw almost that exact wording in an internal email thread from Mr. Reese, in the material we already obtained through OSHA channels."

Clara slid that printed email into the pile. The judge read the highlighted line, lips compressing.

"This isn't one bad log or one sloppy form," I said. "It's a pattern. And the only way to see the full pattern is to follow Mr. Reese's footprint through the systems he controls."

Silence settled. The wall vent hummed. Somewhere down the hall, a copier started and stopped.

Judge Bishop steepled his fingers, then flattened his hands on the desk. "Mayor."

Tessa cleared her throat. "Your Honor, from a legal standpoint, I don't have standing to tell you no." Her eyes flicked to me. "My concern is fallout. If this goes sideways, if you sign this and it doesn't hold up, or it turns out to be less than it looks, folks won't blame the company first. They'll blame the sheriff's office. And city hall. And this bench."

"People are watching either way," I said. "If we do nothing with what we've already seen and it comes out later, that's on all of us too."

He looked at me. "Sheriff, if I give you this, you understand you're pulling on a thread that runs straight through this town?"

I thought of ward hallways and cold shoulders. Of Hal's shop and Rosa's front room. Of Abby's question at the coat rack: Do you?

"Yes, Your Honor," I said. "But right now that thread's tied around a dead man's neck, and we've already seen it in their own books."

The room went still. Tessa's eyes dropped to her pad. Clara sat straight, hands quiet on her knees.

Judge Bishop exhaled slowly. Pen tapped once more, then stilled. He turned a page in the affidavit and picked up his pen. "All right," he said. "I'm not giving you the whole barn. I'm not going to sign a fishing license for every server they own."

He began to write, the scratch of ink loud in the quiet. "Scope is limited to: Mr. Reese's email account and incident reports three months before and after the death; safety bonus records for the same period; badge-swipe logs for the field office and rig satellite office for that week; camera maintenance logs for all rigs where Mr. Reese has sign-off authority."

He paused, looked up at me. "You'll observe strict chain of custody. No midnight surprises on local news. No grandstanding."

"Yes, sir," I said.

He finished the signature, blotted the ink, then slid the warrant toward the envelope near my hand. His pen lay uncapped beside it.

Tessa watched it move like it was a piece of dynamite.

"I expect a copy for the file as soon as you execute," Bishop said. "Mayor, you'll get notified after service, not before."

"Understood," she said, though her mouth tightened.

I slipped the warrant into the envelope with more care than it needed, cardboard edges cool against my fingers. For a second it felt fragile, like it might crumble if I gripped too hard. It was just paper, but it shifted the ground under all of us.

We stood. Leather creaked again. Hands were shaken. Outside his door, the hallway air felt drier, sharper.

Halfway down, Tessa caught my sleeve. "Sheriff, a minute?" she said.

Clara glanced at me. "I'll get the truck," she said, heading for the stairs.

Tessa and I stepped through the side door onto the square. Cold wind pushed against my collar, carrying diesel from a truck idling near the curb. The diner's door chimed faintly across the way.

"You know this is going to hurt," she said, not bothering with small talk.

"So did that fall," I said.

She winced. "I'm not defending what happened out there." Her eyes tracked a company pickup rolling through the intersection, logo bright on the side. "But when that warrant shows up at their office, they'll call. They'll scream about witch hunts and job killers. They'll threaten to move operations. People will lose sleep. Some will lose work."

"I know," I said. My hand brushed the envelope in my coat, making sure it was still there. "But if we let a man die and let his widow be told to shut up because we're scared of their temper, that's another kind of hurt. One we don't have numbers for."

She hugged her arms against the cold. "Just tell me you're sure, Milt. Not just suspicious. Sure enough to bet the town."

"How sure do you need?" I asked.

She met my eyes. "Sure enough to carry it when elections roll around. Sure enough to walk into church and see who won't sit by you and not flinch."

Abby's voice in the hallway rose up: Do you? My jaw worked once before I answered.

"I'm sure enough to bet my own pew," I said. "And that's already happening."

Tessa's gaze softened, not with comfort but with recognition. "If this goes sideways," she said quietly, "they won't just blame you. They'll blame me for not stopping you."

"Then we both better be right," I said. "I'm not asking you to like this, Mayor. I'm asking you not to pretend you didn't see the same ink I did on that desk."

She looked back toward the courthouse windows, where sunlight bounced off glass, making it hard to see who moved behind them. "Do it by the book," she said. "Keep me in the loop enough that I'm not blindsided at a council meeting. And for the love of this town, don't let this turn into a circus."

"I don't like circuses," I said. "Too many clowns."

That got the barest curve at the corner of her mouth. "You know what I mean." She glanced again at the company truck, now a block away. "I'll have to warn them something's coming. Can't not. But I won't tell them you're out of control. Don't make me a liar."

"I won't," I said.

She pulled her blazer tighter. "Okay then." Her breath fogged in front of her. "I've got a budget workshop. You've got...whatever comes next."

We parted at the bottom of the steps. She angled toward the diner, shoulders squared against the wind. I headed for the sheriff's office, envelope a firm rectangle against my ribs.

At the curb I paused, watching a field-office truck roll past on the cross street. The sun glared off its windshield, hiding the driver's face. The lines between courthouse, diner, church, and that building out by the rigs felt like ropes, finally pulled tight.

Behind me, the courthouse door swung shut with a soft thud. Ahead, the badge on my belt felt heavier than it had that morning. I tapped the steering wheel once as I climbed into the truck, the way I did when a decision tipped from maybe to done.

We had a warrant now. Whatever story Colton thought he'd locked behind his keycard, the law had a way in.

Chapter 21

Documents Under Fluorescents

Glass doors sighed shut behind us, my reflection sliding over the company logo like a bad overlay. Fluorescents flattened the safety posters on the wall into washed-out slogans. A few heads popped up over cubicle tops as word traveled faster than we could walk: sheriff in the building.

I handed the receptionist the warrant and my badge card at the same time. She took both like they might burn.

"Mr. Reese is in a meeting," she said.

"He's about to be in this one," I answered. "Have him and your company lawyer meet us in a conference room. We'll wait there."

Clara stood at my shoulder, messenger bag strap across her chest, face calm, eyes busy, taking in doors, keypads, the one closed steel door down the side hall that had to be server or records.

The HVAC hummed overhead, pushing stale warm air down at us. Printer whirr drifted from somewhere back in the maze, spitting out something today that wasn't for us. Yet.

They put us in a small conference room with glass walls facing the bullpen. Coffee and toner scented the air. I set the warrant on the table and left the envelope open so nobody could claim I'd hidden the ball.

Colton walked in with their lawyer two minutes later. His jaw muscle jumped once when he saw the envelope, then went still. He wore a company-branded vest, polo underneath, not a speck out of place.

"Sheriff." He gave me a practiced half smile. "You could've called. We always cooperate."

"Today we're cooperating under this." I slid the warrant out, turned it toward him. "Signed an hour ago. Judge Bishop limited it to safety records, incident logs, emails, and badge-swipe data tied to the rig death and your local operations."

Their lawyer took it, glasses low on her nose, lips moving as she read. Her fingers spun a pen faster than she probably knew.

"What scope of date range are you treating as 'tied'?" she asked.

"The dates on page two," I said. "From six months before Jared Pike's fall through one month after. Specific accounts and servers are spelled out. Digital copies only, plus any hard copies of safety reports, audits, incident logs, and maintenance records that cover that window."

She flipped to the second page, pen still spinning. "This is going to be disruptive. We have operations, "

"I understand. That's why I brought only one deputy." I nodded toward Clara. "We'll work with your staff. But we are seizing what's named. Chain-of-custody starts now."

Colton leaned on the back of a chair, easy. "Sheriff, you're welcome to anything that helps you close this tragic accident and move on."

I let that hang a beat. Behind him, through the glass, a clerk's hands shook just enough to make her stapler chatter against a stack of forms.

"Funny," I said. "Your email doesn't call it a tragedy. We'll get to that. For now, I need IT in here to start a pull from your mail server and access logs. And whoever controls hard-copy safety files."

The lawyer opened her mouth. I raised my notebook.

"You can object later in court," I said. "Right now this warrant is valid. Let's get your people moving before backup tapes cycle and before anyone accuses you of stonewalling."

She didn't like the last word, but she liked the prospect of spoliation hearings less. I watched her decide.

"I'll have IT bring an external drive," she said. "We retain originals. You get mirror images."

"That's exactly what the judge ordered," Clara said. "We'll hash checksums as we go."

The lawyer blinked at her. Not many deputies out here talked that way.

IT arrived with a rolling chair and a hard drive, a young man in a company hoodie whose badge lanyard kept swinging against his chest. His eyes cut toward the closed door I'd already marked as likely server room.

"Let's start with Mr. Reese's mailbox," Clara said. "Then shared safety folders and any distribution lists that include 'rig incident,' 'safety bonus,' or 'near miss.' We'll define more key terms as we go."

He glanced at Colton. Colton gave one of those small nods that pretends not to be permission.

"We'll set up in your server room," I said.

"That's secure," the lawyer objected.

"So are we," I said. "You'll have someone in there with us. My deputy will document what we access. It's all in the warrant."

Out in the main office, staff pretended to work louder than before, keyboard clicks suddenly crisp, phones lifted and set down in busy pantomime. The HVAC hum felt like a second, lower conversation.

The server room door finally opened, a green light blinking above the handle after the IT kid swiped his badge. Racks of equipment hissed and blinked, network lights winking like a nervous heartbeat. Clara went to work beside him, voice low, methodical.

I stayed in the doorway where I could watch both her screen and the hallway. The company lawyer parked herself at the end of a row of cubicles like a sentry. Colton drifted in a slow orbit through the bullpen, stopping behind people's chairs, pointing at screens that weren't about to be more important than the USB cable Clara had just plugged in.

I kept one eye on him. Who he leaned close to. Who he skipped. When he passed the receptionist's desk, her eyes went toward that server-room door before she dropped them back to her monitor. Habit patterns are hard to fake.

The printer out by the copier spat warm paper into a growing stack. A clerk walked by with it to the conference room we'd just left, the pages cupped like something fragile.

I met her at the threshold. "Mind if I see which batch that is?"

Her smile was tight. "Just the incident log index you asked for, Sheriff."

I took the top few pages, scanned column headings, dates. Incidents, near-misses, training notes, sign-offs. Colton's initials dotted through like a rash.

"Thank you," I said. "Deputy Ray will want to match this to digital pulls."

We spread out at the conference-room table, Clara coming back and forth with printed sets as IT's jobs finished. Cardboard boxes appeared from somewhere labeled ARCHIVE. Every time a file drawer clanked open out in the bullpen, one of the clerks jumped.

Time slid down the walls along with the fluorescent light. I kept a running list in my head: log where each box came from, whose hands, which cabinet. Make sure every digital folder Clara copied matched something we could point to in testimony, not a fishing trip.

Colton finally stepped in again and pulled out a chair opposite me. Some of the smooth had worn off.

"Sheriff," he said, folding his arms. "Is this really necessary? You've already talked to us. We gave you everything you asked for voluntarily."

"What you provided voluntarily left gaps," I said.

He raised his eyebrows. "Such as?"

"Such as the maintenance log you produced for Camera 3 that night." I flipped my notebook open to the page where I'd written the time span beside my own weather note: clear, dry, no storm. "Your initials, your timing, bogus weather justification. Such as selective bonus payments in the ledger that stop when a particular hand starts asking questions."

He shifted, arms tightening, then loosening again. "I sign a lot of things, Sheriff. You know how it is. We're busy."

"Busy enough you don't remember calling a man's death a tragedy?" I nodded toward the stack of emails Clara had just printed. She slid one on top, the ink still a hair damp, faint warm smell rising from it.

She tapped a line halfway down the page. "Here."

Under the bed of company boilerplate, one line of plain speech: one of the hands scribbling every little incident like he's auditioning for trial exhibit A. Sent from Colton's account to a regional manager whose name I didn't recognize.

Clara read it aloud. The HVAC seemed to hush a notch.

I checked the time stamp. Dated two months before the fall. Right in the window where Jared stopped getting "safety bonuses" and started carrying a notebook on his hip like a second wallet.

A memory from that diner parking lot slid in against the printed words: Hank's voice sharp with fear, saying he said better one bad fall than a full audit. Wade shushing him. I'd written it down as Hank's phrasing, his fatalism. Now "trial exhibit A" sat in company email, same spine of thought, different clothes.

I let it sink all the way in. I pictured Jared hunched at a man-camp table, copying log pages, maybe thinking if he wrote it all down somebody would have to care. Then Colton at his computer up here, fingers on keys, annoyed enough to write about him not as a man but as a future piece of cardboard on an easel in court.

"You recognize that, Mr. Reese?" I asked.

Colton's jaw set. "People talk about legal risk all the time. It's a figure of speech. We say 'don't turn this into Exhibit A' as a joke, meaning don't make a big deal over nothing."

"Nothing," I repeated. "You sure that's what you meant here?"

"It was a near-miss-heavy quarter, Sheriff. The guys were filling out forms for stubbed toes. That kind of record makes lawyers and regulators circle. I was venting."

Clara slid another sheet over. Same thread. Same frustration. Line: if one more roustabout plays lawyer with my logs, I'll need hazard pay myself.

"You wrote these before Jared died," I said quietly. "And you wrote them about somebody who'd already been hurt once on that rig and kept writing it down."

"How would I know that?" he said, too fast. "You're putting words in my mouth. It could've been anyone."

My pen hovered over my notebook. I didn't write the argument. I wrote the pattern: managers thinking like defendants months before blood hit steel. When you frame a hand as a walking exhibit, it isn't a long step to seeing him as a liability instead of a neighbor.

Colton watched my hand move. For a second, worry edged through the calm on his face. Then it was gone and he leaned back.

"We're done answering questions today," the lawyer cut in. "You have what the judge authorized. We'll challenge any overreach."

"You're welcome to," I said. "In the meantime, we copy what's listed."

By the time the boxes were taped and labeled and the last download bar reached one hundred percent on Clara's screen, the office had gone from rattled to exhausted. Staff kept their eyes on their monitors while not working. The receptionist's stapler lay untouched beside her hand.

Clara slid the email thread into an evidence envelope, the plastic crackling under her gloved fingers. I wrote the case number and "Reese email, 'trial exhibit A' thread" on the outside, then signed across the seal. The plastic bit at my thumb as it closed.

Out in the hallway, Colton stood at his office doorway, arms folded, watching. I held his gaze as I pressed that seal down.

For the first time since I'd met him, something in his eyes gave, a flicker, like someone staring too long into headlights and finally squinting. Then he turned, stepped back into his glass box, and let the blinds fall, slats clattering softly into place between us.

We weren't finished.

The conference room held a river of paper now: incident logs, safety audits, copies of training rosters. Cardboard boxes sat open on the gray carpet like low, brown mouths. Clara had her sleeves shoved up, highlighter uncapped, stacks sorted into piles that almost made sense.

I stood near the doorway with the dolly, watching the IT tech's monitor in the bullpen. Progress bar creeping across as he burned the last chunk of access-control data to the external drive.

"Let's keep hard copies and digital matching," I said. "If it exists in one and not the other, I want to know which way the current runs."

Clara didn't look up. "Already flagging them."

Pages rasped as she flipped. Yellow stripes marched down the right-hand margin. The overhead lights buzzed.

A clerk wheeled in another box. "Older near-miss logs," she said. "Back three years like you asked."

"Thank you," Clara said. "Set them here, please."

The clerk set the box down but her eyes went to Colton's office, blinds still closed. Her blinking sped up when I thanked her by name. People under pressure tell on themselves in a hundred little ways.

I pulled the lid off the new box. Tabs labeled by month. We didn't have the time or the warrant to read their whole history, but we did have an index Clara had printed from the server, a tidy table listing every near-miss by date and category.

She slid that index next to the cardboard, ran her finger down to March. Then frowned.

"Where are March's?" she asked.

I stepped closer. The index listed half a page of entries under March, fall from ladder, tool strike to hand, sling failure. All marked "near-miss." But when she dug to the March tab in the box, the hanging folders gaped empty.

She checked April for misfiles. Nothing.

"Maybe they got moved." The office manager's voice came from the doorway, casual set over tight. Her smile could've left imprints.

"Great," Clara said. "Let's move them back. The index says they exist. So either show us the paper or we'll take digital."

The manager's tight smile didn't waver. "We consolidated some of those into training materials. Efficiency."

"Training materials are covered by the warrant," I said. "If they involve incidents."

She shifted, hand brushing the doorframe. "The way our system works, a near-miss that doesn't meet OSHA criteria can be recoded. It's still in the system, just under a different flag. Pulling all of those will take, "

"Deputy Ray?" I said.

Clara nodded, eyes on the manager. "We'll wait. IT can help."

The manager's gaze went out toward the bullpen. The IT kid had heard enough to turn his chair halfway around, drive in his hands.

"Why are March's near-misses listed here but not in the file?" Clara asked him. Her tone stayed flat.

He swallowed. "Uh. Those got consolidated as training... per safety's request. So they wouldn't skew the metrics."

"Safety meaning Mr. Reese?" I asked.

The kid's eyes went to Colton's shut blinds, then back. "I just do what the ticket says, Sheriff."

"Good," I said. "Then print every one."

He hesitated one second too long, then spun back to his keyboard. Mouse clicks stuttered; the printer out front warmed and started coughing out fresh sheets.

The first batch came in with the same warm-paper smell, black text crisp. "Training module: Ladder Use, Case Study." "Tool Handling Safety, Scenario Review."

The descriptions matched the incidents from the index. Same dates, same locations, same initial-report text buried below new headers. Only the codes in the corner had changed: where "NM" had been, some hand had clicked "TRN" and walked on.

"What's the point of recoding them?" I asked.

The office manager's smile now had teeth. "Near-miss reporting can trigger extra review. These were low-level, and we wanted to use them as teaching tools instead of cluttering the metrics. That's standard. Regulators understand."

"Regulators understand a lot of things," I said. "Jurors, too."

Clara flipped one of the March printouts over. Signature block at the bottom: electronic sign-off by C. Reese.

She pointed with her pen. "These recodes went through you."

Colton's blinds didn't move, but I could see the line of his shoulders in my head.

"Of course," the manager said quickly. "Everything safety-related does. He was just following corporate guidelines about making sure our dashboard reflects true risk."

Out in the hall, somebody's laughter burst too loud, then cut off like a mic killed mid-sentence.

My mind did its own math while Clara laid the pages in order. Near-misses, falls that didn't quite break bone, slings that snapped but missed skulls, had all started as red flags. Then at some point somebody decided they'd look better painted as lessons.

We'd already seen the money trail: safety bonuses that went to guys who played along, then stopped when Jared kept writing everything down. Now here on the table, the paper trail caught up, each recode a small tap on the brakes of reality.

"How far back does this go?" I asked.

The IT kid brought more printouts in, edges warm. "At least the last year. Maybe more. We'd have to query by code changes."

The warrant didn't let us sweep their whole history. But in our six-month window, the pattern was enough.

"Bag these as a set," I said quietly to Clara. "Mark them by original code and recode date."

She reached for an envelope, hands steady. I watched the dates as she wrote: some recodes went through days after the incidents, some weeks later, just before quarterly reports.

"Every time you hit 'training' here," I said aloud, more for myself than for anyone, "you took a nail out of the ladder holding your men up."

The office manager's tight smile slipped, then came back.

We kept going. The IT kid's drive filled. Clara checked each directory list against the warrant language before she let him press "start." Out on the floor, a junior staffer blinked and swallowed when I asked how often logs got recoded.

"It's just how we've always done it," he mumbled. "We don't want to look like a problem site."

I thought of Rosa's front room, casseroles on her counter and an envelope on her table. Of Hank in the parking lot muttering better one bad fall. Men like Colton weren't the only ones afraid of scrutiny; everyone had been taught to fear audits like weather.

Only this kind of weather came from keyboards.

By late afternoon my back ached and the cardboard box nearest the door stood full. I taped the lid shut, the tape squeaking as I pressed it down with my palm. On the side I wrote the case number and, under it, "Rig Incident, Office Records."

The hum of the HVAC chased us down the hall as we rolled the dolly out. Staff watched us go without looking at us directly. The receptionist's eyes were wet but steady.

At the threshold I looked back once. Colton's blinds stayed closed. Somewhere behind them, he was calculating. How to frame this as dark humor, training, clerical error. Which subordinate to blame for clicks he'd electronically signed.

Out in the cold lot, the sound shifted to gravel crunch under my boots and the faint rush of traffic. The sun had sagged toward the mesas; the office's fluorescent glare spilled onto asphalt, but it couldn't follow us to the truck.

Clara lifted the last box onto the tailgate and shut the cap. Her breath fogged in front of her.

"We've got enough to make them nervous now," she said.

"Good," I answered. The box edges dug into my palms, real weight. "Nervous men make mistakes. These," I tapped the cardboard, "already look like a whole set."

Inside, the case had taken on a different shape. Not just one death, not even one rig. A culture where you could right-click danger into training and buy silence with a bonus line in a ledger.

Jared hadn't just been in the way. He'd been in the margins, and somebody in that office had decided to erase him.

I climbed into the truck, set my notebook on the console, and wrote four words under today's date: paper tuned to fail.

Chapter 22

Latches and Lines

Wind cut through my jacket the second I stepped out of the truck. The rig towered over us, metal bones thrumming in the gusts. Work lights glared even in daylight, throwing hard shadows across steel.

Up there, at the level my eye went to without wanting to, the crossbeam still showed a faint stain if you knew where to look. Weather and washings had faded it, but memory sharpened what the elements blurred.

Wade waited at the base of the stair, hands jammed so deep in his pockets his shoulders hunched. His eyes skipped past the beam. They went to the ladder, to Clara measuring rail height with a tape, to the limp training dummy we'd borrowed from a safety contractor.

"Didn't think I'd have to see that thing up here," he muttered.

"It's lighter than a man," Clara said. "We weighted it best we could. We're not asking you to do anything with it yourself, Wade. Just watch, and answer questions."

He shifted his weight from one boot to the other. A nerve tic fluttered at the corner of his eye when the wind whistled through the derrick and made a brace sing.

"Y'all already decided what happened," he said.

"We decided we needed to show our work," I said. "You've walked this catwalk more than any of us. That counts for something."

Oil and chemical smell rose from the pad, mixing with cold metal. I wrapped my gloved hand around the ladder rail, familiar rungs under my boots as Clara and I climbed. Each step took me back to that first morning: dark sky, harsh lights, Jared's body skewered wrong, my gut whispering no before my brain had the vocabulary.

We reached the catwalk; grate flexed under my weight. Clara set the tape along the rail, chalk lines ghosting where she'd measured horizontal distances earlier.

Down below, Wade hovered at the base, neck craned, as small as any man looks when you put steel and gravity around him.

"Okay," Clara said, voice clipped, professional. "Sheriff, start here." She pointed to a spot on the catwalk where the original cleanup photos had shown Jared's boot scuffs.

I stood where she indicated. The rail hit me at mid-thigh, cold leaching through my jeans where it pressed. I looked down to the crossbeam where the stain was. It sat out from the rig structure, a leap zone, not a stumble.

"First run," she said. "Conscious misstep. Sheriff, lean against the rail like you were looking out or shifting weight. I'll push this dummy at shoulder height with the kind of shove you might get if you tripped or bumped."

Wind tugged at my coat. I planted my boots, grabbed the rail with both hands, then forced myself to let go, fingers hovering a hair above it. The grate pattern pressed through my soles.

"Ready," I said.

Clara crouched by the dummy, then heaved it up so its feet lined with the scuffs on the grate. She braced, counted under her breath, and shoved.

The dummy arced over clean, clearing the crossbeam by more than a foot before hitting open air where Jared never reached. It swung on its tether and jolted below, nowhere near where the body had hung.

Wade cursed softly from below.

"Again," Clara said. We repeated with a stronger shove, then with me exaggerating a lunge, leaning my full weight as if a man had leaned too far to look down.

Every time the dummy cleared the beam. Conscious muscles caught, balance fought back, even when foam joints tried to mimic human slack.

My stomach tightened. Part of me had wanted the math to be messier, to leave a little wiggle for accident. The dummy spinning below us made that smaller each run.

"Now dead weight," Clara said quietly.

She climbed back up, unhooked the dummy, dragged it to the mark again. "This time, Sheriff, hold it under the arms for a second, like you're steadying someone who's out. Then let go as I push the legs."

My fingers dug into the canvas under what would've been armpits. Even knowing there was nobody inside, the sag of it did something in my chest.

"Ready," she said.

I nodded. On three I let go while she shoved low. The dummy dropped forward like a sack of wet sand, no muscle tension, no flinch. It pivoted over the rail and slammed into the crossbeam hard enough to rattle metal, exactly where the bruise pattern had ringed Jared's torso in the ER photos.

The sound made my teeth hurt. Wind whipped the dummy, chalk dust from our marks puffing as it struck.

Below, Wade flinched. His hands came halfway out of his pockets, then jammed back in.

"Again," Clara said, voice a shade rougher. "Just to be sure."

We repeated twice more. Conscious, it cleared. Dead, it crashed, each time into roughly the same spot. Physics didn't care about stories; it cared about torque and angle and gravity.

I thought of the ER doctor flipping back the sheet enough to show us patterned bruising across Jared's ribs, saying quietly, This looks like he hit something before the beam.

"What's your read?" I asked Clara.

She checked her notes, chalk smudging her gloves. "If he went over awake, on his own, he should have cleared that beam more often than not. The most consistent way to hit right there is if he was out or near-out, with somebody controlling the drop."

"In your professional opinion," I called down to Wade, my breath steam in the air, "as a supervisor who's walked this catwalk for years, could that have been a simple slip?"

Silence floated up with the wind. The dummy swayed a slow arc where it hung, toes tracing an invisible line.

Wade shifted, boots scraping gravel. For a second I wanted to climb down fast and grab his jacket and shake him. Ask him why he'd stared at that beam that night and still nodded when company men said "accident."

That would get me nothing but a satisfaction I couldn't afford.

I waited.

Finally he tilted his head up. His face looked smaller from up here, color leached by the lights.

"No, Sheriff," he said. The words came low but they carried. "Not if he was awake."

My pen was ready. I wrote the sentence down as he said it, each word its own mark. My gut had been yelling that since the first night. Today, the steel and a foreman's own mouth joined the choir.

Wind stole his words and flung them off across the pad. My notebook kept them.

We hauled the dummy back up, unhooked it, laid it on the grate where Jared had first lain. Chalk outlines ghosted around its limbs, fresh scuffs of rubber lining up with older scratches on metal.

Clara's mouth had settled into a tight line; she didn't waste sympathy as armor against what we were proving. Later, maybe. Not up here.

"Let's go look at the latch," she said.

We climbed another level, boots clanging on grating. Metal bit cold through my gloves when I braced on the rail to crouch. The latch that had "failed" sat where we'd left it, surface pitted and scratched, familiar now as a face in the ward hallway.

I leaned close. Grease smeared the edge, catching dirt where fingers had worked in the dark. Wind gusts made the structure creak; the sound crawled along my spine.

Clara clicked her flashlight on, beam cutting across the metal. She scraped lightly with her gloved fingernail along one side. A bright, sharp-edged groove flashed where grime flecked away, running crosswise to the direction a lanyard would normally pull.

"These aren't from a fall, Milt," she said, low. "This is somebody's practice swing."

I studied the spacing, parallel arcs about as far apart as the teeth on an adjustable wrench. Rust had settled in around them, but the base of each cut still shone brighter, newer than surrounding corrosion.

"They were here the night we first climbed up," she added. "Your early photos show the same pattern if you zoom in. I checked before we came."

I thought back to that first morning, camera in my gloved hand, breath fogging in the viewfinder as I pointed it at everything that looked wrong. I'd captured this scar without understanding it.

"Then they were here when Colton signed his inspection log," I said.

Wade had followed partway up, stopped one level below, as if closer would burn. His gaze kept skittering off the latch whenever we turned it that way.

"Steel gets scraped out here all the time," he said weakly. "Chains, hooks. It ain't pretty work."

"There's random scrape," Clara said, "and then there's this. These cuts go against load. See how the rust rims them, but the groove's edge is still sharper than the rest?"

She turned to me. "State lab's prelims mentioned directional striations. If their microscope images match this spacing and orientation, we'll have strong support for deliberate weakening with a tool like that wrench set we pulled from the office locker."

Wind gusted, making the catwalk shudder. I put a hand out to steady myself and felt the latch's chill through the glove. Somebody had stood right here with a wrench in their hand and turned potential energy into a slow fuse.

I made myself slow down. I noted depth, angle, where rust pooled, where it didn't. Field notes would have to line up with lab reports if we wanted to keep defense from poking holes.

Inside, my mind walked through hands: Wade, sent up under pressure; Hank, drunk and pliable; some company man like Colton in a clean vest, telling himself he was just "tuning" a sticky latch.

"Makes it easier for it to slip under load," Clara murmured. "Then when it does, you get to say steel's bad, not paperwork."

"What do you want me to say?" Wade asked from below, voice flat. "I signed inspections. I should've looked closer, but you don't stand here doing metallurgy. You click through, keep things moving. Guys get mad if they think you're hunting for reasons to shut 'em down."

His honesty, late as it came, carried its own weight. A man who hadn't wanted to look had walked past these grooves day after day. Somebody else had carved them.

"We're not asking you to take the whole fall," I said. "But I am going to write that you signed off."

He didn't argue.

Clara snapped a close-up photo of the exposed groove. The flash popped, turning the scar into a white jagged line in her camera screen before the image shrank into a thumbnail.

I straightened, knees complaining. The pad spread below us in a patchwork of tanks and trucks, lights harsh against the surrounding dark.

"Somebody tuned this to fail," I said, more to the wind than anyone.

I wrote the phrase down for later, same way I'd written Wade's admission. Words and metal both had to line up.

As we made our way back down the ladder, the training dummy lay twisted on the grate where Jared had been, chalk marks scuffed, fresh rubber streaks right where his bruises had been. Physics and file marks had closed ranks.

At the bottom, Wade stared at the dummy, pale.

"He never would've gone over like that on his own," he murmured. It wasn't to me, not really. More like a confession to himself.

I still pulled my notebook out and wrote the sentence as the wind carried his words off across the pad.

Chapter 23

Man in the Glass Office

The glass in Colton's office threw my reflection over his as I stepped inside, two sheriffs ghosting the same man. Outside, the open floor of the field office hummed, keyboards, phones, people pretending not to glance our way. In here, air freshener fought and mostly lost against stale coffee and toner.

Colton rose from behind his desk. Neat stacks of paper squared to the edges, a harness-serial inventory clipped in one corner, family photo turned just so. Everything in order.

"Sheriff," he said. "Sorry about the zoo out there. Have a seat."

I took the chair he pointed at, set my notebook on my knee. The projector on the credenza sat in standby, its fan a low whirr. Office cameras, little dark domes in the corners, looked dead but never felt that way.

"We've both had a long couple of weeks," I said. "I appreciate you making time."

He gave a small laugh, all sympathy. "Anything we can do to help you close this out. None of us want Jared's death hanging over the yard."

"Good," I said. "Because I've got a few loose ends."

I started easy, slid the file open without showing the sharpest pages. I talked about "safety culture" the way he liked to, about training refreshers and near-miss logs. He leaned back, relaxed into his script.

"We take this seriously, Sheriff," he said. "You know that. That's why we have bonus structures tied to safe operations. We're not like some outfits out in the Dakotas."

My pen clicked once. "The safety bonus ledger you turned over, that's company standard policy?"

He nodded, fingers resting on the edge of the family photo. "Discretionary, but yes. We reward crews who go a quarter without recordable incidents. It builds buy-in."

"Including Jared," I said.

He hesitated just long enough you'd need a notebook to see it. "At one point, yes."

I flipped to a tabbed page. Clara's handwriting, small and tight, beside my own notes. "The ledger shows bonus deposits to Jared and a couple others, signed off by you, through mid-month. Then they stop. No more entries under his name. That about right?"

Colton's gaze slid past me to the right, to the camera dome above the door. "Bonuses are discretionary. We have to send signals about appropriate use of the reporting system."

"Meaning?"

"Well." He smiled, tried to soften it. "We want people to log real hazards. There was some...over-enthusiasm. Guys writing up scuffed paint and sticky hinges, like they were building a case. That's not what the program's for."

I let the silence sit. Out in the bullpen, a phone rang, stopped. Highway noise ghosted through the double-glazed windows.

"So you cut him off," I said. "Even though incidents on his rig kept getting logged."

"I wouldn't phrase it that way," he said. "We adjusted. There's a difference between serious issues and clutter."

I watched his hands. No twitch yet. "His widow says he was scared," I said. "Said they'd come after him if he kept writing things down."

He pressed his fingers together, then let them fall apart. "Grief colors memory, Sheriff. I told you at the walk-through, we did everything by the book."

"You did mention that." I flipped another page. "And this email we picked up under the warrant. Ring a bell?"

I read the line. "'One of the hands scribbling every little incident like he's auditioning for trial exhibit A.'"

Color crept up his neck. "You've apparently seen my worst prose. That was a frustrated moment, venting to a regional manager. Off the cuff."

"You were talking about Jared."

He exhaled through his nose. "I was talking about behavior that undermines cohesion. You know as well as I do, constant complaining wrecks a crew. We had a man intent on turning every squeak into a federal case."

"He turned up dead," I said. "On your watch. While cameras you controlled happened to be dark. While a rung you signed off on a week earlier happened to be the one with the bad weld. While a latch you stamped had tool marks running against normal wear. Help me understand how all that stacks up to 'by the book.'"

His nostrils flared, then went still. "You're mixing categories. Weld integrity, camera uptime, human behavior. Different domains. You're a sheriff, not a safety engineer."

"True," I said. "But I know how paper lines up with steel. Let's talk about that camera."

He glanced at the off projector like he'd rather be giving a slideshow. "We've covered this. The maintenance log's in your file."

"You wrote 'static, driving snow' for that ten-to-midnight window," I said. "You remember saying that?"

He nodded, confident again. "That storm was a mess. We had whiteout on the north access. I personally went into the shack before it hit. Checked Camera Three myself."

"My notes from that night say 'clear, stars out, dry cold.'" I tapped the margin. "Road cams from the county show the same. No flakes. Just exhaust in the lights."

He straightened. "Then I must have mixed nights up. We get weather here, Sheriff. Hard to keep them all straight."

I let that pass for the moment. "We'll come back to the cameras. For now, I want to zero in on Jared's gear. You told me at the pad that morning you were in charge of harness inspections. That right?"

"I sign final approvals, yes," he said. "Supervisors do the day-to-day, but it rolls up to me. That's my job. That's why it cuts when anyone suggests we don't care."

I slid the printed harness inventory halfway across the desk. The corner peeked from under his legal pad already; he'd kept a copy where he could see it. "This inventory you provided lists harness tags as of the last pre-incident check. Serial numbers, locker assignments, sign-offs. That list complete?"

"As of that date, yes."

"Any changes to Jared's harness between then and the night he died?"

He spread his hands. "Not that I'm aware of."

"You didn't reassign his gear? Swap tags? Move it to a different locker?"

"No." He smiled, strained. "Sheriff, a harness is a harness. They're interchangeable. We track them, but there's no reason to play games with who gets which one."

"Yet you spent a lot of time with Jared's harness that morning," I said. "More time than anyone else on scene."

He stiffened. "I was doing my job. In a death like that you check equipment. See if there's a recall, a manufacturer fault. You don't want to blame a man if the webbing failed."

"Sure," I said. "But everyone I talked to that day was looking at Jared. Or up at the crossbeam. I've got a note from that morning: 'Colton focused on harness tag, not the body.'"

He laughed, too loud for the room. Heads in the bullpen turned and snapped back to screens. "Sheriff, I examine equipment. That's literally my job description. If I'd stood there emoting instead of checking gear, you'd be asking why the safety guy skipped the harness."

He wasn't wrong about the description. But the picture in my head shifted: gray webbing over my glove, metal tag cool under frost, Colton's breath fogging as he leaned in, eyes locked on numbers while Rosa rocked in the wind behind us.

"How many times would you say you handled that harness?" I asked.

He shrugged a shoulder. "Once? Twice? We bagged it as soon as we could. You had your tech there."

"Before we bagged it," I said, "did you check the tag?"

He went a little still. The air freshener turned sharp in the room.

"I check tags as a matter of course," he said slowly. "Always have. Helps me match gear to inspection dates."

"Did you read the serial off Jared's tag that night?"

"That's...yes. I did. I make it a practice to, "

"What was it?" I asked.

He opened his mouth, closed it. His gaze slid to the printout peeking from under his pad, then to the camera dome, then back to me.

"I don't have it memorized," he said. "There are dozens of tags."

My pen rested. I let the silence drag until the whirr of the projector fan felt loud. He shifted, fingers starting to drum on the desk when I reached for the ledger copy.

"That's the thing," I said. "I never told you which harness Jared was in. I told you there were anomalies in the locker count and in the serial list your office gave us. I never mentioned any tag on him being special."

He swallowed. The little chord in his neck jumped. "You said there were anomalies," he snapped. "So I checked. That's what you want, right? A hands-on safety manager, not some guy who only reads spreadsheets?"

Earlier in the week, standing on the catwalk, Clara had run a gloved fingertip along the latch groove.
"Somebody's practice swing," she'd said. "And it was here the first night. That's on your photos."

Wade had watched the deadweight dummy smack the beam and whispered, "He never would've gone over like that on his own."

Now I had Colton, in his aquarium of glass and posters, volunteering knowledge of a harness tag he shouldn't have singled out unless he'd touched that gear when nobody wrote it down, or known before Jared went up which one he'd wear.

"Walk me through your night," I said. "From when you drove onto the pad to when you left. Use your own words."

He set his hands flat, knuckles blanching. "I got the call about some near-miss chatter the previous shift. So I swung by to do a spot check. Talked to Wade, checked training binders, did a quick walk around. Weather was rolling in; I didn't want to keep guys in the wind."

"Time?"

"Early evening. Before dinner."

"Camera log has you running a 'static check' on Camera Three between ten and midnight," I said. "Maintenance window you initialed. That about right?"

He frowned. "Again, we've talked about this. There was interference. I had techs look at it."

"You wrote you looked at it," I said. "You initialed it. And your badge swipe put you inside the camera shack during the same gap the footage cuts out around Jared's fall."

"Then your logs are wrong." His gaze lifted toward the dark dome. "Sheriff, this has turned into a witch hunt."

Another little flare at the word "homicide" when I'd used it in the warrant briefing. Another note in the margin. He was good at sounding offended for the right reasons.

I flipped my notebook closed without capping the pen. "This isn't about witches. This is about physics and paper. Latches don't grind against themselves in straight grooves. Welding receipts don't backdate themselves. Cameras don't shut off during clear skies because of imaginary snowstorms. And safety managers don't accidentally memorize the tag on one dead man's harness if they're not unusually interested in that piece of gear."

"You're twisting everything I say," he said, voice low now. The charm scraped thin. "You come in here with your mind made up. You want to feed a jury a story about some villain in a suit. You have no idea what it takes to keep these guys in paychecks."

Across the glass, a woman at a cubicle ducked her head when I glanced her way. The posters behind Colton shone under the fluorescents: smiling men in hard hats, slogans in big block letters. ZERO INCIDENTS, FULL LIVES.

I thought about Rosa's dim front room. About Wade's hands jammed in his pockets on the pad, eyes turned from the dried stain on the beam. About Jared's cramped handwriting in the torn notebook: dates, dollar figures, "bonus, colton" penciled in the corner.

Maybe Colton believed his own pitch. A tuned latch here, a shaved log there, one bad fall instead of a full audit. Keep the metrics clean, keep the rigs turning, keep everybody fed. The logic always looks better from the chair behind the desk.

"Here's what I know," I said. "The man who died kept notes on near-misses your ledger stopped paying him for. The rung he went past had a welded repair your supervisor lied about. The latch that should have held him was fresh-cut along the teeth of a wrench. Your initial sits on the maintenance window where the camera went dark. And now you've told me you personally checked the tag on his harness that night even though, by your own inventory, that tag already appears in a list that left your office days before."

His jaw worked. "If you're accusing me of murder, say it."

I let the word sit a second before I answered. The truth of it edged cold through my chest. When I'd first walked this office weeks ago, I'd tagged him in my notes as "corporate functionary. Low physical risk." Easy to think the blood stuck to rougher hands.

"I'm accusing you of lying," I said. "About weather. About cameras. About what you touched and when. The rest will sort itself out in affidavits and at the arraignment."

"You're overreaching," he said. "My lawyer will be in touch with the county attorney."

"Good," I said, standing. The chair legs squeaked on the carpet tile. "They're the ones who'll be reading your tag inventory and your maintenance log side by side. I'd rather not misquote you."

He stared at his hands, fingers pressed so tight the knuckles went white. The family photo sat just out of line with his gaze; the clipped harness-serial printout peeked from under a legal pad like a corner of a confession.

"Sheriff," he said as I reached for the door, "this is bigger than you think. If you tank this yard, you don't just take me down. You take down a hundred families. Including some with your last name."

He meant Joel. He meant GreenSpire. He meant Eve's brother on a rig crew. All the quiet lines that tied paychecks to pulpits.

I opened the door. The outside office dropped its eyes, everyone back to their screens. The air tasted of recycled heat and cheap cologne. Behind me, glass separated us like an aquarium wall. A man in a suit, hands flat on a desk, posters shouting safety over his shoulder. A tag number I didn't know yet, but would.

Out in the hallway, the notebook felt heavier in my pocket. I added a single line as I walked past ducked heads and the dark eye of another camera.

"Colton: 'I personally checked his harness tag that night.'" I underlined it twice.

Not proof yet. Not on its own. But a statement I could test against badges and inventory before I ever let myself treat it as fact.

I didn't sit again. Not in that office.

I turned back from the door, let my knuckles rest on the frame. "One more thing," I said.

Colton glanced up, schooling his face. "Yes?"

"Let's get our skies straight," I said. "Just so there's no confusion later. For the record. You're saying the snow that knocked out Camera Three, the 'driving snow' in your log, hit during that ten-to-midnight window the night Jared died."

"That's what I remember," he said. His foot tapped once under the desk before he stilled it. "A mess. Visibility gone. That's why we had interference."

"Because funny thing," I said. "My notes from the road that night say 'clear, stars out, temp dropping, no precip.' The highway cams show dry pavement. The trooper who rolled through the pad at eleven didn't log weather. Just cold."

His eyes flicked to the window, to the bright blue beyond. A shadow from a passing truck slid over his face and the slogan behind him. ZERO INCIDENTS.

"There have been a lot of storms this winter," he said. "I must have mixed dates. If your notes show clear skies, then I was thinking of another shift. It happens."

"Which shift?" I asked.

He opened his mouth. Nothing came out.

He tried again. "I don't recall off the top of my head. I'd need to pull logs. You've seen how many we juggle."

I watched him, still in the doorway, the backs of my shoulders cool from the outer office air.

The day he'd first fed me the snow story, back in that same room, I'd walked out telling myself it was a small crack, nothing more. Managers misremember. So do sheriffs.

But my notebook doesn't. Neither do road cameras. Neither does the maintenance log with his initials boxed around the same window where Jared's body went sideways through the night air.

"See, I wrote mine in the truck pulling away from your pad," I said. "Ink smeared where my glove brushed it. 'Weather: clear, stars out, temp dropping, no precip.' Your 'storm' lives only in your maintenance line and your mouth."

His mouth twitched hard at one corner. "Then I misspoke. A simple error. You going to put me in handcuffs over confusion about a snow flurry months ago?"

"Not today," I said. "But I am going to write 'lied,' not 'confused,' in my notebook. That tends to matter in front of a judge."

Anger flashed in his eyes, quick as heat above a flare. "You're not the only one with a notebook, Sheriff. I've been documenting my interactions with you too. This isn't my first rodeo with a local trying to make a name."

"Good," I said. "Keep writing. Paper's how we'll sort this."

I stepped fully into the outer office. The soft hum of the vent washed against the murmur of phones. My pen clicked down as I walked.

"Colton repeats storm excuse," I wrote. "Road cams + notes confirm clear. Maintenance window same as staging. Choice to lie > admit 'don't recall.'"

I capped the pen and slid it into my shirt pocket. The act steadied me more than any hymn ever had in that stake cultural hall.

By the time I hit the lobby, faces were turning away hard, heads dipping toward screens that had been still a second before. I couldn't see the eyes, but I felt them anyway, weight between my shoulder blades. The glass of Colton's office shone behind me, blank as a clean page.

Out in the lot, I sat in the truck long enough for the scanner hiss to settle around me like breath. A minor traffic stop crackled, then some chatter about a loose steer.

I opened the notebook one last time before driving off and drew a small box around three words.

"Harness tag. Weather."

Two alleged facts from his mouth. Two leads I'd already started pinning to harder things, badge swipes, inventory lists, sky on my skin.

I'd gone into that glass office thinking of Colton as a man who doctored forms and let line bosses bend steel. Paper harm. Distance.

Driving away, watching the field office shrink in the rearview, I saw him differently. Not just the name on the maintenance log. A body in the camera shack during the dark gap, if the badge data backed it. Fingers on a tag he shouldn't have needed to read, if the serial list proved it out.

He wasn't just rearranging numbers to please some regional manager. He was close enough to the gear to leave marks the lab could later match to his tools.

I shifted into drive, the truck seat creaking under me. Ben Latham's watch sat heavy on my wrist. I rubbed the glass once with my thumb and pulled out into traffic.

Colton Reese had moved to the top of my suspect list before I hit the highway. Not in pencil anymore, but until the logs and lab came back, I reminded myself, not yet in ink the court would call proof.

Chapter 24

Scanner Interlude: Weather Note

The office felt bigger at night when it was just me, the desk lamp, and the scanner muttering to itself.

I'd killed the overheads. Yellow light pooled over my notebook, the rest of the bullpen sinking into shadow and the faint smell of burnt coffee from the pot nobody'd washed. The heating system clicked and sighed in the walls. Every so often the scanner spit a call, loose cows by the river, a possible DUI rolling in from Vernal, and then went back to hissing.

Colton's "driving snow" line had been playing on a loop in my head all afternoon, rubbed raw from the way he'd said it like he was reciting policy. Seasons get into you out here; you remember which winters tried to kill you. I'd driven that rig road enough nights to know when the stars were out and when you couldn't see your hood.

Still. Memory's slippery, especially when you want it to go one way instead of another.

I flipped back through the notebook, past Wade's shaky admission on the catwalk, past Clara's measurements in blue ink, past Rosa's quotes in my crooked block letters. My thumb left a faint trace of oil and dust along the page edges.

The scanner popped. "Unit three, check welfare, trailer park off Highway, " The dispatcher's voice blurred into white noise again while I read my own handwriting.

There it was. The page from that first night. The paper had a slight ripple where a splash of melted snow had dried; the ink on one line spread where my glove must have brushed.

"Rig, clear, stars out, temp dropping, no precip."

Four words. Clear. Stars out. No precip.

I remembered hunching over the wheel in the dark, steam from the travel mug fogging the windshield, the derrick lights behind me turning the windows into black mirrors. My fingers had been stiff in the cold when I wrote that line, pen stuttering, but I'd made myself write it before the heater caught up. Ben had drilled that into me: write what the sky's doing while it's still on your skin.

Road cameras had since backed it up, dry pavement, exhaust in the light, not a flake. Trooper log for his drive-by the same hour: "Cold, clear."

Colton could mix up storms if he wanted. My ink and those pixels didn't.

I stared at the sentence until the letters blurred. Something in my chest unwound a notch. Not relief. More like a knot that had been pulling in two directions finally choosing one.

Years back, in another kitchen, I'd talked myself into trusting a bishop's version of a bad marriage over the bruises I'd seen. Took me longer than it should have to admit I'd let his collar talk louder than my own eyes. The woman paid for that with a broken jaw.

Since then, I'd been careful about who got to overwrite what I'd seen.

Still, when it's a man like Colton, polished, certain, backed by lawyers and a hundred paychecks, it's tempting to second-guess the scrawl of one tired sheriff. You start to wonder if maybe the sky did spit a little, if maybe your brain edited flakes into stars later to fit the story you think you're telling.

The physical fact of the page in front of me cut through that fog. Cramped letters, a smear where a glove had dragged, my breath puffing in the truck cab.

I uncapped my pen and wrote in the margin next to that weather line: "Colton: 'driving snow/static', false (per road cams / trooper)."

The click of the pen sounded louder than it should have. I underlined "false" once, slow.

The scanner broke in with a short burst of laughter from some deputy, then a "Ten-four," then hiss again. Life in the Basin ticked along, drunks, skids, neighbor feuds over dogs and fences, while I sat in the lamp's little circle, turning stars into evidence.

I thought of all the men I'd let have the last word over the years because they had titles or pulpits or fancier offices than mine. Company reps with their laminated charts. Ward leaders with their scriptures open to keep sweet over the hard verse. Me nodding in too many hallways so the room could stay comfortable.

Eve's voice floated up from another night at our table, dishes stacked in the sink. "If it was our name on those papers," she'd asked, "would you keep the peace or tell the truth?"

I turned a few more pages, skimming my older ink. When did we first write Colton's name? When did his question mark harden into a period?

On an early page near the front, my handwriting read, "Colton at pad, eyes on harness tag, not body. Circle? Odd." I added a small asterisk in the margin now and drew a line from it to the weather note a dozen pages later.

Harness. Cameras. Sky.

A pattern you can hold in your hand is harder to argue away than a gut feeling, even when the mayor starts talking jobs and the bishop starts preaching about unity.

I set the pen down and pressed thumb and forefinger to my eyes until little sparks danced behind my lids. Fatigue sat heavy in my shoulders, but under it there was a quiet, stubborn steadiness.

He'd lied. Not misremembered. Not gotten confused in a busy winter. Chosen a storm that didn't exist and built his maintenance story around it. Chosen to mention a harness tag he had no clean reason to know, if the badge and inventory logs landed the way I suspected they would.

The paper in front of me wasn't perfect. My angles could still be off. Someone else's print might show something I'd missed. But this, this line about stars backed by cameras and logs, was real in a way no polished email could erase.

I reached for my notebook again and, below the margin note, added: "Rely on contemporaneous notes / external logs, not later spin (mine or his)."

The building creaked as the furnace cycled off. For a second the quiet felt like the inside of a chapel before a meeting starts, heavy, expectant. No hymn, just static.

"You lied, Colton," I said into the empty room. My voice sounded small against the scanner hiss. Saying it out loud made it more than ink.

I closed the notebook. The covers thumped shut, a little louder than necessary. I leaned back in my chair, let my head rest against the worn cushion, and rubbed my thumb over the face of Ben Latham's watch until the cool glass warmed under my skin.

Through the dark window, the square's streetlights threw thin reflections. My own face looked back at me, ghosted over the night, badge catching the lamplight.

Out there, Colton was probably on the phone already, telling corporate this was overreach, telling counsel about the nosy sheriff with a grudge, maybe repeating that storm story to men who wouldn't bother checking old sky.

In here, it was just me and the pages I'd carried through wind and fluorescent courtrooms and too many casseroles. My notes weren't fancy, but they were mine.

I opened the notebook one more time, underlined the weather line again just enough to darken it, then snapped the cover shut with a final little snap that felt like a promise.

When the time came to sit with the county attorney and stack up bricks, latch grooves, weld receipts, badge swipes, emails, I'd put this thin sliver of sky on the pile too. A clear night against a man-made storm.

The scanner crackled with some deputy's "Code four." I turned off the desk lamp. The room fell back into shadow except for the glow from the radio and the EXIT sign over the door.

On my way out, I tucked the notebook inside my jacket instead of leaving it on the desk. The paper pressed like a spine against my ribs.

Whatever the ward thought. Whatever the company spun. However ugly the politics got.

Ink first. Then the rest.

Chapter 25

Threats in the Parking Lot

The bell over the diner door rattled behind me and the night took its place again. Neon from the Roosevelt Family Diner soaked the gravel in pink and blue. My truck sat off to the right, one of only three left in the lot. The air bit my cheeks and carried grease and fryer oil from the vents.

Bootsteps scuffed near the dumpster.

"Sheriff."

Wade peeled out of the shadow by the metal bin, jaw set, hands bare and red from the cold. Hank hovered behind him, shoulders hunched, a cigarette ember cutting a small arc when his hand moved.

"So this is what you're doing now," Wade said. "Sneaking papers into town and calling it safety."

I stopped where the neon fell off, halfway between them and my truck. Gravel crunched under my soles, diesel idled far up the highway. I kept my notebook zipped in my coat and my badge on my belt where they could stare at it if they needed to.

"What I'm doing," I said, "is following a signed warrant. You two want to tell me why you're waiting for me in a parking lot instead of calling the office?"

Hank drew on the cigarette hard enough the paper crackled. Ash spilled over his boot.

"Man can't talk to the sheriff now?" Wade said. "We got jobs on the line. Kids. Mortgages. You kick in those doors today, you think Colton's the only one that bleeds?"

So that's what this was. Not a bar fight, not a confession. Fear dressed up like anger.

"You heard about the warrant fast," I said. "Colton call a meeting, or did you just feel the wind change?"

Wade's mouth tightened. "Everybody talks. Lady at the courthouse sees you walking past with state boys, she tells her cousin, who tells my wife. By supper I hear you're scooping up every email a man ever sent."

"Only the ones tied to Jared and that rig." I shifted my weight, gravel grinding. "You two sleep better with the file complete, or with Colton's version holding steady?"

Hank worked the filter with his lips. Smoke drifted, then broke in the wind. His free hand trembled more than the cold warranted.

"We're not liars," he said, words soaked in smoke. "We just... we said what they told us to say."

Wade shot him a look sharp enough to draw blood. "You said what was true. Period."

I let the silence fill with the neon hum and a semi's gear change somewhere up Main. Hank stared past me. His fingers jerked the cigarette down again, ash sprinkling his laces.

"Walk me through your worry," I said. "You here to tell me I've got the wrong man, or you here to tell me you're scared to be standing under him when he lands?"

Wade stepped closer to Hank's shoulder, like he'd body-block words if he could.

"We're here," he said, "because you know how this place works. If jobs go, it's our names they cuss in church. Not yours. You'll still have your badge. We'll be the ones they say killed the Basin."

"And Jared?" I asked. "What do they say about him right now?"

Nobody answered that. Hank dragged in smoke until his eyes watered.

In my chest I still carried Rosa's front room, dim light on kids' toys and a crumpled settlement envelope. I carried my own kitchen table where Eve had leaned on her elbows and asked whether I'd keep the peace if it was our name in those ledgers. Men like Wade framed it as jobs. For Rosa the math had been groceries versus telling the truth over her husband's body.

"You already know what I found." I kept my voice even. "Weld receipts that don't match statements. Bonus ledgers with Colton's signature. Camera logs with his initials. This doesn't start and end with one roughneck who missed a step."

Wade's hands opened and closed at his sides. "We did what we were told. Safety meetings. Checklists. We didn't touch those cameras."

"But you heard talk," I said. "Somebody higher up made it clear that incident numbers mattered more than near-misses on a catwalk."

Hank's shoulders twitched. Wade cut his eyes his way again, warning.

"Sheriff," Wade said, "you ask questions in that building, they'll fire ten of us to prove they still can. That warrant says you don't care what happens to the rest of us."

"That warrant says I care what already happened to Jared."

The cigarette shook. A flake of ash landed on Hank's boot and held there, tiny orange coal in the dark.

"He kept writing," Hank said, voice rough. "You know that. Every little slip, every close call. Made the rest of us look like we didn't give a damn." He swallowed. "We gave a damn. Just not the way he did."

"Jared wrote because he thought it'd help keep you alive," I said.

"Yeah." Hank let out a thin laugh. "Look how that turned out."

He flicked the cigarette toward the gravel. The ember tumbled and died.

"Who leaned on you after he died?" I asked. "Colton? Somebody above him? Or a whole crew of supervisors making it clear the story had to stay simple?"

A diesel pickup rolled past on Main, bass line thudding through its doors. Wade let it go by before he answered anything.

"You don't get it," he said finally. "All that paper you pulled, it's what they told us to sign. You come after us, you're punching down."

"I'm not here to punch," I said. "I'm here to know whether what's in that paper matches what came out of anybody's mouth in the yard. Things like, say, how many incidents you could afford before the company took a hard look."

Hank shifted, boots grinding. For a second his eyes met mine, then slid to the far end of the lot.

"He said we were bleeding on the wrong side," Hank murmured. "Too many dings, they'd come in, start pulling rungs, writing men up, shutting down shifts. Said better one bad fall than a full audit."

The words hit like metal on metal. I saw Clara at my desk, holding up the printout from Exhibit A. One line in Colton's email: one bad fall on the books is better than a full audit. His digital voice now in Hank's mouth behind the diner.

Wade's hand clamped onto Hank's arm.

"Shut up," he snapped, low. "Don't you start mixing up what people said with what you remember, not with a warrant in his pocket."

Hank jerked free. "I ain't mixing anything. You were there. You heard him same as me."

"Who?" I kept my tone level. My pulse did its own thing, steady tick against Ben Latham's watch. "Who said that, Hank? Better one bad fall than a full audit?"

I already knew, but a jury wouldn't be sitting in my head.

Wade answered before Hank could open his mouth.

"Nobody said that," he snapped. "He's... he's rattled. Got lawyers talking on the radio, Rosa's crying on the news, bishop preaching about patience from the pulpit. He's mixing things."

Hank looked at the gravel, then at Wade, then at me. Wind pushed diner grease smell around us.

"You know who," he said, just loud enough to cross the space. His jaw tightened like he'd bitten the words in half.

Wade took a half-step in front of him, shoulders broad in the neon spill.

"We done here?" he asked me. "We gotta be back on at six. If we still got a rig to stand on."

"You're done whenever you decide you'd rather be witnesses than shields." I let my eyes rest on both of them. "This doesn't have to end with you in the same folder as Colton. But that's up to you. You've got my office number. You know where the door is."

Hank dragged fingers over his mouth. "We got kids," he said, almost to himself.

"So did Jared," I answered.

Rosa's boy flashed in my mind on that sagging couch, hands wrapped around a chipped Xbox controller, asking if his dad's job had hurt him. Hank's cigarette had shaken that night in the bar when I laid the gas receipt in front of him. His empty hand shook now.

"Come in," I said. "Tell it like it is. The more I know about who said what when, the clearer it's going to be where fault really sits."

Wade's jaw clenched. His truck keys clicked in his fist.

"Fault sits with a man standing on a rail when he shouldn't have been," he said. "Paper can say whatever you want after the fact."

I didn't bother arguing physics in a neon-lit lot.

"You boys drive safe," I said instead. "Snow or not, those roads will kill you faster than I ever could."

Wade's mouth thinned. He turned first, boots crunching, Hank trailing. Their taillights flared red as they pulled out, slowing only long enough to look for traffic that wasn't there. The truck rolled down Main toward the man-camp, glow shrinking and then gone.

Cold dug through my coat. I walked the rest of the way to my own truck. The scanner on the floorboard muttered some other county's unit number when I opened the door.

For a moment I stood there, door open, gravel under my boots where Hank's ash still speckled the ground. I took my notebook out and flipped to a blank page in the wash of the dome light.

Parking lot. Wade & Hank.

I wrote Hank's line the way I'd heard it, underlining what mattered: "better one bad fall than a full audit, 'he said.'" I added: Hank anxious, hand shaking; Wade trying to shut down the quote and rewrite who'd spoken.

Wind pushed along the strip, lifting the edge of the page. Audit in my scrawl sat beside audit in my memory from Clara's copy. Same rhythm. Same cheap math.

Colton's email had gone out under fluorescent lights at the field office. Hank had carried the same song out here to the gravel.

I closed the notebook, slid in behind the wheel, and pulled the door shut. The scanner hissed. Ben Latham's watch sat cool and heavy against my wrist. Somewhere down Main, Wade and Hank drove toward a dawn shift none of us were going to forget.

By the time I got back to the office, the square was mostly dark. Streetlamps painted the courthouse steps a dull yellow. Inside, the sheriff's door stuck, then gave under my shoulder. Familiar smell met me: old coffee burned low on the hot plate, dust in the vents, faint gun oil.

The scanner hissed and popped in the bullpen, one deputy on graveyard mumbling a traffic stop to dispatch. I dropped into my chair. The springs complained, same as always. The desk lamp lit the island of my blotter, everything beyond it shadowed.

My notebook lay beside the thick case folder like it had been waiting.

I uncapped my pen and wrote at the top of a clean page: Parking lot, Wade & Hank.

Jerked cigarette, ash on boots. Wade angry, posture blocking. Hank's phrase exact as I could get it: better one bad fall than a full audit.

I added notes in the margin about tone. Hank's voice, half confession, half excuse. Wade's fast denial, jumping in before Hank could name Colton outright. The way Hank wouldn't quite meet my eyes when he said you know who.

Fatigue tugged at the base of my skull. It would've been easy to throw the whole thing under color, roughnecks blowing off steam, repeating somebody's dark joke about OSHA. But color doesn't get read into evidence. Clean sentences do.

I reached for the case folder. Paper rasped under my fingers, a sound I'd heard so often it almost counted as comfort. Clara had clipped Colton's worst emails into a separate subfile. I slid it free and laid it open beside Hank's quote.

There it was again, Exhibit A. Plain black text on white, corporate letterhead blurred when we'd reprinted it for the warrant packet. In the middle of a paragraph about incident metrics and losing bonuses: "one bad fall on the books is better than a full audit."

I underlined the phrase once, firm. Circled audit.

On my own fresh page, Hank's sentence sat almost on top of it. My hand slowed as I drew a line between the two, pen squeaking slightly on the paper.

"Same song, same singer," I said out loud. The empty squad room didn't argue.

The scanner filled a beat with static, then a deputy checked in from county line, voice tinny. Somewhere else in the Basin someone drifted left of center or came home drunk. I sat in the pool of lamplight and pictured Colton in his glass office, smoothing his tie, those words in his inbox months before Jared hit steel.

This wasn't stray gallows humor. This was policy, passed from a manager behind a desk to mid-levels in hard hats.

I pulled a blank form from my drawer: Supplemental Report. The header boxes waited for date, time, place. My pen felt heavier than it should as I started filling them in.

Statement regarding contact with Wade Garrison and Hank Dillard, Roosevelt Family Diner parking lot, 2200 hours.

I wrote Hank's words as directly as I could, added observations: odor of alcohol present on both; Hank's hand tremor; Wade's attempts to interrupt. I steered clear of nervous and scared. I wrote showed visible signs of anxiety, voice shaking, body positioned behind Wade when prison mentioned. Those are things you can swear to.

In the "relevance" section, I summarized the email line, careful not to overclaim yet. Phrase from email Exhibit A ("one bad fall on the books...") echoed in Hank Dillard's reported statement regarding supervisory guidance on incidents and audits.

The act of writing steadied me. The pen moved easier as the lines stacked up. Intuition is fine when you're alone in your truck. It doesn't do a thing for you under oath if you never pinned it to paper.

I stopped once, rubbed thumb and forefinger over my eyes, then went back to the forms. Tired or not, this was the window. By morning, memory would already be sanding the corners off Hank's tone.

When I finished the narrative, I dated and signed it, then flipped back through earlier pages in my notebook. The old weather note from the night of Jared's death looked up at me from its underlined line: clear, stars out, temp dropping, no precip.

You lied, Colton, I'd told the empty room earlier. Tonight's line turned the volume up. You didn't just lie once; you taught other men how to talk about killing risk as bookkeeping.

I slid the supplemental report into the case folder, behind Clara's email printouts and ahead of Hal's weld receipt. Then I pulled the pushpins from the edge of the corkboard by my desk and freed a strip of blank index card.

Crew coached: "one bad fall", source: Hank.

Block letters, thick ink. I carried it to the board and found the space where Wade and Hank's names sat, pushed a little away from center. Colton's card, maintenance log, bonus ledger, camera gap, held the middle now.

I pinned the new card between them. Stepped back until the lamplight caught the whole web. Lines on paper, arrows in my head. Bonus scheme, weld, harness tag, weather lie, now the phrase itself threaded from email to parking lot.

In my chest, something small and stubborn settled. I wasn't dealing with a tragic incident smoothed by panic. I was dealing with a man who'd decided one human body was an acceptable price to keep his numbers pretty.

Rosa's question in her dim front room came back: "You gonna let them say he was careless?" Eve's kitchen question sat in the margin of another page, underlined twice.

If I kept calling this negligence, I'd be lying the same way Colton had, only softer.

I turned off the lamp. The board held its silent geometry in the dark, case cards glowing faintly in the spill from the hallway exit sign. Outside, the river moved under ice somewhere beyond town, indifferent.

On my way out I paused by the window. My reflection and the square beyond overlapped, ghost of a badge over a line of neon. My shoulders squared without me telling them to.

Tomorrow I'd walk this new line into the county attorney's office. Tonight, I had done the only thing I could: write it down so it couldn't be wished away.

Chapter 26

Breathing at the River Bend

Headlights washed over cottonwoods and the dull sheen of water before I killed them. The world shrank to starlight, the faint glow of my dashboard, and the murmur of the river around the bend.

The scanner in the cab mumbled a call sign, then dropped back to static when I shut the door. Gravel settled under the truck tires in a soft cascade.

My breath hung white in front of me as I walked to the edge of the pullout. Boots crunched. Somewhere upstream a dog barked once, then went quiet.

I hadn't really decided to come here. The road had turned my hands down on its own, past the last streetlight, through the dark gap where fields gave way to willows and the river's curve. This was where I ended up when the job and the ward and my own house blurred into one humming knot.

Water hissed around a snag below, steady as a long exhale. Cottonwood leaves whispered above in the intermittent gusts.

I leaned both hands on the cool hood and flipped my notebook open. Pages fluttered in the breeze, earlier entries catching bits of starlight: rig notes, Rosa's kitchen, Hal's receipt, Colton's weather line with false scribbled next to it.

Halfway back, near a coffee stain, my handwriting slanted thinner. Eve's words I'd jotted the first night she said them at the sink. Peace or truth if our names were on those papers.

I'd drawn a box around it then, like a question on a test I meant to come back to.

Now it stared off the page at me in the dim light from the open truck door.

Cold bit through my jacket sleeves. I shoved my free hand deeper into the pocket, thumb finding the familiar edge of Ben Latham's watch.

Out here it was easier to remember why I'd written half this mess down in the first place. Not for judges or reporters. For Rosa, on that sagging couch with kids climbing in and out of her lap. For Hank's shaking hands. For the roustabout at the man-camp door who'd said if I disappear, it wasn't the ladder.

The river slid past in the dark, and I thought of all the men I'd heard talk themselves into bad choices with numbers. One drink. One shortcut. One lie in a bishop's office because the facts would be a mess. One bad fall instead of a full audit.

It always sounded tidy. One contained loss instead of a sprawling crisis. I'd believed it once or twice myself, younger, standing in cramped hallways while leaders told me they'd "handled it," and I'd let a report die in a drawer.

"Not choosing is still choosing," I said into the cold.

My own voice startled me, louder in the open quiet than it would've been in the squad room. Breath clouded, then vanished.

If I backed off now, softened affidavits, called this an incident with contributing negligence, I'd be making a choice as clean as any Colton had made. Just with smoother language.

Rosa would get a better check. Wade and Hank might keep a version of their jobs. The company flier on the ward bulletin board would stay up with its glossy pictures of donations. The ward would breathe easier in the foyer. Eve's brother would sleep a little better before his next shift.

And Jared would live forever as the careless hand who went where he had no business, drunk or sloppy depending which story folks preferred.

I flipped to the back of the notebook where I'd taped scraps: Rosa's refusal to call it an accident, Hal's note about rushed weld work, Clara's quick line about badge logs and Colton in the control shack. Hank's phrase from the parking lot sat in my handwriting now like a verdict.

Water kept moving. Stars hung above the cottonwoods, cold and distant. It would've been easy to say the river and sky didn't care what we did with each other down here. Might even be true. But Rosa cared. Abby cared. God, if He still listened to any of us, had made plain what He thought of false balances in more than one verse.

I thought of Ben Latham again, the one case he'd half-told me before the cancer got too loud: a woman who'd come to him scared and the bishop who'd promised it was handled. The later hospital photos. The years Ben carried that in his eyes.

He'd rubbed this same watch then. I pressed my thumb against its face now till the metal dug into skin.

"This is it, Ben," I said under my breath. "This is the one I don't walk soft on."

The rush of water answered in its own language.

I pictured Eve at our table, margin of light from the kitchen fixture on her hands. How she'd asked her question and then stood there, dish towel in both fists, waiting to see who I was going to be.

She hadn't married a man looking for a fight. Neither of us had wanted that. We'd wanted a house on this river, two kids, some church callings, a sense that the Basin's hard edges could be sanded down around us.

Instead we'd landed in a place where work killed a man on a derrick and the same institutions that brought us casseroles also told Rosa to keep things in the family.

The river hissed against a rock, steady. Wind rattled dry leaves across the gravel behind me, tiny bones skittering.

"I'm going to walk it through," I said to the dark. "Charges that fit what he did. No finessing."

Saying it out loud didn't change anything practical. The warrant was already signed. The evidence sat in the vault. The county attorney would still have her own thresholds. But something in my chest shifted from maybe to yes.

I trace-counted in my head the people who'd be angry when the Chronicle printed the complaint. Roman Hale at his ranch, fuming over breakfast. Bishop Cade working the phrase tragic accident into prayers. Joel running numbers on tax revenue and calling it stewardship. Tessa Kline checking donor lists and town budgets, eyes on me across the square.

Abby would be mad at me for some other reason if I didn't follow it through. For once, my daughter and I lined up.

I stared down at the notebook again. Eve's question in the margin. Rosa's name, circled three times in other notes. I wrote one more line under the box around Eve's words: Truth, even if it cuts our own name.

The river didn't stop. Trucks on the highway far off didn't stop. The scanner in the cab crackled once with some deputy's routine radio check and then settled back.

Resolve didn't come with trumpets. Just a man with cold hands and a notebook accepting there was no clean way back to how things were.

I snapped the cover shut and let my palm rest a second on the worn cardboard. The hood under my other hand felt solid and cold. Somewhere in town, Eve was probably rinsing mugs, turning off the porch light, checking that Abby had put her phone away. She didn't know yet that tonight at the river was where I'd picked my side all the way.

Truth was the noble answer under the stars. It would feel a lot less pretty when we were eating alone at ward potlucks.

I pushed away from the hood and walked to the driver's side. The dashboard glow spilled faintly onto the page when I opened the door, enough to show the edge of the next blank sheet.

I flipped the notebook back open on the hood before getting in. If I was going to live with this choice, I needed more than a feeling. I needed a plan.

New page. I printed a short heading: Colton, chain to Jared's death.

Then I started listing, leaving space between each bullet.

1. Maintenance log, "camera 3 static," initialed C.R., spanning death window. Inconsistent with my weather note (clear, stars out).

2. Payroll ledger, selective "safety bonus" payments signed by C.R. for Jared, stopped weeks before death. Amounts match Jared's notebook.

3. Email to regional manager, "one of the hands scribbling every little incident like he's auditioning for trial exhibit A." (Jared.)

4. Backdated weld receipt from Hal, rung repaired week before death, contradicts Wade's statement of untouched structure.

5. Harness-tag comment, Colton said he "checked Jared's harness tag that night" when not asked. Suggests foreknowledge or post-incident tampering.

6. Badge-swipe logs, C.R. entering camera-control shack during footage gap despite claim he'd left hours earlier.

7. Harness-tag swap, inventory shows tag change after incident for Jared's harness.

8. Hank's quote in parking lot, "better one bad fall than a full audit" (echo of email phrasing), attributed to "he," context: coaching on incidents vs. audit risk.

I stepped back, pen hovering. The pattern looked different all in one place. This wasn't my resentment drawing lines where none existed. This was a man using his authority over logs, cameras, money, and mid-level supervisors to turn safety into a numbers game that ended with a body.

Negligent homicide. Evidence tampering. Maybe more, once the county attorney got her teeth into the statutes. I could hear her voice already, picking at the weakest link, asking where the jump from sloppy to criminal lay.

"Walk her through it in order," I told myself. "No sermons. Just the spine."

I tapped the numbered list with the pen, underlining the numbers, not the adjectives. Sequence and proof. Let the moral part ride under the surface unless someone asked what it cost.

The river hummed on. The cold worked through the seams in my coat. Fear hummed under my ribs, low and constant. Fear for Abby at school, for Eve in the halls at church, for Rosa getting flat tires in front of the only grocery store in town.

Still, my hand didn't shake when I capped the pen and slid the notebook into my inside pocket.

I climbed into the truck. The scanner came back to full murmur as soon as I turned the key. A deputy reported clear on a house check. Another car asked about a stray dog on the highway.

I pulled away from the river slow, taillights catching dust in the mirror. The bend and its cottonwoods disappeared behind me. Ahead, a scatter of town lights grew, square taking shape like always.

For once, the story I'd been telling myself in the dark and the one I was going to tell in that courthouse felt like the same thing.

Chapter 27

Prep with the Prosecutor

The conference room off the courthouse hallway always felt like a closet someone had left a table in. Scuffed wood, one buzzing light, dry air leaking from a vent overhead. Footsteps and voices in the hall slipped under the door like they belonged more than we did.

I set my thick manila folder in the middle of the table. The edges had gone soft from being opened and shut too many times. Clara pulled a little projector from her bag, plugged it into her laptop, and a close-up of Jared's harness latch flared onto the portable screen. Tool marks haloed the metal like a rash.

County Attorney Carol Henley sat opposite, legal pad ready. Blue suit, hair pulled back. No small talk this time.

"All right, Sheriff." She clicked her pen. "Walk me from the rig floor to whatever you think justifies negligent homicide and tampering. Assume I'm a jury that doesn't care about oil jargon."

"That's why Clara's here," I said. "She keeps me honest on the tech."

Clara lifted a hand in a half-wave but let the photo talk first.

"The latch from Jared Pike's harness," she said. "This is not what normal wear looks like. These cuts here, here, consistent with somebody backing off the spring tension with a hand tool."

Carol's pen moved. "You have lab confirmation on that, or is this opinion?"

"Prelim from the state tool-mark guy," Clara said. "Full report pending. We can live without it for charging because of what stacks around it."

I opened the folder, slid out the first divider. "Scene photos, then paper. I'll spare you the scanner logs unless you ask."

She almost smiled. "Mercy appreciated."

We walked through the early pieces: Jared impaled on the crossbeam, angle of impact, the doctor's note on bruising that implied he went over limp. I watched her more than the photos, the pause in her scribbling when Clara paired bruise locations with rail height, the way her gaze drifted to the little window when I mentioned Bishop Cade pressing Rosa to accept the company's version.

"This stays a work-incident file if all you have is a bad ladder and a grieving widow," she said.

"I know." I reached for the next stack. "That's not all."

Hal's weld receipt went down between us. Grease smudged the top corner where his thumb had rested the day he handed it over.

"Hal Briggs did a weld on the exact rung Wade claimed was untouched," I said. "Receipt's backdated. Date lines up with a near-fall the crew talked about later."

Clara clicked to a photo of the rung, close, showing fresh bead under old paint.

"Supervisor lied about no work being done," Carol said. "Why?"

"Because admitting it raises questions about why that rung failed under Jared and not before," I said. "Keep that in the back of your mind."

Next tab: payroll ledger copies. Clara slid one page across, her finger resting by a column of numbers.

"Company safety bonuses," she said. "Authorized by Colton Reese. Jared gets them on and off for months, then they just...stop. Same weeks he starts copying logs. Figures in his pocket notebook match these."

"Stopping a bonus is not a crime," Carol said. "It may be petty, but."

"It's motive," I said. "If you're a safety manager whose promotion depends on low incident numbers, and one hand stops taking hush money and starts compiling a personal log, he's a problem, not an employee."

Her pen hovered. "All right. Incident logs?"

Clara pulled up the maintenance entry for Camera Three. I set the paper copy beside her pad.

"Colton's initials on a 'static check' covering the exact window the footage goes to snow," I said. "He told me it was a storm. My note from that night says dry, clear, just cold. We confirmed weather with the state. No storm anywhere near that pad."

Carol's jaw tightened once, a little jump under her ear. "So he lies about the reason for the gap."

"He lies," I said. "And he's the only one with authority to schedule that maintenance window."

She flipped back a few pages. "All this still gets me to negligence. Sloppy, maybe reckless. I'm not yet at homicide."

"That's why we kept digging," Clara said. She tapped a key. A screenshot appeared: an email header with Colton's name.

"We seized this in the first warrant," she said. "Colton to a regional manager. He complains about 'one of the hands scribbling every little incident like he's auditioning for trial exhibit A.' No names, but time period matches Jared, and we've got co-workers repeating the same phrase."

I added Hank's line from the parking lot in my notebook, slid it over. She read the quote, "better one bad fall than a full audit", and looked back at the printed email, where near enough the same words lived in black and white.

"That exact phrasing came out of Hank's mouth in the diner lot," I said. "He attributes it to 'he,' which, in his world, means Colton or Wade. Only one of those has regional managers in his address book."

She leaned back, pen stilled. The vent hummed above us, dry air on the back of my neck. Out in the hall, a door shut hard enough for the frame here to shiver.

"Walk me the night," she said. "From when Jared went up that ladder to when Colton claims he was home in his pajamas."

Clara nodded, almost to herself. This had been her late-night project as much as mine. She laid out the timeline like beads on a string.

"Twenty-two hundred, crew rotation. Jared off scheduled task." She clicked; a badge-log list appeared. "Twenty-two twelve, his badge hits the shack door by the base, normal for log copying. Twenty-two seventeen, Colton's badge opens the camera-control building. That's right when the feed cuts to snow. He told Sheriff Kingston he'd left the pad 'hours earlier.' His truck doesn't hit the gate camera until twenty-two forty-one. That's twenty-four minutes unaccounted for."

"And the harness?" Carol asked.

"Inventory report logged the morning after the death." Clara pulled a printed sheet from a plastic sleeve. "Jared's assigned harness tag number crossed out, replaced with another serial. Initials match Colton's on every other maintenance form. No reason listed for the change. That's the only harness swapped that day."

I added the memory that had bothered me since his office.

"When I met him alone," I said, "he volunteered that he'd 'checked Jared's harness tag that night.' I'd never mentioned tags. No one else did either. That's the kind of detail you focus on if you've already been in the system changing numbers."

Carol rubbed a thumb along the side of her pen, eyes on the harness sheet, then the screen, then the email. My pulse thudded in my neck.

"Sheriff," she said, "if this goes all the way to trial, can you look a jury in the eye and say you believe this wasn't an accident? That somebody made decisions that killed him?"

"Yes, ma'am."

The yes came easy. The next part took a breath.

"I can also look Rosa Pike in the eye if we don't bring it," I said, "and I know which of those would keep me up more."

She grimaced, like I'd made her bite down on something sour. But she didn't look away.

"Jobs are going to take a hit," she said. "Roman and the mayor will say I'm helping you destroy the local economy over one death on a dangerous job."

"Jobs are already part of the math," I said. "So is a man on a beam who didn't have to be there. So is a pattern of lying on paper. If this was just rust and bad luck, I'd have signed the incident line myself."

Clara's finger tapped a slow rhythm on the table beside the badge printout. I thought of the river the night before, the murmur like static from the scanner, and the note in my own margin: not choosing is still choosing.

Carol inhaled, then let it out through her nose, eyes on the evidence fan between us, the latch photos, the weld receipt, ledger copies, email, badge logs, harness report.

"All right," she said. "Put them in order for me."

She pushed her pad into the middle, drew a quick vertical line. "Timeline on the left, elements of the offenses on the right. We're talking negligent homicide, not intentional murder. And evidence tampering."

"Failure to maintain safety equipment you know is compromised," Clara said, "coupled with falsified logs and deliberate disabling of surveillance."

"And post-incident alteration of key physical evidence," I added. "Harness tag swap, plus coached statements."

"Plus the 'better one bad fall' remark," she said quietly. "That's going to sing to a jury. Ugly song."

We talked through jury instructions, what a judge in this county might allow in on motive, how much ward pressure language she thought she could touch without blowing up voir dire. She circled the email twice, underlined the badge swipe time.

"It's not just sloppy," she said, more to herself than to us. "It's a pattern that leads to a body."

The weight I'd been carrying since Jared's name first crackled over the radio shifted, not off me but into the room.

"Okay," she said, brisk now. "You want negligent homicide and evidence tampering. I'm comfortable endorsing both. We'll frame the narrative clean, keep the technical underpinnings in exhibits. No sermons. Just the spine."

The back of my neck went warm. I hadn't told her that line. I'd only whispered it over my own notebook under cottonwoods.

"We'll also need an emergency preservation order on corporate data," Clara said. "The first warrant got us a slice. He's going to start scrubbing as soon as he feels charges coming."

Carol capped her pen, uncapped it again. "Draft me a supplemental summary with that timeline, cite your sources. I'll sign off on charges and on a second, tighter warrant for his office and whatever servers you can justify. We'll route any ward records through a judge for supervised copies."

She slid the folder toward me, then stopped and left it there, her hand resting on the cardboard a beat.

"I'll take the political heat," she said. "You keep your chain of custody spotless. If we're going to crack the Basin over this, we do it right."

I gathered the papers back into the folder. The latch photo on the screen glared down on us, harsh and bright.

"Yes, ma'am," I said.

Clara and I stepped out of the conference room into the courthouse hall. Footsteps echoed, somebody's laughter bounced off tile and faded. The air out here was no better, dry heat rising from the old radiators, but at least it didn't smell like stale coffee.

"You all right?" Clara asked, low.

"Ask me after the next warrant," I said.

We pushed through the heavy front doors into thin winter light. Cold cut up under my collar. Traffic noise from the square rolled over us, diesel idle from a pickup at the curb, a horn off down Main, the soft slap of a flag rope against its pole.

Mayor Tessa Kline waited off to the side of the steps, coat pulled tight, a leather bag on her shoulder. Her eyes went first to the folder in my hand before they came up to my face.

"Sheriff. Deputy." She gave Clara a polite nod. "Busy morning?"

"Always," I said.

She glanced at the courthouse doors behind us, then toward the diner across the street where grill smoke and coffee smell drifted in the cold.

"Walk a minute?" she asked.

Clara flicked her gaze at me. The question there, want backup or not? I jerked my chin toward the sidewalk. She fell in beside us.

We went down the steps onto the square's cracked sidewalk. Flyers on the community board near the door rattled in the wind, youth dance, ward potluck, a GreenSpire stewardship talk that someone had half torn down.

"I won't pretend I don't know why you were in there," Tessa said. "Roman's been in my ear already. So have three shop owners and a pastor."

"Occupational hazard," I said.

"Of mine or yours?" She tried for lightness, but the line of her mouth stayed flat.

"Both, I guess."

The wind funneled between the brick buildings, bringing the smell of grease from the diner and exhaust from the idling truck. My hand tightened on the folder until the cardboard edge bit my palm.

"I'm not here to tell you how to do your job," she said. "But I'm trying to see the edges of mine." She looked at the traffic, not at me. "Some of our biggest donors are already on edge. If this case goes sideways, we could be looking at cut jobs, cut services, empty storefronts. People will blame somebody. Likely not the company."

"Likely the sheriff," I said.

"And the mayor who 'let' the sheriff push it this far," she said. "They'll say we killed those jobs."

"People can say what they want," I said. "I didn't put a man on that catwalk with a weakened latch and a dead camera."

Her breath puffed white. She watched it drift, then vanish.

"I'm trying to gauge how much is rumor," she said. "There's talk you're chasing ghosts, that this is about your cousin and GreenSpire more than one rig hand."

"It's about Jared Pike," I said. "It's about paper that says one thing and bodies that say another. The rest is just where the threads run."

She shifted her bag higher on her shoulder. "Are you sure you want to push it this far? There's a version of this where it's a tragic incident and we fight for stricter OSHA compliance and move on. No criminal charges, no headlines, nobody's name in the Chronicle except in the obits."

Out of the corner of my eye, Clara's brows ticked up, just once.

"There's also a version," I said, "where we pretend not to see the pattern because it's easier on the budget. I drove out to the river last night and tried that story on. It didn't fit."

Tessa gave me a long, sideways look. The truck at the curb revved, then settled back into a low rumble.

"What do you have?" she asked. "Really. Beyond what the paper already sniffed at."

I thought about the prosecutor's pen pausing over the email, the badge log on the screen, the harness inventory with its crossed-out number and familiar initials. I didn't owe Tessa specifics. Anything I said here would ride in her next phone call to Roman, to Carol, maybe to Bishop Cade.

But I also didn't want her thinking this was just my hunch and Rosa's grief.

"We've got company emails," I said slowly, "where Colton complains about one of his hands taking notes like 'trial exhibit A.' We've got maintenance logs with his initials covering the camera gap. And now we've got badge swipes that put him inside the control shack right when those cameras go to snow."

Her fingers cinched tighter around her bag strap. Wind tugged a strand of hair across her cheek.

"Along with harness inventory changes after the fact," Clara added, voice mild.

Tessa stopped walking. We stood near the crosswalk, the diner's plate-glass window throwing back a warped reflection of the three of us.

"So if I go to Carol and suggest maybe this stays on the administrative side," she said, "I'm going to sound like an idiot."

"I wouldn't use that word," I said.

"I might." She almost smiled. "Roman keeps telling me this is one sheriff's crusade. That if we just let the safety people handle it in-house, we can protect jobs and avoid a circus."

"This isn't in-house anymore," I said. "You saw me come out of there with that folder because you timed it that way. You also know what it means that she called us in at all."

She stared across the square at nothing in particular. The courthouse door thudded shut behind us. Someone laughed over at the diner, a quick bright sound that didn't reach us.

"I grew up here," she said softly. "My dad worked turnarounds on those rigs. I'm not blind to what they buy us. I'm also not blind to what they take." She looked back at me. "I need to know whether I should be bracing for an arraignment or for you coming to me later saying, 'Sorry, it all fell apart.'"

"Brace for an arraignment," I said. "We're not hanging this on a bad bolt and a prayer."

She held my gaze a second longer, then nodded, short, sharp motion I felt more than saw.

"I'll make my calls," she said. "Try to keep the council from lighting their hair on fire before we even have a charging document. I won't lean on the county attorney to go light. That's the best I can give you."

"It's more than I expected," I said.

"Don't thank me yet," she said. "If those layoffs come, your name and mine will share the headline."

She turned then, heading toward the diner. Her shoulders squared as she walked, steps steady, like she was already rehearsing whatever speech she'd need at the next council meeting.

I watched her go, then turned back toward the sheriff's office. The square between us felt wider than it had an hour ago. The courthouse brick at my back felt less like a backdrop and more like a wall I'd chosen to stand on the wrong side of.

I shifted the folder under my arm and started across.

Chapter 28

Harness Tags and Swipes

The Utah State Police substation sat near the highway like every other state building I'd ever been in, low, beige, humming. Inside, radio chatter crackled from the main room, a steady layer under keys clicking and printers whining.

A trooper named Jensen waved us to a central workstation. "You're the rig death, right?" he said. "Badge logs and CCTV grab?"

"That's us," Clara said.

We pulled up chairs. Monitor glow washed our hands blue. Ventilation rushed through the ceiling vents, smelling of disinfectant and burnt coffee.

"System logs everything?" I asked. "Ins and outs?"

"For the badge doors, yeah." Jensen's fingers ran across the keyboard. "Camera stuff depends what they set up, but we've got the raw feed they sent OSHA before your warrant hit. Somebody over there is a neat freak on backups. Lucky for you."

Rows of numbers streamed down the screen, dates, times, card IDs. Dry as dust until you remembered each line was a person passing a door.

"Filter to the night of the death," Clara said. "Twenty-one hundred to twenty-three hundred."

He tapped, narrowed the timeframe. The list shrank. Crew names I knew by badge number slid past: Jared, Hank, Wade. Then another string.

"Here." Jensen highlighted a line. "Badge ID ending in seven-four-three-five. That's, "

"Colton," I said. "That's his."

"You sure?" he asked.

"I am," Clara said before I could. "Same number from the maintenance log access."

Time stamp: 22:17. Location: CAMERA CTRL BLDG EAST.

Jensen whistled under his breath. "And you said your cameras went to snow when?"

"Twenty-two fifteen," Clara said. "OSHA copy was time-stamped."

My fingertips dug into the edge of the desk. We'd guessed. We'd argued it out on paper. Seeing it here, bare, dried my throat.

"He told me he'd left the pad by twenty-one hundred," I said. "Said he hit town 'before the weather really came in.'"

"No weather," Jensen said. "We checked the logs after your call. Clear enough I could've seen my dog on the porch from Vernal."

Clara scrolled further. Twenty-two forty-one: same badge at the main gate. Twenty-four minutes from shack to gate, not counting whatever he did in-between.

"Can you print that slice?" she asked.

"Already on it." Printer behind us chugged to life, paper smell mixing with sour coffee.

"Now the harness tags," she said. "They sent inventory records with the badge logs?"

"Yup. Somebody packaged it all nice. Again, lucky."

He opened another window: a table of serial numbers, dates, remarks. Clara leaned in, eyes narrowing. I thought of Colton's fingers on Jared's harness tag at the scene, the way he'd palmed the plastic like he was checking a number he already knew.

"Here." She pointed. "This line. Harness H-23, assigned to Pike, J. Status: reassigned. Date stamp, the morning after the death. New serial substituted. Initials on the change: C.R."

"Colton Reese," I said.

"Any reason for the change listed?" Jensen asked.

"Blank," Clara said. "No damage, no inspection fail, nothing. Just swapped."

Jensen shook his head. "That's...odd. Most folks don't keep that clean a paper trail when they're pulling tricks."

"That's his hubris," I said. "He believes in systems. Thought logging it made it look routine."

The printer spit out the badge-log sheet. I took it, the paper warm and dampening under my hand. Names, numbers, times. Story laying itself out.

"Can we get a copy of the raw CCTV backup too?" Clara asked. "Just that gap segment."

"You can get the whole dump," Jensen said. "Our server guy already burned it to disc per the warrant. It'll be noisy, but your techs can isolate the period."

"We are the techs," she said. "But we'll manage."

While he dug in a cabinet for the disc, I kept my eyes on the cursor blinking over Colton's badge ID, that tiny pulse like a heartbeat waiting on orders. I remembered standing on the rig grating with him, his polished boots too clean for that deck, his attention not on Jared's body but on the harness tag still clipped and useless.

Back then the moment had just felt wrong. Now it sat in my chest with weight and shape.

You coached them, I thought. You ordered the maintenance window, cut the feed, fiddled the tag, then walked out under a clear sky and called it a storm.

Jensen handed over the disc in a clear sleeve. Clara slipped it into her case. She pulled out her phone, snapped a photo of the screen with the 22:17 entry, in case a printer jam or file crash chewed the record later.

"You're good," Jensen said. "Chain-of-custody forms are on the desk. Sign here, here. We'll keep the originals. You get certified copies."

We signed, date and time. The ceiling vent draft cooled the sweat at the back of my neck.

On the walk back to the truck, Clara held the harness printout up to the winter light slanting through the substation's glass door.

"You see why that bugged you at the scene?" she asked.

"Yeah," I said. "He touched the tag like he already knew it mattered. That wasn't curiosity. That was checking his work."

She let out a breath that was almost a laugh, no humor in it. "Well. His own swipe card and his own initials just made our day."

"It's making his arraignment," I said.

We drove around to the side lot and went back in to a quieter corner table, just a laminate surface with laminated ID charts trapped under the plastic. Other troopers worked at desks further down, their voices a low murmur under the steady tick of a wall clock.

I spread our notes and the fresh printouts like a small case board. Badge logs, harness sheet, email copy, maintenance log, ledger excerpt. The spine, like I'd told myself. Like I'd promised Carol.

"Let's try to break it," Clara said.

"Break what?"

"The case against him. Assume we're wrong. Who else could this be?"

I rubbed my thumb over Ben Latham's watch where it sat on my wrist, the crystal cool under the pad of my thumb. He'd have approved of that question.

"Underling borrowed his card," I said. "Somebody else tapped in and out of the camera shack. Colton signed the change because that's what bureaucrats do."

"Okay," she said. "Who had access to his card?"

"Policy says nobody." I flipped through my notebook. "Practice says maybe his admin. But she was at a ward thing that night. We checked photos. Plus she wouldn't know how to run the camera system."

"Could Wade or Hank have done the harness swap under his login?" she asked.

"To log into the inventory terminal, you need his password," I said. "We pulled the access log; only his username touched harness records that week."

She tapped the harness sheet. "Alternative: the system misattributed the change. Glitch."

"We already had IT walk through that," I said. "They'd love to blame it on a bug. It's not."

She sat back, chair squeaking. The clock on the wall ticked loud in the pause.

"What about motive?" she said. "Assume for a second this is all random. Backdated weld, stopped bonuses, maintenance window, camera gap, badge swipe, harness swap. Give me a world where that much lines up by accident."

"There isn't one." The answer came faster than I liked. I didn't want to skate on outrage.

I looked down at the papers, made myself slow.

"Hal's weld receipt puts Wade in the picture early, knowing the rung's weak. Hank's gas receipt shoves him off the pad during the key window. Wade's in briefing at the time we think Jared went over. If either of them did the physical push, they did it outside the window the badge logs and reenactment support. But Colton? He shows up in the only building that can take the cameras dark at the exact minute they go out. He has his initials on the maintenance window. He has power over bonuses and over harness assignments. And he's the one who parrots the company line about storms and family companies."

"And he's the one who uses the same 'trial exhibit A' language we hear from Wade and Hank," she added.

"Right." I pointed to the email. "If somebody else cooked that phrase up, we haven't met them."

Clara studied my handwriting in the margin next to Hank's quote, then my tighter script under the email, same words underlined in both.

"If we're wrong about him," she said slowly, "we're going to have to invent a phantom, someone else with his height, his access, his badge number, his initials, his writing style, his management role, his motive, and his habit of coaching language into the crew, and then prove that guy exists without ever having seen him."

"Which is a longer shot than just accepting the man we've got," I said.

She smiled, a small, grim thing. "Good. I like Occam's razor."

Radio chatter spiked briefly in the main room, a burst of codes that had nothing to do with us. The clock kept ticking above our heads.

Inside, a memory drifted up: Bishop Cade in the clerk's office, warm smile, telling me saving the ward from scandal was a kind of stewardship. Then Colton's email, dressing his safety metrics up in the same language. If you say "family company" and "trust" often enough, maybe you start believing paper can forgive gravity.

"Numbers and initials," I said, tapping the badge log. "That's what this is now. Feelings got us to the river. This is what gets us to a verdict."

Clara's pen started its staccato against the table, then stilled.

"You're going to have to testify like it is math," she said. "Not like it's about Bishop Cade or ward gossip or Roman's handshakes."

"I know." I stacked the pages, squared their edges. "Math, not sermons."

She huffed that almost-laugh again. "Then let's go write it up like math."

Outside, through the high window, a patrol car eased out of the lot and turned toward the highway, lights off, just another unit going about its business.

For the first time since Jared's body swung under the rig lights, I could picture another drive clearly: Clara's cruiser and my truck heading to Colton's glass office not to ask for logs or polite clarifications, but to read this neat little column of times and initials off the page and watch his face when he realized the system he trusted had finally taught him the truth.

Chapter 29

Office Lights Burning Late

The glass doors sighed shut behind us and the air changed.

Fluorescents flattened everything in the lobby. The receptionist's fingers hung over her keyboard. A laser printer pushed out half a page and stopped. Somewhere in the back, an HVAC unit breathed steady.

Colton stood in the hallway outside his glass-walled office, framed by laminated posters: ZERO INCIDENTS, SAFETY IS LOVE. Tie straight, badge on his belt, expression pleasant enough to put on a brochure.

I walked toward him with Clara at my side and a trooper behind us, the folder under my arm heavier than paper ought to be.

"Sheriff," Colton said. "Didn't know we were on for today."

"We are now," I said. "This is Trooper Ames. We've got a warrant signed out of county. I need you in your office, sir, and I need everyone else to stay at their stations."

The receptionist swallowed. Keyboards went quiet in the open office beyond the glass.

Colton's gaze went to the trooper's shoulder patch, to the folder at my elbow, back to my face. "Of course," he said. "We always cooperate. What's the scope this time?"

"Your office, your computer, your email, badge logs, and safety files for the Roosevelt rig," I said. "You'll get a copy in a minute."

We stepped into his office. Quiet click as the door shut. Coffee and toner and some plug-in air freshener sat on top of recycled air.

I set the folder on his desk and opened it slow. Tessa and the prosecutor had drilled the next part into me. Facts, not speeches.

"Before we start," I said, "you're not under arrest at this moment. You're free to leave the room unless or until that changes. But you are not free to interfere with the search or tell your people to move records. We clear on that?"

"Crystal," he said. Hands on the blotter, pen between two fingers. "I'll have to notify our counsel."

"You can do that from that chair," I said. "Line stays open. No shredders, no mass deletes. Trooper will sit in."

Clara slipped back out to the hallway. Through the glass I watched her talk to the receptionist, then move down the row of cubicles with yellow evidence tags in her fist. A printer started again somewhere and stopped when she reached it.

I pulled out the first sleeve: the badge-swipe log from the state system. Blue rows of numbers under a header I already knew by heart.

"You remember telling me you left the pad before the storm rolled in," I said.

He gave the hint of a smile. "I remember telling you I headed out when the weather started to look bad, yes. It was late. Long day."

I laid the printout on the blotter where he couldn't avoid it. "This shows your card entering the camera shack at ten-seventeen that night. Right in the middle of the footage gap."

He looked down. Not looking would have been stranger.

His pen shifted a hair when he reached the line with his own badge number. The muscles along his cheek jumped once, then went still.

"Sheriff," he said after a beat that ran long, "that night was months ago. I'm not going to pretend I recall every minute. If I walked into a shack to check a breaker, or to see what the static looked like, that isn't a crime."

"You didn't mention that before," I said. "You said you were in your truck headed off-site when the snow started."

"It was chaotic." His voice caught on the first word and he smoothed it out. "Crews calling, weather shifting. I told you my best recollection."

The night had been clear and dry. My notebook said so in my own writing. The state weather station said so. I let that sit between us.

I pulled the next sleeve: harness inventory printout. Columns of serial numbers and initials.

"You're proud of your systems," I said. "Your logs. Your tag program."

"They keep men alive," he said. That one came quick, automatic.

I slid the printout forward and stopped where the entry changed: Jared's assigned harness number, then a line through it and a new number with the same set of initials as half the other safety entries.

"You see this?" I asked.

His fingers tightened around the pen when they passed over the new tag number, tiny movement, then eased again.

"That's routine," he said. "We rotate gear. If something's worn or out of spec, we issue a new harness. I sign off on a lot of those."

"Day after he died," I said. "His old number swapped. No corresponding purchase order. No note that the old harness was taken out of service and bagged. Just a change."

He blinked once. "You're the one who told me at the scene his harness had a cut strap. Remember? If there was a defect, of course we'd issue a replacement."

"You told me at the scene you'd 'checked Jared's tag that night,'" I said. "That was before anybody had described where the body hit, or what condition the strap was in. You zeroed in on that tag in the middle of a dead man and a panicked crew."

His eyes went to the office door, quick toward the hallway, then back. "I check a lot of tags," he said, lighter now. "That's my job."

My job was to listen to the things a man couldn't keep out of his voice.

I pulled the third piece: the email thread Clara had dug out of their server during the earlier warrant, arrowed to one paragraph for the judge. I'd underlined it last night at my kitchen table while Eve dried dishes.

"I want to read part of your own email," I said. "This went to your regional manager two weeks before Jared died."

I read it out: "One of the hands scribbling every little incident like he's auditioning for trial exhibit A. Need support to rein that in before it spooks the crews."

The line hung in the air with the same oily shine it had on the printout.

He stayed quiet. The pen had stopped moving.

"That hand was Jared," I said. "You cut off his safety bonuses right after you sent this. Ledger reflects it. His notebook, which I pulled from his trailer, matches the amounts."

"You're piecing things together that don't belong together," he said. "We adjust bonuses all the time. Production, attitude. This is a complicated operation, Sheriff."

"Let's keep adding pieces, then." I slid the maintenance log out, the one for Camera 3: STATIC CHECK, initialed CR over the same window Jared took his last walk.

"You wrote up a static check and blamed the gap on a storm," I said. "Weather station ten miles from the rig reads clear and cold. My own note from that night does too."

"You know as well as I do those towers can get microclimates." He raised his chin half an inch. "Ground fog, inversion. I'm not a meteorologist. We saw snow bands all week."

"You also told me you were off-site," I said. "This log says you were at the console, doing a 'static check,' at the same time your card hit that badge reader. That's not fog. That's time and place."

He opened his hands finally, palms just off the blotter. "I sign off when crews report problems. That doesn't always mean I happen to be right there. Maybe a tech, "

"The badge system doesn't know who a tech is," I said. "It knows the card that opened the door. This one was yours."

Outside the glass, you could have heard a dropped staple. Staff sat fixed at their monitors. Clara moved through them, tagging tower cases and file drawers, yellow stickers blooming like bright weeds.

HVAC hummed around us. I let it fade. All I listened for was his breathing and mine.

"Colton," I said. "You told me, in this room, you'd be happy to walk me through every procedure, every log, every policy. I took you at your word. What I need now is not policy. It's how you can say you'd left that pad when this says you were in the shack. And I need you to explain why Jared's harness tag got swapped the day after his body hit steel."

His face settled into something polite. Too polite.

He set the pen down with care. "Sheriff, I understand you're under a lot of pressure," he said. "Widows, lawyers, elections. People want a villain. But you're turning administrative work into a crime because it fits a story you've already sold yourself."

"That story is made of your initials, your badge number, and your words," I said. "This isn't about what I want to believe. It's about what I can put in front of a judge."

His gaze slid off the printouts and found the framed certificate on the wall: some regional award for incident-free quarters. My own brother-in-law had bragged about the same plaque at a barbecue once.

Eve's question in our kitchen rose up, steady as a hymn line: what would you do if it was our name on those papers?

"Here's where we are," I said. "Hank and Wade both tried to carry your water. They're in their own swim now. The weld receipt says somebody knew that rung was a problem. The tool marks on the latch say somebody weakened it. The bruises on Jared's body say he didn't go over that rail on his own two feet. Your badge and your log put you where the cameras went dead. Your inventory record puts your initials on his harness swap the next day. And your email gives you a motive: one bad fall instead of a full audit."

The phrase struck him harder than the rest. A beat of recognition moved across his eyes before he caught it.

"You're twisting, "

"I'm quoting," I said, and set the last page on the stack. The printout from the thread where he'd written: better one bad fall than a full audit, in black ink.

He inhaled, shallow. That was the first time since we'd walked in that something like real fear showed.

Through the glass, Clara paused at his assistant's desk with a drive box in hand, looked in at us long enough to see his face, then turned away with that tucked inside her.

I gathered the pages into a neat pile and squared them with the edge of his blotter, the way my old sheriff had taught me when he wanted a suspect to feel every millimeter closing in.

"This is your chance to tell me where I'm wrong," I said. "On any of it."

He stared down at the stack. Office sounds outside seemed to retreat, like we were under glass.

Long seconds.

"I want a lawyer," he said.

Not angry. Not indignant. Flat as the desk under his hands.

That was its own kind of answer. The man who'd spent weeks offering me guided tours through his systems had decided more words could only hurt him.

"Okay," I said. "You'll get one."

I pulled the Miranda card from my pocket and read it: right to remain silent, right to an attorney, anything you say may be used.

He signed the acknowledgment line with a careful hand. The pen left a tiny streak of ink at the end of his name.

"You understand these rights as I've explained them?" I asked.

"Yes," he said.

"Want to keep talking to me without your lawyer present?"

"I said I want a lawyer." His eyes cut to the door again, toward where company counsel would be hurrying from her own office, shoes sharp on tile.

"Then we're done with questions for now," I said. "But we are not done."

I opened the door. The printer out front had finally gone quiet. Most of his staff had their eyes on their screens and their attention on us.

"Clara," I said. "Tag his tower. Get copies of everything we listed. Trooper, you're with me."

The trooper by the window unhooked his cuffs, metal clicking in his hands.

I looked once more at Colton, now just a man in a chair with his own paper turned against him.

He stared back, jaw set, hands resting too neatly on the blotter.

The polished safety man in the posters still smiled down from the walls. On his own side of the glass, surrounded by slogans and certificates, he finally looked like what he was to me now: a defendant.

Chapter 30

Rosa's Choice

Rosa's porch light glowed dull against the late afternoon. Cold air slid under my collar as I stood there with the manila folder in my hand.

Cartoon noise leaked through the thin door. Beans or something like them simmered inside; the smell came through a seam in the frame along with cheap detergent.

Eve and Marie stood just behind me. Eve had her own folder tucked under one arm, Marie a legal pad and a stack of forms.

Rosa opened on the second knock. Her eyes went to my badge, then to the folder, then to the two women at my back. What strength she had in her shoulders drained all at once.

"You already did it," she said. Not a question.

"Yes, ma'am," I said. "He's in custody. I wanted you to hear it from me."

She stepped aside. "Come on in. Kids are in their room. TV's loud, so they don't have to hear grown-up talk."

The living room was as I remembered it: sagging couch, small lamp on an end table, a cluster of school papers and settlement envelopes on the coffee table. Laundry piled on a chair, half-folded. The air carried that mix of soap and cold seep from the door every rental on this side of town seemed to share.

We sat. The couch creaked when Rosa settled on the edge. She wiped her hands on her jeans, then set them on her knees.

"Tell me," she said.

I opened the folder, laid out the bare bones. Badge swipes. Harness tag. Email. The arrest. I kept it simple, stuck to what was already going to leak in the Basin by dinnertime.

"Charges are negligent homicide and evidence tampering for him," I said. "There'll be others on the paperwork for his supervisors. It won't bring Jared back, but the law's not going to call this an accident."

She closed her eyes for a moment. When she opened them, they were wet but clear.

"So he goes to prison," she said. "Maybe. Years from now. In the meantime they still paying my rent, Sheriff? Or do they take that back because you made him the bad guy?"

"That's part of why we're here," I said. "Marie knows more about that contract than I do. And Eve's been talking with other folks in your shoes."

Rosa's mouth pulled sideways. "I don't know anybody in my shoes."

"You do," Eve said quietly. "They just don't all admit it out loud yet."

Marie slid her folder onto the coffee table, careful not to knock over the stack already there. She waited until Rosa nodded before she pulled the top envelope free.

"I brought the draft they sent you," Marie said. "And a version with some changes we'd like to walk you through. Your choice, Rosa. Our job is to tell you what each one really means, so you can decide."

Rosa blew out a breath. "Go ahead."

We went clause by clause. Marie translated phrases like "non-disparagement" and "general release" into plainer language.

"This part," she said, tapping one paragraph, "says you agree never to say anything in public that could be taken as negative about the company, its officers, or employees. That includes telling your own story if they decide it hurts their reputation."

"So if somebody at church says Jared was drunk and I say no, he wasn't," Rosa said, "they could...what? Take the money back?"

"They could try," Marie said. "Or threaten to. More likely they'd use it to scare you into backing down. We can't promise what they'll do. We can promise what this paper gives them grounds to claim."

Rosa's fingers started a fast rhythm on her knee when Marie mentioned dollar amounts. They went still when Marie read that clause again.

I listened and watched, kept my mouth shut when my temper wanted to break in. This was Marie and Eve's lane more than mine. My job here was to be the man who would still show up if Rosa chose the harder road.

Eve leaned forward, palms light on her thighs. "They wrote this to sound like it protects you," she said. "But it mostly protects them. There's another way."

"What way?" Rosa asked. "Bills don't care about ways."

Marie flipped to the second version. Pink highlighter marked some lines. Others had neat strikes through them.

"This version keeps the financial terms the same," she said. "Same amount, same schedule. But we strike or narrow the pieces that would gag you about certain things. You'd still agree not to share exact settlement amounts or confidential HR information. But you would keep the right to speak about Jared's character, what he told you, and your own experience. It's a smaller target they'd have if they tried to come after you later."

Rosa studied the pages. Her lips moved just enough to show she was reading along.

"Why would they ever sign that?" she asked. "They're not dumb."

"No," Marie said. "They're not. But they'd rather wave a signed agreement in public and say 'we took care of the family' than take the risk of a jury with no settlement at all. And they don't want to be seen bullying a widow in front of a judge. If you come back with this and we're standing with you, odds are good they swallow the edits and tell themselves it's close enough."

"You say odds like this is a game," Rosa said. No heat, just tired.

"It's not a game to you," Marie said. "It is to the people who drafted this. That's why we're here, to make sure you're not the only one playing without a rulebook."

The kids' cartoon punched through from the back room, a sudden shout of fake danger. Then music. Then quiet.

Eve looked at Rosa, then at me. I heard the kitchen question again under everything else: what do you do when the truth costs somebody else more than it costs you?

"Let me ask it a different way," Marie said. She slid both sets of papers aside so the wood of the table showed. "Ten years from now, what do you want your kids to be allowed to say about their dad?"

Rosa's gaze drifted past us to the hallway.

"I don't want them growing up hearing he was careless, or drunk, or that he tripped because he was lazy," she said finally. "He was careful. He was scared. He talked and talked about how scared he was."

She looked back at me. "You know he was careful."

"Yes, ma'am," I said.

"So if I sign their paper the way they want, I'm telling them they can say what they like, but I can't stand next to them?" she asked. "Because some lawyer somewhere can drag us back on this?"

"That's the risk," Marie said. "If they decided to push it."

"Is there any way," Rosa said, voice low, "I can take enough to keep my boys in this house and still be able to say he wasn't what they're going to call him?"

"Yes," Marie said. "That's this version. You initial here", she tapped the narrow changes, "not here." She tapped the broad gag lines. "You'll still get pushback. They may try to talk you out of it. But you won't be alone in that room."

Silence settled for a beat. Refrigerator hum from the kitchen filled it.

Rosa's eyes went to Eve.

"If I don't sign it their way," she said, "if I say out loud that they lied about him...are you still going to be there when they get mean?"

"Yes, ma'am," I said before Eve could. "The case is ours either way. What you sign or don't sign doesn't change what I put on the stand. This just decides whether anyone gets to tell you you're not allowed to remember your own husband."

Eve nodded, throat working.

"And you won't be the only one," she said. "We're putting a circle around you. Women who've been where you are. We'll sit in that room if you want us. We'll help with rides. Groceries. Homework when court days run long."

Rosa looked down at the ink. Her fingers smoothed the edge of the page, then stilled.

"Bring me a pen," she said.

Marie handed her one.

Rosa signed on the line by her name. Her hand shook once, then steadied. She drew a neat line through the broad non-disparagement paragraph and initialed the margin where Marie had marked.

"There," she said. "They can pay for what they did. But they don't get my mouth."

She set the pen down and pushed the signed stack away from her, as if it might burn if she held on.

We let the room breathe for a moment.

"Second thing," I said. I pulled a simpler form from my folder. "This is a sworn statement. It's not the same as testimony in court, but the words can become that later. It's voluntary. You're allowed to stop anytime."

"More paper," she said, half a laugh that wasn't one.

"Yes, ma'am," I said. "But this one is yours. In your words. Nobody from the company gets to edit it."

She studied the blank lines. The refrigerator clicked on and off. A car hissed past on the road.

"I'm tired, Sheriff," she said. "Feels like I been talking since the day he died and nothing changes."

"I know," I said. "We can do this another day. Or not at all. We've got a case on the numbers and the metal. This would help us tell the full story, but I won't say it doesn't cost."

"What do you need to know?" she asked.

"Only what he told you," I said. "In your kitchen. In your bed. On the phone. The parts that stuck because they scared you too."

That landed. She blinked, once, slow.

Marie slid the statement form closer, along with her pad. She uncapped a ballpoint; the scratch when she tested it sounded loud in the quiet room.

"I'll write for you while you talk," Marie said. "We'll read it back. You can change anything you like. This is not a test. There's no wrong answer."

Rosa leaned back against the couch, feet slipping out of her shoes to tuck under her.

"Okay," she said. "Okay."

We started simple: full name, address, date. Then the night before the death.

"He came home off his shift, sat right there," she said, pointing to the end cushion. "Didn't even take his boots off at first. Said his legs were jelly."

"What did he say about work that night?" I asked.

She closed her eyes, chased the memory.

"He said, 'They're going to get somebody killed if they keep going like this,'" she said. "I asked who, and he said, 'Could be me. Could be Hank. Could be some kid they hire next month. They don't care which one, as long as the numbers stay pretty.'"

"Did he ever say a name with that?" I asked. "Of a person pushing him?"

"Colton," she said, soft. "He always called him 'that man in the tie' when the kids were around. But when it was just us he said his name. Said, 'That man don't care if I walk off that rig as long as the line on his chart stays green.'"

The way she echoed him, low and steady, raised hair on my arms.

"We're going to put that exactly how you said it," I told her. "If that's all right."

"That's what he said," she replied. "It's the thing I keep hearing when I try to sleep."

Marie wrote, pen scratching along the lines. Rosa went on in starts and stops. About the night Jared sat at their wobbly kitchen table, copying pages out of a log book, circling one line with initials next to a "safety bonus" he wouldn't sign for.

"He said he wrote it down because no one believes a hand over a man in a tie," she said, glancing at my notebook. "Said if he disappeared, not to let them say he just didn't watch his step."

We anchored dates as best we could. I nudged away from anything that started with "I heard someone say" and back toward "He told me." It would matter later, in a cold courtroom where lawyers liked to peel things apart.

Now and then Rosa's voice cracked. Marie paused then, hand resting just above her forearm until she nodded to go on.

When we reached the blessing from Bishop Cade, the part about trusting family companies and keeping things in the family, I watched her face harden.

"He stood in my front room and said God wanted Jared to trust the brethren," she said. "God didn't put that ladder there." She opened her eyes and looked straight at me. "You tell me, Sheriff. Whose hands put Jared up there that night?"

"I can tell you what the logs say," I said. "And I will. In front of whoever tries to say otherwise."

We finished the statement. Marie read it back, slow, including the direct quotes.

Rosa corrected one date, added one sentence: "Jared was not drinking that week. He promised me, and I saw it."

When she was satisfied, she took the pen again. Her name came out as a small, shaking scrawl at the bottom of the page.

Marie blew on the ink, slid the original into an envelope, then handed Rosa a photocopy.

"This one's yours," she said. "You keep it where you like."

Rosa looked around for a place. Her eyes landed on a chipped ceramic angel on a side table, standing guard over funeral programs and school photos. She lifted the angel, tucked the paper under it, then set the figure back on top.

"Now it's with him," she said.

We stood. Eve reached out and held Rosa's hand for a heartbeat longer than polite.

"Call us when the company comes back around," Eve said. "We'll be there before they finish their first rehearsed line."

Rosa nodded, already pulling her shoulders back into something like readiness.

At the door I paused. One of the boys lay asleep in the back room, visible through the cracked door, toy truck tucked under his arm. Cartoons still flashed across the screen in front of him, sound turned down now.

He had no idea his mother had just traded some safety for a promise.

On the walk back to the truck, gravel crunched under my boots. The scanner in the dash muttered about a stray cow and a fender-bender out on Main.

Eve slid into the passenger seat beside me. Her hand rested a moment on the file between us, then on my wrist. The old watch Evie had pressed on me "for as long as you need it" sat cool against her fingers under my cuff, heavy as ever.

"You did right bringing the paper and not just the cuffs," she said.

"I still feel like I talked a widow into a harder road," I said.

"She chose it," Eve said. "All we did was show her the map."

Out past the rentals, the refinery flame licked at the dark. Somewhere between there and Rosa's little house, a man in a suit would be reading the same logs I'd just quoted and praying for loopholes.

I started the engine.

"Let's go home," Eve said. "You can write. I'll start a list of who else we haven't heard from yet."

Justice, I reminded myself, wasn't a moment at an office desk or a signature on a form.

It was a stack of paper and a terrified woman who had decided her boys needed know what happened more than they needed quiet.

Chapter 31

Diner Eyes and Cold Shoulders

The bell over the diner door jingled when Clara and I walked in, same as it always had. Coffee and fried eggs wrapped around us, but the room changed shape all the same. Forks paused. Conversations flattened, then picked back up in new lanes.

Our usual booth sat open along the window, already cleared. Somebody had made space, and somebody else had suddenly remembered somewhere else to be.

"Full house," Clara said under her breath.

"Looks it."

We slid in. My badge pressed against the vinyl when I sat. I kept my hands flat on the table instead of hooking them at my belt.

The server, Trina, been here since I was a kid, took an extra beat before coming over. She dried her hands on her apron, eyes flicking from my face to the patch on my shoulder and back.

"Morning, Sheriff. Deputy." Her voice sounded careful, like she was reading from a script she hadn't practiced enough. "You want your usual?"

"Yes, ma'am," I said. "Appreciate it."

She made a small sound that wasn't quite agreement and wrote it down. When she moved off I watched whose heads tracked her path and whose eyes stayed welded to their hash browns.

At the counter, an old roustabout named Gene planted both elbows and stared into his coffee. Behind him, two younger hands from the rig kept talking about a basketball game like nothing around them had changed. That hit me more than the silence. Some folks were already deciding the case was above their pay grade.

"You counting votes?" Clara asked.

"Habit."

"What's the tally?"

I let the room settle into shapes. A rancher from out toward Diamond lifted a hand in a short wave. Another man, small-engine shop, big donor, looked straight through me like he hadn't seen the booth.

"Mixed," I said. "Could be worse."

She breathed out once through her nose, eyes moving the opposite direction from mine, catching people who made sure not to look our way.

"Folks back home tended to save the shunning for after the potluck," she said. "Efficient bunch here."

Trina brought coffee. Steam curled up out of the chipped mugs and fogged the bottom edge of the front window, putting a smear of haze over Main Street.

"You two doing okay?" she asked quietly. "Heard it's been...a lot."

"It has," Clara said. "We're all right."

Trina's fingers tightened on the pot handle. "My brother says you did right by that Pike boy." Her eyes shifted toward the corner booth where two business owners sat over ledgers. "Not everybody agrees. Just so you know, there's folks that do."

She topped off my cup and walked away before I could answer.

"That's one in the column," Clara said.

"Careful," I told her. "You're going to make me optimistic."

I lifted the mug. The coffee was a little burnt, same as every late breakfast in this place. Still tasted like home.

The bell over the door jingled again. The sound cut through the radio's soft country song and the low murmur of talk.

Mayor Tessa Kline stepped in, crisp jeans, blazer, hair smoothed into a safe shape. No entourage, just a smartphone in her hand and a tightness around her mouth that didn't fit any campaign flyer I'd seen.

She scanned the room quick, clocked us, then wound her way through the tables. The business owners at the corner booth watched her pass. One of them set his jaw and looked away when she glanced down, like he wanted distance in case the sheriff's curse rubbed off.

"Milt," she said when she reached us. "Deputy Ray."

"Tessa."

"Mayor." Clara gave her the professional half-smile I'd come to know: polite, distant, measuring.

Tessa rested both hands on our table and bent close enough that her words didn't have to carry. Her fingers tapped once against the Formica when she stopped moving.

"I just spoke with the judge," she said. "He says everything's clean on the warrant and arraignment."

"I'm glad to hear it."

"He also says his phones have lit up since the charges hit." She looked at me, not Clara. "Some of our biggest employers are...concerned."

"About?" I asked, though I already knew.

"Optics. Stability. Jobs." She slid the words out like beads on a string. "They're worried what kind of message this sends to investors. Whether it looks like we're hostile to development. You know the talking points."

Clara stirred her coffee, spoon clicking slowly. "Or," she said, "maybe it sends the message that when a man dies on a rig here, somebody looks twice instead of slapping 'accident' on it."

Tessa's mouth tightened. Not a frown; something smaller, controlled.

"I understand your position," she said. "I'm not here to argue the case. That's the court's job. But there's more at stake than one arraignment. We've got budget hearings coming up, infrastructure bids on the table. If this turns into a circus, people pull back. It happens."

She shifted her weight. A faint tremor ran through her fingers before she stilled them.

"What are you asking me for?" I said.

"Nothing formal." She let out a short breath without warmth. "Just...let things cool before any big statements. Maybe don't feed Lorna too many dramatic quotes."

"County attorney already talked to me about that," I said. "Trial's not going to be in the Chronicle. That's not what worries him."

"What does?"

"Whether we start telling folks not to come forward because donors get spooked."

Her eyes flicked down to my badge, then back up. "No one's saying that."

"They don't have to." My gaze went past her to the corner booth, to the men watching their numbers instead of the room. "They just call your office."

She straightened a fraction. "My job is to keep the lights on, Milt. I'm not trying to undercut you. I'm asking you to help me manage the fallout."

"By slowing down?" Clara asked. "By picking cases that won't upset anybody?"

Tessa's jaw worked once. "By being aware that every headline hits more than one ledger. That's all."

I thought of Rosa's coffee table covered in papers, of a little boy sleeping with a toy truck under his arm while his mother signed away less than the company wanted.

"Tessa," I said, "I can't uncharge a man because somebody's nervous about investors. We're past that now."

"I know." She stepped back half a pace, smoothing her blazer. "Didn't expect you to. Just, if you can keep things...measured. At least until we see where the jobs land."

"We'll do our jobs," I said. "Same as you'll do yours."

Her shoulders eased. "All right." She gave Clara a nod that looked more like apology than command. "Deputy."

When she turned away, the two business owners in the corner booth watched. One gave her a look that asked a question. She lifted her palm in a way that said, Later. The little scene played like silent theater.

Clara's spoon rested against her cup. "Well," she said. "That was subtle."

"Basin-style subtle," I said. "Words under the noise."

"Think she means it as a threat?"

"I think she's counting votes too. Same as us."

The food came. Eggs, bacon, toast, the kind of meal that fits both celebration and wake. We ate in stretches, letting the sound wash back to normal. A regular at the counter said something about the Jazz, loud enough to float back. Someone else answered with a joke about ref calls. Life's muscle memory kicking in.

I watched faces. A roustabout I didn't know well gave me a short, deliberate nod when he caught my eye, then turned back to his plate. Two women from the ward, still in scrubs, pretended not to see me at all on their way to pay.

"You look like you're back on the catwalk," Clara said quietly. "Cataloging tool marks."

"Probably am."

"See anything useful?"

"I see who's making distance and who isn't," I said. "That's going to matter when we're picking a jury pool. When we knock on doors for the next one."

She wiped her mouth with a napkin. "The next one being GreenSpire?"

I didn't answer that straight. My mind had already gone there, to the green tree logo on email headers, glossy in Colton's seized folder.

The bell chimed again.

Hal Briggs came in with a streak of grease along his forearm and a to-go coffee cup already half-drained. He spotted us, hesitated, then altered course like the decision hurt a little and felt good too.

"Sheriff," he said when he reached the booth. "Deputy."

His shop rag hung from his back pocket. The smell of oil and cold air rode in with him.

"Hal," I said. "You off the clock?"

"Truck alignment." He jerked his chin toward the window, where his battered shop pickup sat at the curb, hood darker than the rest of the body. "Thought I'd refuel."

He turned, making sure his voice carried beyond our table without outright shouting.

"Hey," he said, loud enough that Gene at the counter and both women in scrubs could hear. "Just wanted to say thanks."

"For what?" I asked, though I knew.

"For not letting them call Jared drunk and be done with it." Hal's shoulders loosened a little as he said the name. "He was a careful hand. Folks might argue about a lot of things, but that ain't one of them anymore."

Some heads turned. The women in scrubs froze mid-step. Gene's grip on his mug eased. A worker at the back booth, who'd been pretending not to listen, let his chin lift a notch.

"Appreciate you saying that," I told Hal.

He grinned, quick and crooked. "Figured if the big shots can whisper in corners, the rest of us can say things out loud." His gaze ticked toward the corner booth where the business owners sat, then back. "Anyhow. I got rotors waiting."

He tapped his cup against the table once like a toast and walked out. The bell jingled again. Through the grease haze on the glass I watched him cross to his truck, coffee lifted, steps lighter than when he came in.

Clara's mouth pulled into a half-smile. "That man," she said. "Not subtle."

"Sometimes that's useful."

The diner noise shifted. One of the younger rig hands at the back turned to his friend and said, not quietly, "Jared always double-checked my harness."

"I know," the friend answered. "Saw it."

Those words filed themselves in the same mental drawer as Hal's receipt, Rosa's signature, Colton's email.

We finished eating. When the check came, I slid cash under the plate. As we stood, eyes pressed on my back, some heavy, some weighing, some light.

On the way to the door, a courthouse clerk coming off a break dipped her head and murmured, "Heard about the arrest. Tough call. Glad you made it."

"Worth doing," I said.

Outside, cold air knifed in. The bell gave its tired jangle as I pushed the glass door open. Across the street, traffic rolled by under a low gray sky.

Hal was just climbing into his truck. He caught my gaze through the window and lifted his coffee in a small salute, grease-slick fingers circling the cardboard. I gave him a short return, nothing big, just enough. Behind me the diner door swung shut, leaving the smell of coffee and split opinions at my back as we stepped into the thin winter light of Main.

By the time the din settled behind us and we'd walked halfway down the block, my shoulders had that familiar ache that comes from holding them square too long.

Clara fell in beside me, coffee still in hand. The courthouse sat ahead across the square, brick catching what passed for sun.

"We got a minute?" she asked.

"Before the scanner drags us somewhere?" I checked my watch. "Maybe."

We turned back toward the diner lot and leaned against my truck. The metal was cold through my jacket. Across the street, the ward building steeple poked over the roofs, white against the washed-out sky. Between here and there, the Chronicle office window reflected both steeple and courthouse like they belonged in the same frame.

"Place feels different," Clara said.

"How so?"

"Back when we came in here months ago, this was just breakfast." She jerked her chin toward the diner. "Today it was a town meeting with hash browns."

She tapped her mug in a slow rhythm.

"You thinking about jumping ship?" I asked, half-kidding, half-not.

"And miss all this?" She snorted softly. "No. Just...taking stock. That's the first arrest that hits this many pressure points at once. Company, ward, donors. You know it's not the last."

GreenSpire sat between us without being named at first. Colton's emails. That folder in evidence with the little tree logo and talk of "regional stewardship partnerships." Eve's little circle around the word in her notebook the night before.

"You know this isn't the end of it, right?" Clara said. "Hale and his people aren't going to just shrug and go home because we took down their safety guy."

"I know." The answer came out before I thought about it. Saying it tightened something and eased something else.

She watched my face. "You sure?"

"I'd like to pretend otherwise," I said. "Go back to DUIs and bar fights. Let somebody else worry about land deals and bonus schemes."

"But?"

"But if we treat this like a one-off, that's a lie. The ledger, the emails, the minutes Eve heard about? All the same handwriting."

Memory slid in: Eve at our kitchen table, hand resting over Rosa's, asking what she wanted her kids to be able to say about their dad. Evie Latham's story about Ben passing up a hard case once and how it sat on him until he died.

"Eve's not going to let me pretend it's over," I added.

"Good." Clara took a sip. "I transferred out here for the view, not for early retirement."

I let out a quiet sound that might have been a laugh on a warmer day.

"County attorney's already chewing on GreenSpire's name," I said. "Those mentions in Colton's threads. The folder. But he wants us to stick to what we can charge clean."

"Which is the rig," she said. "For now."

"For now," I agreed. "But those emails aren't going away. Neither are the folks Eve and Marie are talking to. Wives scared about new leases, water deals, bonuses tied to callings."

I pictured Eve and Marie at our table with her spiral notebook, little circles of ink around names and fears. A separate case file nobody at the courthouse had numbered yet.

"You start pulling on GreenSpire," Clara said, "you're not just taking on a safety manager. You're poking at the whole way this county pays its light bill."

"Light bill or not," I said, "if the record shows harm and cover-up, we're not going to pretend it's none of our business."

She lifted an eyebrow, then let her shoulders loosen that same small fraction I'd seen back in the office the night the judge signed our first warrant.

"Good," she said. "I needed to hear you say that out loud."

"I needed to say it," I admitted.

We stood there a while, watching a pickup roll by with a GreenSpire logo on the door, a neat green tree on white sliding along the curb.

"Think they're watching us?" she asked.

"Probably." I dug my thumb into the worn edge of Ben Latham's watch under my cuff. "But we've got a few watching back now."

"Rosa," she said.

"Rosa," I echoed. "Hal. Maybe Trina. Maybe some roustabout two tables over who just heard Hal say Jared's name like it mattered."

She hummed in agreement.

"The office is going to feel smaller," she said. "Every warrant from here on out, every jury pool, this case is going to be in the room with us."

"Then we write like it," I said. "Reports that stand without gossip. Clean chains. Witnesses that know we won't walk off when jobs get threatened."

"Eve and Marie can help with that last part more than we can," Clara added. "People talk to them I'll never get in a room."

"I know." The admission sat heavy and right. "Which means we treat their notes like gold when they bring them in. Not as gossip. As leads."

She nodded once, slow. "Scanner'll call us soon enough," she said, echoing her own joke from earlier breakfasts.

I looked toward my truck. Through the windshield the scanner sat dark on the dash, quiet for the moment. Between it, the courthouse, the ward, the little newspaper office, the lines I'd been pretending were separate started to blur into one map.

"This isn't going to get easier," I said.

"Nope."

"But we're in it."

"We are," she said. "Long haul, Sheriff."

We peeled away from the truck. Clara headed toward her cruiser. I crossed toward the square, coffee cooling in my hand, the little green tree on that passing truck lingering in the corner of my eye like a mark on a map I'd have to come back to.

Chapter 32

Ink on the Chronicle Proof

The bell over the Chronicle's glass door gave the same tired jangle as the diner's, just pitched higher. Inside smelled like old ink and dust and whatever cleaner Lorna used on the scuffed tile.

Stacks of back issues leaned against one wall, headlines I half remembered from other fights. The front room held two desks and an aging couch. From the back came the tap of keys and the low buzz of fluorescent lights that never stopped flickering.

"Back here," Lorna called.

I threaded past the stacks. She sat hunched over a monitor, glasses catching the blue glow, fingers moving in quick bursts. A line of text marched across the screen as I came up beside her. Jared's name in bold, my own a little farther down.

"Hope you brought red ink," she said without looking away.

"I was thinking pencil," I said. "Red makes people nervous."

"Good. Nervous people read closer."

She finished the sentence, hit save, then swung the monitor so I could see better.

"I know the ground rules," she said. "You don't edit my work. I don't write your press releases. But given the county attorney's heart rate on that last call, I thought we'd run this one by you for factual landmines."

"Appreciated," I said. "He used the words 'tainted jury' three times this morning."

"He's not wrong to worry." She pointed with her pen at the top of the screen. "Here's the lede."

Sheriff's Office Alleges Staged Rig Death Amid Safety-Fraud Pattern.

Under it, smaller type: Prosecutors charge company safety manager in Roosevelt derrick case; internal records suggest systemic bonus scheme.

"You're putting the pattern up front," I said.

"Where else would it go? You've spent weeks telling me this isn't just about one bad fall." Her voice went softer, not unkind. "You still okay with that part being public?"

I let my mind run through the lenses I'd been using all morning. Defense attorney turning every line into a motion. Rosa at her kitchen table, Chronicle on the placemat. Some roustabout at the man-camp scrolling the website on his phone.

"If we leave it out," I said, "somebody else fills in the gaps."

"Exactly."

I read on. She walked me through tight paragraphs about latch tool marks, badge logs, "selected internal records," Rosa's civil settlement without naming the amount, the charges filed. No mention of how Jared's body had sat on that steel, no gore.

"Appreciate you keeping the...details out," I said.

"People don't need me to paint that picture," she said. "Their imaginations are bad enough."

She scrolled farther. A new subhead: Ward Leaders Urge Patience, Jobs Cited.

"That's the part the county attorney will sweat," she said. "But it happened. You got leaned on in those halls."

"There's a way to say it without turning it into a ward-bash," I said.

"That's the plan." Her cursor blinked beside a line that read: "Local religious leaders encouraged members to 'trust family companies' and avoid 'public contention' as the investigation unfolded, according to multiple attendees."

"'Multiple attendees,'" I said. "Here being..."

"Eve. A couple of others. I don't have ward minutes; I have people's recollections. I'm not naming titles or quoting one man like he issued an official proclamation. I'm describing a climate."

I pictured Bishop Cade's hand on Jared's head, words about trusting family companies, then Colton's email with almost the same phrase. How those lines had braided through this case like barbed wire through fence posts.

"Can we anonymize that just a hair more?" I asked. "Same idea. Less of a bulls-eye on any one calling."

She thought, then typed: "Some local church leaders encouraged members..."

"Better," I said. "They still know who's who. But you're not hanging a name before it's in a transcript somewhere."

"Speaking of transcripts." She scrolled again. "Here's the email paragraph."

The draft read: Internal emails reviewed by the Chronicle include one in which the charged safety manager refers to "one bad fall" as preferable to a full safety audit he feared would hurt production metrics.

"That's the line giving your attorney hives," she said.

"It is," I said. "He'd rather see 'an email expressing concern about audits' than the words we found on the page."

She tapped the pen against her teeth. "Can he gag you from confirming that phrase is in an exhibit?"

"He can ask me not to hand the defense an argument that the whole jury pool read it and made up its mind."

"Fair." She backspaced over the quotation marks and rewrote: "...one email in which the charged safety manager suggests that enduring a single serious incident would be preferable to a broad safety audit he believed might harm production metrics."

"Same idea," she said. "No exact wording. Anyone who wants the quote can wait for discovery."

"He'll sleep better," I said.

"So will Rosa," she added. "Less chance some lawyer waves my headline under her nose and asks if she remembers exactly how it read."

We went through the section on Rosa next. Lorna read out loud: "The widow, whom the Chronicle is not naming to protect her children's privacy, accepted a narrowed civil settlement and has provided a sworn statement to investigators about her husband's concerns."

"You all right with the 'not naming'?" she asked. "You've said her name in public settings."

"She sat beside Eve at Jared's remembrance," I said. "Half the ward knows who she is. The rest could figure it out in two clicks."

"But a line here can still mark a line," Lorna said. "I'm not obligated to hand her name to every distant cousin and internet crank with a comment login."

"Leave it as is," I said. "She's been asked to carry enough of this case."

Lorna nodded once, fingers pausing above the keys longer than they had for anything else.

She scrolled to a sidebar box on the right.

"What's that?" I asked.

"Context piece," she said. "Shorter. 'Safety Bonuses Halted Before Death.' I'm tying the ledger entries you and Clara pulled to the month Jared died."

The sidebar listed dates, amounts, Colton's initials, and a line about payments stopping weeks before the fall. At the bottom, in smaller type: GreenSpire development was referenced in some internal documents reviewed by the Chronicle, but no charges have been filed related to that project.

"You're putting GreenSpire's name on the page," I said.

"In a footnote," she said. "As something already present in seized records. Not an accusation. A breadcrumb."

"Breadcrumbs draw birds," I said.

"The right ones, I hope."

I ran my thumb along the edge of her desk, feeling the grooves where someone had carved initials years back.

"You planning to quote me?" I asked.

"That depends," she said. "You got something worth quoting?"

"What are you thinking of asking?"

"Same thing my readers will," she said. "Why push this when everyone around you told you not to. That's not a yes/no question."

She opened a new line, cursor blinking. "Can I quote you on why you pushed this past 'accident'?"

I watched the empty space a second. The words that came weren't polished; they weren't meant to be.

"Put it this way," I said. "When the numbers, the tools, and a dead man's notebook all point the same direction, my job isn't to keep the peace. It's to write down what happened and let the chips fall."

She typed it. Didn't clean it up, didn't swap "chips" for something fancier. Just set my name under it.

"That'll do," she said.

We sat quiet a moment. Keyboard tapping from the front desk carried back, the only other sound.

"You know you've made yourself part of the story," she said finally.

"Never had any illusions otherwise," I said. "We both did. Different sides of the net."

She smiled without much humor. "Yeah. Well. I'd rather be on record about why we wrote what we wrote than pretend we're just neutral ink."

Her fingers hovered over the keys again. "You ever get burned?" I asked. "By trusting the wrong source."

"Once," she said. "Statehouse story. I ran a quote from a woman who thought she was off the record. She lost her job. I kept mine. Been trying to even that scale ever since."

"That why you called about Rosa?" I asked.

"That, and I don't like getting ambushed by defense attorneys in motion hearings." She shook her head. "They love to pretend the paper is the one on trial."

"So do bishops," I said, before my filter caught up.

She caught the slip and filed it away with her eyes.

"I'm not out to burn the ward as an institution," she said. "I'm out to tell the things how they intersect with power and money in this place. If that makes some men in suits uncomfortable, they can start with their own minutes."

"Careful," I said. "You'll get invited to sacrament meeting."

"Hard pass," she said. "I've got my own pews to sit in."

She turned back to the draft, made final tweaks, changing "some employers" to "some large employers," softening one adjective about corporate spin. Then she hit save, the tiny click feeling bigger than the sound.

A printer whirred in the back corner, warming up to spit out a proof. We waited while it fed the pages through.

"You know Roman's already tried to lean on you," I said. "Ads, quiet visits?"

"Of course," she said. "Front-page photo ops. Sponsored content dressed up as features. We run the ads; it's how I pay my one part-time reporter. We don't run the fluff as news, and that's where they get sore."

She plucked the warm printout from the tray and smoothed it on her desk. The headline sat there in black: Sheriff's Office Alleges Staged Rig Death. Under it, a photo of the derrick against gray sky I remembered from our first morning out there.

She slid the proof toward me. I laid my hand flat on the page for a second, feeling the raised ridge where the ink sat thicker in the bold letters.

"You're sure you want to use that photo?" I asked. "You've got others."

"It was yours," she said. "Your deputy's, anyway. State lab shot for the record. I pulled it from the public filing. No silhouettes of grieving widows, no kids by a graveside. Steel and air. That's enough."

"Jared's mom might not agree," I said.

"She might not," Lorna said. "And if she calls me, I'll talk to her about it. But I'm not going to pretend the rig doesn't exist because it's hard to look at."

I folded the page carefully, lining the edges up.

"One more thing," she said as I tucked it into my notebook. "GreenSpire. I kept it to a line this time. But if their name keeps popping up in documents, that story's coming."

"I figured as much."

"I'll need you on the record again," she said. "Not as my PR. As the sheriff who can say whether what we see on paper matches what you see on the ground."

"You get the records, we'll talk," I said. "Within what the law lets me say."

"Fair enough."

I stood. The old newsprint smell followed me back through the stacks, the way diesel followed me off the rig.

At the door, with my hand on the bar, she called my name once more.

"Milt."

"Yeah?"

"Whatever else anyone says," she said, "this article is about Jared. Not about you, not about me, not about Colton's bonus. About a man who wrote things down because he thought nobody would believe him otherwise."

"I know," I said. "That's why we're here."

The bell over the door jingled when I stepped out, cooler air washing the ink smell off me. Sunlight glanced off courthouse windows and the ward's steeple down the block. Between them, the square waited, the folded proof a new weight against my ribs.

I crossed the street. Fluorescent glare from the courthouse spilled through the glass even at midday. Somewhere inside, a clerk shuffled papers, a judge checked a calendar, a prosecutor weighed which email to introduce first.

Halfway across the square, a clerk coming down the courthouse steps met my eye.

"Tough one," she said quietly as we passed each other.

"Worth doing," I answered.

She glanced around before she nodded and kept going.

I stopped by my truck, resting my hand on the door frame. Inside, the scanner sat where it always did, silent for now. I slid the proof deeper into my notebook, paper rustling, then tucked both into my jacket.

Across the square, the ward building rose, steeple poking into a pale sky. The Chronicle's glass front reflected it and the courthouse together, like they shared a wall instead of just a street.

For most of my life, I'd drawn lines between those buildings, law over here, faith over there, paper in the middle. Now they'd all been written into the same story: a rig death turned homicide, a mayor counting donor calls, a reporter threading emails into ink, a widow narrowing what she wouldn't sign away.

Cold air slid past my collar. Breath steamed once when I exhaled. My fingers tightened over the folded paper in my pocket, then eased.

I opened the truck door. As I climbed in, the scanner crackled to life with some minor call, loose livestock on a back road, nothing that would make a headline. Just the Basin humming along, same as before, except it wasn't.

I started the engine. The radio's low murmur filled the cab, mixing with scanner static and the distant echo of printing presses already turning my words, and Lorna's, into something the town couldn't unsee.

Chapter 33

Charges and Call Logs

The bailiff's keys chimed ahead of us as we went down the courthouse hall. Tile smelled like wax and burned coffee. I held the heavy door while he walked Colton past me, orange jumpsuit, wrists belted to his waist, ankles chained close enough that the metal kissed every few steps.

He kept his chin up, same as in that glass office. Only difference was cotton instead of pressed denim.

The courtroom wasn't full, but it wasn't empty. Rig hands and ranch jackets on one side, a couple of suits and a company lawyer on the other. Tessa Kline sat near the back with a legal pad in her lap. A woman from the Chronicle slid into a back bench, pen ready; not Lorna, one of her stringers.

I sat behind the prosecutor's table with a stack of manila. Colton went to the defense side, his lawyer smoothing his sleeve before they sat. The cuffs clinked when he settled.

The clerk called the case. Hearing Jared's name read into the record still landed like the first time I saw him hanging in the work lights.

"State of Utah versus Colton Reese," the clerk finished.

The judge adjusted his glasses. "Mr. Reese, you are here on an information charging negligent homicide, a second-degree felony, and evidence tampering, a third-degree felony, arising out of an incident at the Roosevelt Rig Site. Have you had a chance to speak with counsel?"

His attorney stood. "We waive formal reading of the information, Your Honor, and enter pleas of not guilty on both counts."

The judge looked at Colton. "Do you understand the charges against you?"

Colton turned his head just enough that the room could hear him. "I understand I followed company policy."

Not "yes." Not "I understand the charges." I wrote the words exact in my notebook. That line would show up later, when somebody tried to move the blame from him to some faceless "system."

The prosecutor walked through probable cause in broad strokes: latch marks, the ledger bonuses, the camera gap, the badge logs, Rosa's statement. No one argued much over facts. This wasn't the trial; this was putting the official stamp on what we'd already done in conference rooms and on catwalks.

Colton kept his eyes on the judge. The only sign of strain was a flutter at the edge of his mouth when the prosecutor said "deliberate weakening."

Defense kept it standard. "Longtime employee," "no criminal history," "deep ties to the community." He pointed once, very gently, at the benches where company folks sat. "He is no flight risk. The incident reports themselves, which we will address in due course, show bad luck and a tragic fall, not a crime. We intend to challenge the state's interpretation of the physical evidence, including the so-called tool-mark analysis."

So-called.

I thought about the first day on that rig, that latch rough under my fingers, the worn teeth more chewed than used. Back then all I had was a line in my notebook: mark pattern odd. Today I had state-lab case numbers and an envelope waiting on my desk.

The judge went through bail conditions. No contact with witnesses, no travel out of state without permission, surrender of passport. Release to pretrial services, supervised, if he could meet the bond. Company counsel and the defense attorney traded looks like they'd already gamed it out.

When the judge finished, he asked, "Anything further at this time?"

Defense took a breath. "Your Honor, we'd ask that my client be allowed to continue in administrative duties that are non-field related."

The prosecutor shook his head. "We'd object. The charges stem directly from his exercise of authority in safety matters."

The judge didn't take long. "Given the allegations, Mr. Reese is not to engage in any employment or consulting that involves supervision of safety equipment or personnel. Conditions of release will reflect that."

That was the first real hit I saw land on Colton. His shoulders shifted, slight, like he'd braced for a punch and misjudged where it would land.

Gavel, shuffle of papers, talk of the next hearing date. People rose. The bailiff came around again, clipped the chain to the belt. On the back row, Tessa's fingers dug into the leather cover of her planner. A guy in a Halliburton cap tapped a boot faster when "negligent homicide" was said on the record and then made a point of not looking at me as he left.

Out in the aisle, Colton's path took him close enough I could smell the cheap detergent in county laundry.

He didn't turn his head, but his eyes slid my way for half a beat. Not rage, not fear. Calculation. He had already moved from this morning's hearing to some future jury, some appeal judge, some corporate conference call where his name turned into "unforeseen event" on a slide.

His lawyer leaned in, lips near his ear, probably telling him not to say one more word. The deputy steered them toward the side door.

I stayed seated until the benches cleared a little. Habit from years of small-town courts; no sense in forcing people to choose whether to say hello.

When I finally stood, the bailiff handed me back the packet we'd filed. The paper rasp felt heavier than it ought to. One more set of forms to walk upstairs, one more number on the docket.

The hallway outside carried its own murmur: boots on tile, a clerk's laugh, someone on a cellphone talking about hay. Roman Hale wasn't there. Men like him let lawyers and managers be seen in handcuffs; their work stayed in offices with leather chairs.

Clara came off the bench near the drinking fountain, file folder tucked under one arm. "Judge left your language mostly intact," she said. "Pretrial said they'll want a fresh copy of our evidence list this week."

"Good." My voice came out rougher than I meant. "Lab called?"

She held up a pink slip. "While we were in there. State lab. Says urgent, tool-marks. I grabbed the message before the clerk lost it in the stack."

I took it from her. Thin carbon paper, the kind that tore if you bent it wrong. The tech's name was scrawled across the top with a case number and the words: "latch tool-marks / wrench comparison, urgent callback."

The words slid me back to cold steel and wind and the first smear of metal under floodlights. Months of interviews and emails and ledgers had dressed the case up in sentences. This was bare metal again.

"Let's get back," I said.

As we stepped aside to let a family by, three kids in Sunday shoes and a woman with a casserole carrier, two men from the rigs ducked their heads and went past us like we were furniture. A clerk I knew from records met my eye and then glanced down fast. "Tough one," she said under her breath as we passed on the stairs.

"Worth doing," I answered.

In the lobby I held the door for Clara. Cold air off the square tasted like exhaust and paper dust. Across the street, the stake center steeple poked up past the courthouse roofline, like it wanted to see who came out which set of doors.

I slipped the pink slip into my notebook and headed for the truck.

Back at the sheriff's office the fluorescent lights hummed a little too bright. The scanner rattled about a traffic stop out near the truck stop and then went quiet. My desk looked like somebody had parked the whole case on top of it: files from the rig, Rosa's affidavits, copies of the ledger, the bag-and-tag log.

I flattened the pink slip beside the phone and punched in the state lab number from memory. Clara perched in the doorway with a mug, shoulder against the frame. Her coffee sent up a burnt smell that matched the pot on the warmer.

Three rings. Then, "Forensic services, this is Dray."

"Sheriff Kingston, Basin County. Returning a call on tool-mark case", I read the number, "Roosevelt latch."

"Right. Give me just a sec to pull that up." Keyboard rattled faintly. Pages shifted. In the little pause, my fingers tapped once on the blotter. Years in this job, and every time you wait on a lab result feels the same: a long hallway with doors that might open to something or to nothing.

"Okay," he said. "We finished the comparison work on your latch segment and the adjustable wrench set you sent in from that locker."

I pulled my notebook closer and uncapped my pen. "Go ahead."

"Under reflected light and comparison microscope, the pry marks on the latch tongue and keeper show striation patterns consistent with the tool jaws on one wrench in that set. We're talking machining flaws, tiny chatter marks from manufacture, and subsequent nicks that line up. We assigned it high-confidence individualization."

"Tag number?" I asked.

He read it off, slow. Same digits I'd circled weeks back copying the evidence log off the locker bag: 27-59-B.

Clara mouthed it along with him from the doorway and let out a breath when he finished, shoulders easing; I hadn't realized until that second she'd been carrying that number around too.

I wrote it in the margin: 27-59-B, match.

"Sheriff," the tech went on, "we also tested exemplar marks with that wrench on similar steel. Those striations align with the damaged areas on your original latch to a degree we don't see by chance. Think barcode. This wasn't just any adjustable off the shelf. It's that wrench."

Outside the office, a deputy laughed at something down the hall. The sound came through muffled. In here, his last sentence hung in the air a second.

"Could another wrench of the same make and model, brand new out of the box, produce the same pattern?" I asked.

He paused. Paper slid. "We pulled a control from our own tool rack. Manufacturing chatter differences were obvious. The defect we're keying off on yours looks like damage from use. Combine that with the dimensional match on the jaw spacing and angle, and we're in that 'reasonable certainty' range the court likes."

"So your opinion," I said, "is that the pry marks on the latch were made with that specific wrench, not just a type."

"Yes, Sheriff. Within the limits of tool-mark analysis, that's my opinion. I'll have a formal report emailed and a hard copy in the mail today."

My hand tightened around the pen, ink blotting a dark spot by the case number. Months of guessing, arguing, and ledger reading snapped into a straight line: locker to bag-and-tag to lab bench to my desk.

"One more thing," I said. "Timeline. You got our submission on..." I flipped back through pages until I hit the intake note. "...the third. Today's the nineteenth."

"We ran it as quick as we could," he said. "You must have some friends in the capital leaning on our supervisor."

"Nothing but my sunny disposition." I managed a dry sound close to a laugh. "We'll look for the report. Thanks again."

I hung up. For a second the dial tone seemed louder than the scanner, then that dropped away and the room filled back up with the soft sounds I knew: printer fan, hallway phone, the rattle of the air vent.

"Barcode," Clara said. "I like that."

"So-called tool-mark analysis," I said, thinking of defense counsel. "Add 'high-confidence match' to the list."

She stepped into the room and tapped the edge of the message slip. "You going to write that down in courtroom words or in notebook words?"

"Both." I pulled a fresh legal pad toward me. On the top line I put: Latch → wrench 27-59-B (locker, Colton). Under that: "Those striations line up like a bar code. It's that wrench." Dray's sentence, exact. When the time came, I wanted to say where I'd heard it, and how.

I ran my thumb along the page, back through the chain in my head. Locker search on a gray morning; me kneeling in front of Colton's metal box while he stood in the doorway trying to seem casual. Clara holding the evidence bags open. Tagging each piece: date, time, initials. Driving them to the state substation so the chain wouldn't get cute in court.

Defense would still try to pull at it. They'd say another wrench could have been swapped. They'd suggest some deputy miswrote a number. That was their job.

Our job was to make those arguments sound as thin as they were.

"Any holes?" Clara asked.

"Not in the steel," I said. "They'll go after chain-of-custody. So we make sure the log is clean." I flipped to the inventory sheet, checked each handwriting line: my initials, Clara's, the state trooper's when we turned the box over, the lab intake stamp. No gaps. No mystery time where the bag took a walk.

From the evidence-room window, the shelves showed in a slice: cardboard boxes, labeled, stacked neat. The box from Colton's locker sat on the second shelf, taped, "RIG, TOOLS / EMAILS / LATCH" in my block letters across the side. Beside it, wired through the plastic, the outline of a wrench in a clear bag. Just beyond, partly behind a stack of printed emails, gloved fingers crumpled in another bag, soiled gloves we'd grabbed in the sweep and never fully looked at.

"Still thinking?" Clara asked.

"Thinking ahead. Trial. Appeal." I capped the pen and slid the message slip under the clip in my notebook. The margin around Jared's name had more ink than white now: arrows and lines and words like "bonus," "ladder weld," "camera 3," "better one bad fall."

Along one edge, in my wife's hand from a night at the kitchen table: Tell the truth even if it costs.

When we'd first opened a homicide file instead of closing an accident, I'd written "suspicious fall" with a question mark. At the bottom of the page I put question marks again, three of them. Today, under the lab quote, I drew a square and printed in it: FORENSIC LINK CONFIRMED.

"Go home yet?" Clara asked, half-teasing.

"After I update the evidence log." I pushed my chair back. "And return a call to the county attorney. He needs to know he can say 'state lab match' out loud now instead of 'pending.'"

She raised her mug. "I'll get you fresh coffee for that."

"Mercy," I said. "Just water."

She drifted away, footsteps soft on worn carpet tiles. I opened the evidence-room door and cooler air wrapped around me. The smell changed in here: gun oil, cardboard, plastic.

I signed the lab notation into the log, case number and date, then stood a second looking at the shelves. The wrench sat there quiet in its bag, metal dulled under fluorescent light. A man had used it once to shave steel off a latch so a fall would happen just right. Today, that same pattern of scars meant his world had gotten smaller.

At the back of the shelf, the GreenSpire folder's green edge stuck out from under other files. That trail would wait. For the moment, the rig case had gone as far as it could in our hands.

I closed the log and turned out the light.

Chapter 34

Remembrance in the Cultural Hall

The cultural hall door stuck halfway, as it always did when the weather turned. I leaned my shoulder into it and stepped into bright gym light and the squeak of my boots on the waxed floor.

Rows of folded metal chairs leaned against the cinderblock wall. A long table near the stage already wore a white cloth that didn't quite reach the ends. Eve stood there smoothing one corner, hair pulled back, a roll of tape between her fingers. The smell of chicken casserole and brownies slipped in from the kitchen.

Rosa's kids chased a loose balloon between chairs, their laughter a half octave too high for the room. Rosa stood by the table with the cloth, moving a framed photo of Jared an inch this way and that. Hardhat, safety glasses, shy half-smile in the picture. Someone had printed his name in blue marker on a card in front.

I crossed to them, chair legs scraping as I pulled the first stack away from the wall.

"Where do you want these?" I asked Eve.

She eyed the length of the room. "Three rows here, three there. Leave an aisle down the middle. We're not filling the stake center, just the cultural hall."

Her voice sounded steady. Her shoulders were not.

I set chairs in the pattern she sketched, metal knocking as they unfolded. Each one hitting the floor made a small, hollow sound, like a muted gavel.

Rosa stepped back from the table, hands worrying the edge of the cloth. "They wrote 'accident' on the first paper they gave me," she said, not looking at me.

"We changed that," I said. "The new papers don't."

She lifted her eyes. Whatever she found in my face eased something there. Her hand left the cloth alone for a second. "I know. I just needed to say it out loud."

"That's fair."

Eve nudged the picture frame, aligning it with the vase someone had brought. "We put 'In Remembrance of Jared Pike' on the program," she said quietly to Rosa. "No cause language."

"That's fine," Rosa said. "Cause is in my head already."

A folding table to the side held stacks of foam plates and crockpots. Evie Latham sat near the stage on a metal chair, cane leaned against the leg, a plate of brownies in her lap like a shield she'd forgotten to lower. Her eyes tracked me over the rows.

I grabbed another table and dragged it into position. The metal legs shrieked against the floor.

"Sorry," I said to the room.

Evie's mouth quirked. "Don't worry about the floor, Sheriff. It's survived worse than a remembrance."

I walked it into place with more care.

As I straightened, a memory came uninvited: Ben Latham and me setting up chairs in this same room for a youth fireside, him telling me stories about fights in bars and funerals in these walls, his hand resting on the back of a metal chair just like this. "These rooms remember more than the walls let on," he'd said. Back then I heard it as folksy talk.

Evie watched me now with the same eyes that had watched him.

"Need any more tables?" I asked her.

She tapped her fingers once on her cane. "I think we've got enough places to sit. Question is what people will hear while they're in them."

My glance slid to the small portable podium someone had dragged in from a classroom. It sat a little off center at the front, cord from the microphone curling across the stage like a lazy snake.

"I'm just here to move chairs," I said.

"If you don't say it plain," Evie answered, her voice mild, "they'll just tuck it away, same as always."

The words settled heavier than the tables. From anyone else, I could have brushed them off. From the woman who'd watched my mentor wrestle his conscience in the same town, they sounded like another kind of warrant.

Across the gym, people drifted in: ward members with funeral potatoes in foil pans, a few roughnecks in clean shirts who didn't quite know where to put their hands. Some hovered by the kitchen pass-through instead of sitting. Two men I recognized from the rig came in together, paused when they saw me, then peeled off toward different sections of chairs without speaking.

I kept setting up rows. Counting seats settled my mind. Twenty-four, forty-eight, seventy-two. Enough for everyone who'd likely come. Not enough to feel like a spectacle.

As I worked, I cataloged faces. Who came early: the Pikes' home teachers, two Relief Society sisters who had sat with Rosa that first week, Hal Briggs in a shirt that still carried faint shop stains. Who stayed at the doorway: a counselor in the bishopric, a foreman my cousin Joel had once praised from the pulpit. Who didn't show at all.

Eve met my eye once as she carried napkins to the food table. The same question sat there I'd heard in the kitchen months ago, when this all started: What really matters?

I looked away to the podium. My hand drifted out, half-formed, toward the wooden edge as I passed to straighten one last row, then I pulled it back and grabbed another chair instead.

When the work was done, the room looked less like a gym and more like a little courtroom: straight lines of metal and vinyl facing a focal point. A photo on a table instead of a judge on a bench. But the feeling was the same, a place where people would decide what words to use for what had happened.

At the back of the hall, I paused, eyes tracing the row down to the podium. Evie caught my glance and lifted her chin once. Not a push. A knowing.

I saw then that whatever plan I'd had to sit by a back wall and let other people talk had already failed. I didn't know yet what words would come, but I knew that when there was an open mic and Jared's picture staring out over it, my silence would say as much as anything.

I took a breath that tasted like gym varnish and casserole and walked up the aisle to find a seat beside Eve.

"You're going to be fine," she murmured, fingers brushing the back of my hand.

"I haven't said I'm talking."

She looked at the program, not at me. "You don't have to." Then, quieter: "You'll be fine."

The hymn number went up on the board at the front. People rustled into their places. The gym's fluorescent hum grew louder as the chatter dropped.

By the time the sister leading the service stood at the microphone, page shaking in her hand, the chairs were mostly full.

The last note of "Where Can I Turn for Peace?" faded off the cinderblock and into the rafters. Folding chairs groaned as people shifted.

The sister at the front cleared her throat. "We've asked a few folks to share memories of Jared," she said. "And then we'll open the time if anyone else feels impressed. We'll start with Brother Hal Briggs."

Hal walked up, shoulders hunched like he'd rather be under a hood than under a light. He told a story about Jared staying late to help with a stuck bolt on a ladder, then another about him bringing doughnuts to the shop on payday. Simple, kind things. No one breathed much when his voice caught around the kids' names. He swallowed it back and stepped down.

A sister from Rosa's Relief Society talked about casseroles and moving days and Jared showing up in work boots to help push a couch. A counselor in the elders quorum used words like "good provider" and "quiet faith."

Nobody used the word "killed."

Eve's hand had found mine on the seat between us. The second time she squeezed, there was nothing gentle about it.

The sister at the front looked down at her list, then up. "At this time, if anyone else would like to share, the microphone is open." Her gaze passed across the room, brushed me for half a second. "Sheriff Kingston, would you like to share a few words?"

The room turned as one body. Rustle of fabric, a cough near the back, the faint click as someone shut off the projector on the cart.

I could have pretended not to hear. But Eve's fingers tightened, and Rosa, three rows up, had both hands on her son's shoulders like she was bracing him for something.

I stood before I'd fully decided what to say.

The stage came up fast. The microphone cord lay across the floor, then up the short steps, then into my hand. Feedback squealed when I tapped it, then settled.

From up there, the room looked different. The chairs reached back farther than they had from the floor. Faces I knew from Sunday School, from the rig, from the diner, watched me with a mix of expectation and wariness.

Safe was right there. I could have talked about community pulling together and the Lord healing hearts and the importance of family. The kind of thing you could hear at any funeral and forget by the time the cookies were gone.

My mouth opened on something like that. Then my eyes hit the photo on the table. Hardhat, safety glasses, shy smile, name in blue marker. Behind that, Rosa, fingers dug into her boy's shoulders, knuckles pale.

Words I'd heard in conference rooms came up instead, like they'd been waiting their turn.

"Most of you know me from Sundays or from the square," I said. "For the past few months, I've mostly been seeing your husbands and brothers and cousins in other settings. The rig. The office. The courthouse."

A couple of people shifted in their seats. Bishop Cade, sitting toward the side with the other ward leaders, kept his expression careful, eyes on his lap.

"We've used a lot of language around what happened to Jared," I went on. "Accident. Tragedy. An awful thing. All of that is true in parts. It was awful. It was tragic. But it wasn't random."

My hand closed briefly around the edge of the podium. I let go so it wouldn't look like I was clinging to it.

"Jared did everything right," I said. "He wore his harness. He logged what he saw. He trusted the people paid to keep him safe. Someone decided that was a problem and chose to change steel so it would fail when it needed to hold."

The word "chose" dropped into the room like a wrench into a toolbox. Chairs creaked. In the third row a child whispered; his mother hushed him sharp.

"We've filed charges in court," I said. "I won't argue that case here. That's not what this is for. But I can say this without crossing that line: Jared didn't die because God flicked a finger or because some blind fate picked his name out of a hat. He died because of human choices that put numbers on a safety report ahead of a man's life."

A murmur started near the back, then swallowed itself when people remembered where they were.

"I know there are folks in this room who worry about jobs," I said. "So do I. Eve and I have family who depend on oil checks. I know there are folks who worry that saying what happened out loud will hurt faith. I've sat where you're sitting and wondered that myself."

I thought of Eve's note on my notebook, of Evie's words about tucking things away.

"What I've learned the hard way this year," I said, "is that pretending something was an 'unfortunate accident' when we know it was more than that doesn't keep peace. It just moves the hurt onto the people who can least afford to carry it. Widows. Kids. Workers who decide, next time, not to speak up because they saw what happened when Jared did."

At the edge of my vision I caught Eve's thumbs rubbing together in her lap, the way they did in tense ward councils. Rosa's grip on her son eased by a fraction.

"I'm not here as your bishop," I said, and that pulled a thin line at the corner of Bishop Cade's mouth. "I'm here as your sheriff, and as your neighbor. My job isn't to keep everything quiet. It's to write down what happened and bring it into the light where it can be answered for."

I took a breath. "If we can't tell the truth about how Jared died in this room, where we talk about God and His laws every week, then we've got bigger problems than one case."

Silence now. No rustle, no cough. Just the faint buzz of the lights and the soft whir of the drinking fountain in the hall.

"I loved seeing Jared at the river pullout with his kids," I said, surprised at myself for using the word "loved" that way. "He'd nod, say he was fine when it was clear he was worn clear through. He was trying to do right in a hard job. He deserved better from the people above him."

My gaze landed on Hal. His jaw had gone tight. Past him, a couple who'd been loud about "not judging" online sat stiff, their eyes fixed on some point above my head. On the side bench, Bishop Cade's foot, which had been bouncing a gentle rhythm, went still.

"If there's anything I hope we take from tonight," I finished, "it's that telling the truth about what happened to Jared doesn't dishonor him. It honors the care he took with his own safety and with his work. And it tells his kids, and everyone else's, that we value their lives more than we value quiet."

I let the words sit a second. Then I added, softer, "That's all."

I stepped back from the podium. For a moment, no one moved. Then the sister at the front said, "Thank you, Sheriff Kingston," into the mic, voice thinner than before, and invited anyone else to come up if they felt to.

No one rose. The gap stretched until she glanced at the clock and suggested we close with prayer and then eat.

I walked back down the aisle. My legs felt heavier than they had when I'd carried tables.

Sliding into the chair beside Eve, I became aware of the wooden edge of the stage I'd bumped with my knee going up. An odd thing to fix on, but the mind grabs what it can in moments like that.

Eve squeezed my hand under the program. "You did what you needed to," she whispered.

Across the room, Rosa met my eyes and gave me a tired, small smile. Not joy. Not relief. Something like release.

Near the back, a couple in work shirts and Sunday slacks stood up before the closing prayer and walked quietly out, their footsteps loud against the gym floor. As the amen sounded, more people rose, some moving toward the food, others toward the exits.

Conversations restarted, but softer. Pockets of people leaned close, talking in low tones. A few ward members came up to grip my arm and say things like, "Hard but needed," or, "You're brave saying that here." Others walked past, eyes sliding off mine as if I were a picture on the wall.

Bishop Cade approached eventually, hands folded in front of him. "Thank you for coming, Brother Kingston," he said. "We appreciate your service."

His face stayed careful. Too careful.

I nodded. "Appreciate yours, Bishop."

There was a thin pause where another conversation could have started. It didn't. He inclined his head and moved on to Rosa, offering a blessing for "continued comfort" that never touched the word we'd just argued over.

At the food table, kids lined up for brownies. Hal handed plates down the line, telling a joke about the church owning stock in funeral potatoes. People laughed, a little too loudly.

I drifted to the back wall, plate in hand, more for camouflage than hunger. From there I could see the whole room: podium, photo, scattered knots of people.

Evie Latham ambled over, cane tapping. "Ben would've been proud of that," she said quietly, nodding at the microphone.

"Ben liked his quiet," I said.

"He did. Regretted some of it, too." She looked up at me. "You just saved yourself a few years of that kind of regret."

I let the words in, let them hurt, let them settle.

Across the hall, Abby sat with a cluster of youth, listening, her face set in that intent way she had when deciding whether adults were shining her on or not. I wondered how my words had sounded in her ears.

The gym lights hummed on. Outside the high windows, the sky over the square had gone from pale to full dark. Somewhere out there the scanner in my truck would be murmuring about stray dogs and fender-benders.

In here, the noise was a different kind of call log, stories, whispers, new lines drawn in a ward that had just heard, from its own microphone, that "accident" wasn't big enough to cover what we'd done.

I finished what was on my plate, tossed it, and went to find Eve, ready to go home and see what pieces of this night would follow us there.

Chapter 35

Witness Names in Eve's Notebook

I dropped my keys in the ceramic dish by the back door and listened to them settle. The dishwasher in the kitchen churned steady, covering the low hiss of the scanner in the living room. Coffee floated warm on the air.

Eve and Marie sat at the table under the yellow light. Eve's spiral notebook lay open between them, flipped sideways so the spine ran like a river between their mugs. Names curved across the page in her careful hand.

I scraped my boots on the mat and hung my jacket before they could tell me to. Habit. Also a way to take three extra breaths.

"Hey," Eve said. "You still up for coffee?"

I pulled a chair at the end of the table. "If it's legal."

Marie gave a faint smile. "It's decaf. I checked."

"You a cop now?" I asked.

"School counselor," she said. "We're bossier."

The washer door clicked in the next room; a plate shifted and clinked. Outside, the river pushed against its banks, just noise through glass this time of year.

Eve had sectioned the notebook with pencil lines. One column said "Rig." Another, "Pump/Water." A third, "Meetings / Land." Under each she'd written first names, sometimes just a house number or "Loretta, nursery, sister of Hank?" in the margin.

Marie tapped the page. "We were just going over who actually said what. No stories we don't both remember hearing."

She looked tired but clear. The remembrance had eaten something out of all of us. Her cardigan sleeves were pushed to her elbows. The skin along her forearms showed little half-moons where kids had grabbed her this week, holding on through bad dreams.

"What are we doing with this?" I asked.

"Right now?" Eve said. "Just not losing it."

Her pen rested across the spine. The tip was stained blue; the margin was a nest of arrows and tiny circles.

"The women who brought food after the arraignment," Marie said. "They talk while they're in the kitchen. You know that."

"Some of them talk in your office," I said.

She gave a small nod. "Different tone. In the hall it's 'jobs' and 'blessings.' In my chair it's 'he won't sleep' and 'they told him not to write it down.'"

She hooked a finger at one name. "Jolene, husband was at Jared's pad six months before, near-miss on a fall. Same kind of harness."

Jolene came back to me from the line of crockpots. Long braid, eyes on the floor. Her husband's name sat in my own notebook under "near-fall, resolved?"

"Has she filed anything?" I asked.

"Not where it would stick," Eve said. "She told me over potato salad that her husband got a lecture about 'not talking like that in front of the bishop.'"

"So this is gossip," I said, but not harsh.

"This is pre-report," Marie answered. "The part that never makes it to you."

She laid both hands flat on the table. The dishwasher droned. The furnace snapped on and pushed warm air up through the floor grate under my feet.

Eve turned a page back. On the inside cover, she'd scribbled a word weeks earlier and left it: "GreenSpire?" jagged at the edge.

Tonight she circled it, slow, like she was finally willing to look straight at it.

"You remember when Joel first started using that name in talks?" she asked me. "All the 'stewardship' and 'future cabins for youth' stuff?"

"I remember the brochures," I said.

"More women talked to me about their husbands being nervous over those new land meetings than about the rig," she said. "They just didn't have a word for who they were scared of."

"Land meetings like ward things?" I asked.

"Some at the church, some out by the project office," Marie said. "Couples-only evenings. Joel, Brent, sometimes Roman. Lots of maps. Lots of promises."

She slid a folded flyer from her bag and smoothed it out. Green trees in glossy ink, river shining like chrome. GreenSpire at the top in a font that pretended it cared.

"You see the list of 'advisory volunteers' at the bottom?" she asked.

I scanned past the slogans. In small type were names I knew from calls and reports and donation ledgers. A couple I'd interviewed over a cattle theft. A man who'd once begged me not to write up a DUI because "the bishop's depending on me."

"Half those people have husbands who've already come to me about panic attacks," Marie said. "They're scared of losing land, or water, or both. But when it comes time to say it in front of a recorder, they clam up."

"Because if they're wrong, I ruin people," I said. "If they're right, I still ruin people."

Eve's pen tapped the notebook margin. "Nobody's asking you to kick doors on GreenSpire," she said. "Not yet. This is just... keeping track of who's hurting, and why."

Her hand moved as she talked. The same hand that had pressed a dish towel into my palm when I came home from the rig the first night. The same hand I'd promised, more than once, I'd keep out of the way of the worst of it.

My thumb slid under the table to the watch band on my wrist. Ben's old watch, cool at the edge where metal had worn thin.

"You start putting names in a lawman's book," I said, "it's evidence. Or it wants to be. Which means somebody can ask for it."

"That's why they're here and not in your book," Marie said. "At least not yet."

Eve glanced up. "Marie and I can hold things that you can't. Confidences, questions. They're not affidavits until people want them to be."

"And when GreenSpire hears you've got a list?" I asked. "When the company or the stake decides you're building some kind of file?"

Marie's fingers tightened around her mug handle, then eased. "Then I'll do what I do now. Say I'm making sure people know their rights. That's my job. The rest is yours."

The dishwasher hummed on. I could make out the scanner under it now, little rise and fall of traffic: a stop, a welfare check on the south end, somebody's smoke alarm chirping.

"Look," Eve said, turning the notebook back to tonight's page. "Some of this already lines up with things you've seen."

She pointed: Rosa, rig safety, NDA pressure. Under that, "Jolene, harness near-fall, bishop blessing." Then: "Shawna, pump, 'water tasting funny,' meeting with Brent." Another name, underlined twice: "Anna, GreenSpire meeting, land gift rumor, doesn't want kids there."

I recognized three out of five. Their husbands' names sat in my own case files under "statement taken" or "declined to comment."

"You're building a parallel board," I said.

"Not parallel," Eve said. "Upstream."

She gave me a look that asked the question again. I had thought that question was about Jared. It landed now in a different place.

Marie blew across her coffee. "If we're going to write names," she said quietly, "we have to promise them more than casseroles when the blowback comes."

"That's why we're writing them here first," Eve answered, just as soft. "Not on county letterhead. Not in any ward minutes."

I let that sit. The paper under her hand made a faint rasp when she shifted.

This was not the sheriff's incident room downtown. It was my own table. My own wife. A counselor I'd called once to talk a ranch kid out of the back of a squad car. And between them, the beginnings of something that looked an awful lot like a witness list.

"You two planning to hide this from me?" I asked.

Eve met my eyes. "No. But we're not handing you something you can subpoena from us later and feel holy about."

"If they ever want to talk official," Marie said, "we'll bring them to you. With their say-so. Until then, this is about making sure nobody hangs out there alone."

Her words brushed against a memory: the first time I'd walked into Rosa's front room, the stamped envelope on the table with the company logo, her kids' shoes piled by the door. She'd been alone then, except for Eve and the casserole rota and whatever she could get from me across a badge and a recorder.

"Who else knows you're doing this?" I asked.

"Evie," Eve said. "She told me once that if Ben had had women's lists, he might have seen some things sooner. I figured I'd listen."

Of course she had talked to Evie. The old woman who'd watched two sheriffs carry different versions of the Basin on their shoulders.

I traced a finger along the edge of the table where varnish had worn down to dull wood. "You realize Roman and Joel and whoever else is running GreenSpire are used to being the ones who keep lists."

"That's why this one scares them if they ever hear about it," Marie said. "They can't control whose kitchen we're in."

The river outside sounded louder for a moment, like wind had shifted. Or maybe that was just me.

Under my hand, the table felt the way the rig rail had felt the first night, solid, scarred, bearing weight it hadn't asked for.

"All right," I said. "You keep your notebook. I'll keep mine. When something crosses the line from 'hurt' to 'crime,' we talk."

Eve drew a box around "GreenSpire" where she'd circled it. Not dark, just enough to mark it. Then she flipped the notebook shut and laid her palm on the cover, as if it might slide away on its own.

Marie dug in her bag and tucked a trio of folded pamphlets beside the mug tree: counseling referrals, legal aid contact cards. She slid a couple into her own purse as well.

"If anyone from that list needs to talk where it's privileged," she said, "you send them my way or Eve's. If they're ready for your office, you'll know."

She stood. Her chair legs rasped against the tile. For a second the kitchen felt cramped, full of unseen women and their half-told stories crowding the corners.

At the door she paused. "Sheriff? One thing."

"Yeah?"

"When the next one hits," she said, "don't act surprised."

I wanted to say I wouldn't. I'd been on the square long enough to feel patterns coming before they hit. But my throat stayed tight. I gave her a short salute with my coffee mug instead.

After the door closed behind her, the house adjusted. The furnace clicked off. The dishwasher changed cycles and then whirred to silence.

Eve slid the notebook into the top drawer by the stove and shut it gently.

"You okay?" she asked.

"No," I said. "But I'm glad you are who you are."

She came back to the table and stacked the cups, her shoulders sagging for a heartbeat before she eased them straight again.

"You knew Jared wasn't a one-off," she said. "This just gives that feeling a shape."

The shape, from where I sat, looked a lot like a growing shelf down at the office. One spine labeled "Rig Death." Another, empty, waiting for Diamond pasture grass and pump schematics and whatever came after that. A third, sometime down the line, heavy with black dust and Bonanza paper.

Eve dried her hands on a dish towel and glanced at the drawer. "We'll keep writing," she said. "You keep writing. And we'll see where they cross."

The scanner in the other room hissed out a call I didn't need to answer tonight. I listened anyway.

I rinsed the last coffee cup and set it in the sink. Without Marie's voice or the dishwasher's churn, the kitchen felt too big, too empty. The house made itself known: a creak in the wall, the muted mutter of the scanner in the living room, the faint vibration when the furnace fan kicked once and then settled.

Eve sat where she'd been, elbows on the table, fingers laced without touching anything. She stared at the wood grain like she was reading a map hidden there.

I dried my hands and hung the towel, then pulled my chair around so I was beside her instead of at the end.

"That drawer have a lock?" I asked.

"Just my hand," she said.

I set my palm on the edge where the notebook now lay unseen. The wood was warm from where it had been.

"You worried I'm going to grab it and run?" I said.

She let out a breath through her nose. "I'm worried about what happens to the people in it if you treat them like a list before they're ready."

"I know," I said. "I hear you."

Silence settled between us, not angry, just heavy. From the living room, the scanner gave a short burst: unit clear, no report.

"I'm tired," I said.

"I know that too."

She rubbed her temples with both hands, then dropped them and looked at me. The skin under her eyes was darker than it had been in months. The remembrance, the arrest, the sideways looks at church, they'd carved lines on her face that hadn't been there when the snow first melted off the rig.

"If we're going to keep doing this," she said finally, "I need you to remember this is our work, not just your job."

The word slid between us and stayed there. Our.

I thought about all the times I'd come home and tried to leave things at the threshold. Keys in the dish, boots on the mat, cases in the truck. Pretended the scanner was just background noise, not a metronome for our days.

"That's not what you signed up for," I said.

"It's exactly what I signed up for," she answered. "You just didn't read the rest of the contract."

A small, unwilling smile tugged at my mouth. "Fine print, huh?"

She didn't smile back. "I don't want to hate this town, Milt. Help me not hate it by not lying about it."

That landed harder than any speech in the cultural hall.

Abby came to mind, stiff in her folding chair, listening when I'd called Jared's death what it was. Caleb pretending to be focused on his phone while really counting every time someone looked away from us in the foyer. Eve carrying casseroles into houses where people muttered about "troublemakers" between hymns.

"I can't promise easy," I said. "But I can promise honest."

She slid her hand across the table. I met it halfway. Our fingers interlaced, then settled, palms warm, skin a little dry from soap and winter air.

"Honest," she repeated. "Even when it's ugly."

"Especially then," I said. "Otherwise it just rots."

We sat like that while the house around us quieted one piece at a time. The dishwasher clicked into rest. The furnace stayed off. The scanner in the other room hissed low, more breath than voice.

Inside my head, I walked the square I'd been crossing all year: courthouse, office, stake center, diner, Chronicle. Each building lit or dark. Each with people inside who now knew me as the man who'd broken something open, not the one who smoothed it over.

I pictured future nights at this same table. New folders at work. New names in Eve's notebook drawer. Maybe men in suits from somewhere else sitting where Marie had been. Maybe tribal elders. Maybe no one but the two of us and a pot of coffee, deciding whether to push a warrant or leave it be.

Protecting my family had always meant, in my mind, building a wall between them and all that. Tonight it twisted into something else: not walling them off, but making sure we weren't each holding different ends of the same live wire alone.

Somewhere down the hall, Caleb turned over in his sleep and the mattress springs complained. Abby's door showed a line of light at the bottom; she'd be up scrolling, reading comments on whatever the Chronicle posted tomorrow.

"I keep thinking about Rosa's kids," I said quietly. "If I let up now, it's them who pay, not Roman. Not Colton."

"I know," Eve said. "I hear that too when you come home."

Rosa at the remembrance rose in my mind, her hand on her boy's shoulder, the way his eyes hunted the room when people said "tragedy" and "accident" and then looked away when I didn't.

"Honest," I said again, mostly to myself.

We pushed our chairs back after a while and killed the kitchen light. The hallway felt narrower in the dark, walls close, pictures on the plaster just shadows. We stood there for a moment, not moving, listening to the scanner's low murmur from the living room.

No urgent tone. Just a routine traffic stop on the south side, a deputy calling in clear.

I took Eve's hand again. She squeezed once, hard. Agreement, not comfort. Then we walked down the hall toward bed, the faint glow from the streetlamp tracing thin lines across the floor like another kind of map.

Chapter 36

River Glass and Scanner Noise

The truck's headlights cut off when I twisted the key. The dome light bathed the cab in soft yellow for a second, then faded, leaving only the low hiss of the scanner between the seats.

The river was a dark ribbon under a sky that had finally decided to show a few stars. Our breath fogged as we stepped down onto the gravel. It crunched under our boots in slow, familiar rhythm.

I'd driven this road enough times that the dips and frost heaves lived in my hands. Tonight there wasn't any reason to hurry. No body waiting, no witness pacing.

The GreenSpire folder in the evidence room. Eve's notebook in our kitchen drawer. Colton locked up and arraigned, his file thick with tool marks and badge logs. The town sitting in the uneasy quiet that comes after an arrest and before trial.

A flat stretch between climbs.

I shut the truck door gently and clicked the lock out of habit. The scanner murmured inside, a low thread. Dispatch called out a welfare check; a deputy asked if anyone had eyes on a stray cow near the highway.

Eve hugged her coat closer and tucked a strand of hair behind her ear as the wind came off the water. We walked down the short path toward the bank. Cottonwood branches brushed overhead, bare and black against the sky.

The river made its usual sound against the rocks. Not loud, not quiet. Just there. It smelled faintly of silt and melt, even in late summer.

Something slick nudged my boot, a piece of broken glass worn cloudy by the current. River glass. I picked it up and turned it between my fingers. The edges had gone dull from being rolled and tumbled longer than I'd been sheriff.

"Remember when you used to bring Abby down here to skip rocks?" Eve asked.

"She still out-throws me," I said. "She cheats though."

"How do you cheat at skipping rocks?"

"Natural talent." I flicked the glass once, low, and watched it flash and vanish.

We stood side by side, watching the dark water slide past. The truck sat up on the pullout behind us, cab light faint, scanner still whispering.

"Feels like another world from the courthouse," she said.

"Until you think about where this water's going," I answered. "Whose wells it runs under. Whose pumps touch it."

She made a small sound that wasn't quite agreement or disagreement.

My mind, unhelpfully, lined up the last months like slides: Jared on the derrick at first light. Rosa in her front room with that envelope on the table. Colton in his glass office, fingers on a laminated safety poster. The judge's pen dragging across the bottom of the warrant. My own voice at the microphone in the cultural hall, saying the word "chose" where people wanted "tragedy."

And the things ahead, blurry but already forming shapes: pump houses on Diamond land. Joel's neat signatures stacked in assessor files. GreenSpire maps with rivers redrawn.

"I used to think," I said slowly, "that if we could just get the truth on paper once in a while, that would be enough."

"And now?" Eve asked.

"Now it feels like writing it down is the easy part."

The water slid around a midstream boulder and gurgled. Somewhere a frog gave a lonely croak.

We didn't talk for a while. The cold worked through my coat in thin fingers. Gravel shifted under my boots as I moved my weight. My shoulders eased down on their own.

"How's Abby?" I asked.

"Angry," Eve said. "But not at you. At all of it."

"That's fair."

"She's been reading comments on Lorna's story. Some people think you're the hero of the Basin. Others think you've sold it out."

"Both groups are wrong," I said.

Eve's breath made clouds in the dark. "She asked me last night if it was worth it."

"What'd you tell her?"

"That I don't know yet," she said. "That it might feel worse before it feels better. That's not what she wanted to hear."

"It's the only true answer," I said.

I thought about Marie at our table, her neat lists of names and fears. About Hal in the diner, raising his coffee in my direction loud enough for the whole place to hear. About ward members who'd stopped catching my eye in the hall.

"Town's going to split more before it settles," I said.

"Maybe it never settles," she answered. "Maybe it just keeps... moving."

Like the river. Never the same water twice, but still one river.

She threaded her fingers through mine. Heat moved up my arm from that small contact, more reliable than the furnace at home.

We listened to the scanner's faint murmur behind us and the river in front and the wind over both.

"I don't want them growing up on lies," she said after a long time.

"Abby and Caleb?" I asked, though I knew.

"Yeah." Her fingers tightened. "I'd rather our kids grow up with hard truths than comforting lies."

There it was. The compass point. Same kitchen question, different words, same line drawn.

I looked out over the black water and tried to picture the path from here to wherever that choice would take us: to Diamond's gate, to GreenSpire's office, to some hearing room about Bonanza I hadn't even pictured yet.

"That's what we'll give them then," I said. "Even if it means they look at some people different than we did."

"Maybe that's the point," she said.

Stars pricked sharper overhead. A truck rushed by on the distant road, headlights a moving smudge between cottonwoods.

I bent and picked up another piece of glass, smaller this time, and pressed it into her palm. "Souvenir," I said.

She rolled it in her fingers. "From what?"

"From tonight. From remembering we said this out loud."

She tucked it into her pocket. "You going to remember when it's three in the morning and somebody's yelling at you at a meeting?"

"I'll write it down," I said. "You know me."

We both looked back toward the truck. The scanner voice, barely audible, called out a road name I knew by heart. A deputy answered, calm. No sirens.

"I used to like the nights when nothing happened," I said. "Now I just wonder what we're not hearing yet."

"That's why we've got names in the drawer," she said. "And why you've got that folder in evidence. It's not nothing anymore. It's... not-yet."

I let that word sit. Not-yet. Whole court calendars could be built out of that.

The wind shifted colder. Eve shivered, and my knuckles answered with their own ache.

"Let's head back," I said. "Before I lose feeling in my ears."

We climbed the bank, gravel grinding underfoot. The truck's shape grew against the sky, familiar dents catching what little light there was. I set my hand on the cab for a second, covering that old ding near the door handle, and felt the metal's chill.

Inside, the scanner hummed. A brief tone cut through, then settled.

We got in. I turned the key. Headlights speared the dirt road, catching dust and a scrap of plastic. The engine's rumble wrapped around us like a coat.

"Same buildings," Eve said when we crested the last low rise and the square came into view. Courthouse brick, stake center steeple, diner neon, Chronicle window dark.

"Different eyes," I said.

We looped the square once, out of muscle memory. The courthouse's second floor glowed harsh and fluorescent. Somebody working late, or a janitor with the radio going. The sheriff's office was mostly dark except for dispatch.

The stake center sat in shadow, only a light above one side door marking it. The diner's sign hummed pink at the corner, a couple of trucks in the lot even at this hour.

I steered us past the Chronicle last. Its front window showed only the reflection of our headlights, but I could picture Lorna inside earlier, leaning over a draft, choosing which words would make it to print.

Each building had stopped being one thing this year. Courthouse not just law, but politics and land. Stake center not just worship, but pressure and, sometimes, courage. Diner, half café, half jury box. The paper, a mirror we didn't always like looking into.

"Where do you feel at home in all that now?" Eve asked softly.

"In the truck," I said. "And at our table."

"And out by the river," she said.

"Yeah. That too."

The scanner muttered a unit number and then slid into static. I reached over and spun the volume down until it was only a ghost of a sound.

We turned off onto our street. Porch lights dotted the block, warmer than the square's glare. Kids' bikes lay tipped in one yard. A dog lifted its head and let it drop again as we rolled past.

I pulled into our drive and killed the engine. The sudden quiet rang in my ears.

For a moment we sat there, hands still on our laps, eyes on the house.

"This is going to cost us," Eve said. No drama, just statement.

"Already has," I said. "Will keep costing."

She looked over at me. In the reflection of the dash, her eyes were dark and steady.

"Then we pay it together," she said.

I reached across the console and set my hand on hers. The river glass in her pocket clicked against the seat buckle when she shifted.

We climbed out into the cool night. Down the block, a sprinkler sputtered to life then choked off. A porch light snapped off as someone inside went to bed.

Behind us, the square glowed faint over the rooftops. Ahead, our front door waited with its worn paint and crooked welcome mat.

I listened one last time for the scanner's hiss drifting from the cracked window of the truck. There would be other calls. Other cases. Rig. Ranch. Something black and old out near Bonanza.

I couldn't see what they'd look like yet, not in detail. But standing there under the thin wash of the streetlamp with Eve's hand in mine and the taste of river air still in my mouth, I knew I wasn't done.

Not with the law. Not with this town. Not with the long work of telling the truth on paper and in rooms that too often focused on smoothing the edges.

We walked up the path together and went inside.

THE END

Keep reading

— Uintah Basin Mysteries —

The story continues in

— Death at Diamond Ranch —

Summer dawn on Diamond Mountain brings Sheriff Milt Kingston another "accident." Rancher Tom Diamond lies crumpled against a pasture gate, boot tracks scuffed, chain shining fresh in the early light. The pump up on the hill hums in the wrong key, and ditch water runs thin on a day it ought to be full. Neighbors blame a spooked horse and old grudges. Milt's notes say otherwise.

When he follows the water, the trail runs straight into the heart of the Basin's new hope: the GreenSpire retreat project. Forged deeds, batch-filed easements, and a shell company with its hands on multiple laterals all thread back through the county assessor's office—and Milt's own cousin, Joel. Ward councils pitch "stewardship" and tax breaks while ranch families quietly fear losing land their grandparents bled for.

Under fluorescent lights in the courthouse and church cultural hall, Milt and Clara pick apart alibis and numbers. Jake Diamond's debts, Dale Harper's old water theft, Molly's secret meeting in town: each looks bad until the records say different. The one story that won't quite hold is the smooth one from GreenSpire's field attorney, Brent Carrow. To prove Tom's death was staged and not fate, Milt must subpoena his own blood, lean on a whistleblower who could lose everything, and stand in front of a full chapel while emails and maps flicker across a ward projector.

\#\#\#

THE END

Look for the next installment of the Uintah Basin Mysteries

at **https://tsjensen.com**

About the Author

T. S. Jensen grew up on a farm five miles out of a two-stoplight town in the heart of Utah's Uinta Basin, where most directions were given by wellheads, fence lines, and stack yards. His father worked in his own glass and paint shop in town and ran the family farm in Hancock Cove while serving in every lay church calling in the list on Sundays; his mother kept books for the farm and made wedding cakes and dresses.

As a boy, Tyler listened from the hallway while adults lowered their voices over layoffs, bad accidents, and quiet marital troubles. Summers were spent trailing friends along irrigation ditches, into cedar and sage brush covered hills, and past a shuttered alum mine, where family stories about "how things really happened" never quite matched the official plaques.

As an adult, Jensen studied English at Utah State University and spent 30 years in the technology sector on the Wasatch Front.

Church meetings and work all began to blur together as different rooms where the same arguments about loyalty, livelihood, and truth played out. Jensen now writes full-time from his home in Utah County, within easy driving distance of all the places that capture his imagination. He shares a home kept clean by his lovely wife and enjoys spending time with his four adult children and two grandchildren.

His stories grow out of a conviction that landscapes remember what communities try to forget, and that ordinary people, caught between family, faith, and the law, are where the most enduring questions live.

9 781972 052006